PRAISE FOR NICOLAS ROTHWELL

'A caster of spells.'
Australian Book Review

'Masterful and unforgettable.'
Pico Iyer

'Rothwell's calm wondering…left me with
a feeling of enchantment.'
Robert Dessaix

'As moving and eloquent and imaginative…
as contemporary writing can be.'
Peter Craven

Nicolas Rothwell was educated in European schools before becoming a foreign correspondent. He is the award-winning author of *Heaven and Earth*, *Wings of the Kite-Hawk*, *Another Country*, *The Red Highway* and *Journeys to the Interior*. He lives in Darwin.

nicolasrothwell.com

BELOMOR

NICOLAS ROTHWELL

TEXT PUBLISHING MELBOURNE AUSTRALIA

textpublishing.com.au

The Text Publishing Company
Swann House
22 William Street
Melbourne Victoria 3000
Australia

First published in 2013 by The Text Publishing Company

Cover and page design by WH Chong
Typeset by J&M Typesetting

Cover image: *Belomor Thoughts (Crisis)*, by Helgy Karpenko, 2012
Frontispiece: *The Belomor Channel*, by Alexander Rodchenko, 1933; supplied by Art Sensus, London, with thanks to Tosca Fund

Printed in Australia by Griffin Press, an Accredited ISO AS/NZS 14001:2004 Environmental Management System printer

National Library of Australia Cataloguing-in-Publication entry:
Author: Rothwell, Nicolas.
Title: Belomor / by Nicolas Rothwell.
ISBN: 9781922079749 (pbk.)
ISBN: 9781921961953 (ebook)
Dewey Number: A823.3

This book is printed on paper certified against the Forest Stewardship Council® Standards. Griffin Press holds FSC chain-of-custody certification SGS-COC-005088. FSC promotes environmentally responsible, socially beneficial and economically viable management of the world's forests.

In memory of
Tjinawima Napaltjarri

'Vidi ego odorati victura rosaria Paesti
sub matutino cocta iacere Noto.'

I

BELOMORKANAL

EARLY IN THE SUMMER of 1747, as soon as the Alpine passes had begun to clear, the Venetian painter Bernardo Bellotto set out on a journey northwards from his home, travelling for several weeks, through settled Hapsburg lands and wild, picturesque valleys, until he reached the capital of the kings of Saxony—Dresden, on the banks of the river Elbe.

The city, with its spires and gleaming monuments, was famous at that time throughout Europe for its elegance and splendour: the sight of the imperial palaces and churches, seen from across the wide, smooth-flowing river on certain summer days, when the light was at its loveliest and most golden, called to mind the grand views of Italian cities then much in vogue at princely courts—and this was the reason for Bellotto's journey. He was known already for his ability to record a scene, and capture its finest details: much like his uncle Giovanni Antonio Canal, whose gifts he seemed to have concentrated and refined in the minute grain of his own canvases, Bellotto could survey and set down a teeming urban spectacle, singling out its individual features and recomposing them with such harmony the resultant image had the look of a natural, inevitable pattern. Yet his painted cityscapes were chill and solemn where Canaletto's had a warmth and gauzy softness: in his brushstrokes, for all their finesse and painstaking precision, there was a tone quite absent from the works of his more celebrated master; he reached beyond the mere description of the components of a landscape; he seemed inclined almost to pass judgement on the worlds he delineated with such exactitude; he was in love with fate, and mutability—and these characteristics made him the ideal artist for the court on the river Elbe. For the region of Saxony was unstable in those days; its future was uncertain—it had been convulsed by the military campaigns, skirmishes and power struggles that were near constant throughout Central Europe in the century's first decades. Its air of well-founded solidity was deceptive: the majesty of its new buildings had come at a cost, in guns and men; they bore the stamp of its ruler, Augustus the Strong; they were his artifice, the product of his stern, unbending will. Bellotto had been summoned to record the dream of an autocrat, a dream turned into light and stone. That royal Dresden soon became known as Florence on the Elbe—writers and scholars from the nearby cities of Bohemia and Moravia would come to wonder at its beauties, and imagine that they stood amid pavilions of Quattrocento grandeur. But the true model for the king had been Venice: elusive, potent Venice—the Venice of views, the Venice reflected in lagoon waters, which

Bellotto, who would never again see his own homeland, now set about recreating in the cold perfection of his paint.

There is no doubting the gifts of the young artist: even his earliest scenes of Dresden are resolved, and their ornateness has a terrifying edge. The groups of figures scurry like ants, oblivious of the great forces shaping their environment. The squares and public spaces dwarf them, the façades of palaces and the church elevations rise like tombs above them.

These disquieting qualities in Bellotto's work have gone largely unremarked in our time because of a circumstance that the artist himself could not have foreseen. His reputation grew; he travelled widely between the court cities of the Saxon kingdom. The sweeping panoramic views he made during the last years of his life were painted in Warsaw, where he worked for another ruler with an eye to posterity, who commissioned another series of grand vistas, designed to hang in the royal castle. This idyllic Warsaw, rich in parks and fountains, was destroyed, down to the last building, in the course of World War II: the post-war communist regime, in need of some grand project that might absorb Polish nationalist sentiments, decided to rebuild the capital in the image of the old city, stone by stone, brick by brick. Bellotto's paintings were the only systematic blueprint. They became the model, and secured him a late-dawning international fame: for the documentary precision of his work, which derived from his relentless use of a camera obscura to guide his hand, allowed the specialist teams of labourers and architects charged with the reconstruction of Warsaw to build a city in his image, and the recreated avenues and palaces of the Polish capital retain in their aspect to this day something of Bellotto's own cool temperament.

He could not have known. And yet, in some sense, he already knew: and knew very well. There is a famous painting of his, *The Ruins of the Former Kreuzkirche*—it exists in a pair of versions: one in Dresden; one, the more beautiful, in Zurich, in the incongruous setting of the modernist Kunsthaus, where I often used to see it during my schooldays. I can feel even now the thrill of horror it awoke in me when I set eyes on it for the first time. The canvas depicts the remains of a Dresden landmark, largely destroyed during the bombardment of the city by Prussian troops. The church tower dominates the image, though it is set slightly off-centre, to the left. Rubble spills from the main structure: beams of timber, masonry, dust. Intense activity fills the square before the ruined edifice, though whether it is a story of rebuilding or clearing remains, at first glance, quite uncertain: either task amounts, in the fullness of time, to the same thing. Crowds of onlookers survey the spectacle: dignitaries, society ladies, a pair of lovers. The surrounding palaces stand untouched—how inscrutable those powers are that decide where the projectiles fall. The sky is almost clear: a soft, pinkish light is in the clouds. Tiny figures can be made out, standing just beneath the damaged tower's pinnacle, almost on the same level as a stone saint. The entire inner structure of the church is exposed to view: its stairwells and galleries, its vaults and buttressings—the whole hidden wonder of its engineering stripped bare, much like the convolutions of a half-eroded seashell tossed up on a sandy shore.

*

Of all the monuments of Dresden, there was a single one to which Bellotto was drawn back repeatedly: the flamboyant church of Our Lady, the high-domed Frauenkirche, which he painted and sketched, from varying angles, in varying lights, and which the modern generation knew for many years only from these painted recollections. As one stares into those elusive works of his—they hang, for the most part, still, in the city where they were made—one can sense the artist's careful eye, transposing the impressions before him into a style of permanence. How did he decide to give the team of white carriage horses in the forefront of this vista such a springing step? What made him set down in his brushstrokes two dogs at play at the edge of a cloud shadow, one leaping up above its companion, front legs outstretched? Each view snatches the breath of the moment, the rushing race of life; each is a memorial, drenched by the painter's awareness that nothing he sees and makes fixed will ever be fixed, or come again. In every one of these canvases, the eye is drawn by the dome of the Frauenkirche, which Bellotto knew in minute detail: the scars and discolorations on the curved stone flanks can be traced in his different renditions; they are consistent; the artist is proclaiming the complete absence of fantasy from these works. Here is that great stone bell seen from the Moritzstrasse; here it is from the angle of the Judenhof, in different light. The sky, though, is always tinged by a faint quality of haze, which lends the image field a veiled aspect; and, try as one might, the eye cannot strip this filtering away. The figures—they are clear; more than clear, they are distinct from far off, the painted view is accurate far beyond the point where a human gaze would blur and fail: the red court coats beneath the distant palace arcade, the individual spokes on the coach wheels at the picture's vanishing point, the pale shadows cast by tiny cornices and columns—they are all present, rendered in a detail so sharp they hinder the mind's capacity to see. And who are those workmen, their lithe silhouettes picked out by the sunlight on the roof of the Frauenkirche, where the façade leans up towards the dome's fringing balustrade? Three together, and a fourth, close by, bent over, engaged in some elaborate task of repair. This, too, we may be sure, is historical—for the church was always an uncertain building, weakened by the overload of its vast superstructure pressing upon its slender piers. It was, in fact, an ambiguity in every sense: a Lutheran church in a Catholic-ruled city; a cathedral dedicated to the Virgin, whose name it bore, though she was wholly absent from its decorative program; a grand Venetian cupola, made from sandstone instead of marble, and rising not from the lagoon beside the Doge's steps, but over the lush water meadows of the Elbe.

By good fortune, an account survives of the Frauenkirche as it seemed in its time of greatest glory, just after the last battles of the Seven Years' War, when the dome stood proud and high over the half-ruined city. Charles Burney, the eighteenth-century British musician-traveller, records in some detail in his two-volume *German Tour* the impression Dresden made on him after his long journey upriver through the rough, romantic Erzgebirge. 'The city itself has suffered so much that it is difficult for a stranger to imagine himself near the celebrated capital of Saxony, even when he sees it from the most favourable eminence in the neighbourhood, so few of its once many cloud-capt towers are left standing.' The prevailing tone was one of oppressive melancholy: 'From being the seat of the Muses, and habitation of pleasure, it is now only a dwelling for beggary, theft and wretchedness.' Even the opera Burney saw performed at the little Kurfuerstliches theatre left him quite indifferent, though he did note the musical gifts of the street gangs of 'singing boys' who hired themselves out for funerals. The sole distinctive feature of his visit was the church, 'a very noble and elegant building, of white stone, with a high dome in the middle'. It was now the emblem of the city; it had been proof against every attack: the cannonballs and artillery shells aimed at it had rebounded harmlessly from the great stone vaulting's 'orbicular form'. The service Burney attended there filled him with strong emotion, so fine was the singing, 'some three thousand persons, one of the grandest choruses I ever heard'. And it is true that the great church, in its first incarnation, was often regarded as an intimate religious space, despite its overwhelming scale: the preacher's pulpit jutted out towards the congregation pews; the eyes of all those seated in the high surrounding galleries were concentrated on the altar, and on its sculpted group—a vivid treatment, in the round, in the most advanced manner of the day: Christ kneeling in the garden of Gethsemane, an angel appearing to him from the heavens, overhead the eye of God, imperturbable, staring from a knot of cherub-infested stucco cloud. It was an illustration of the central place in life of silent prayer; it also highlighted the strange receptiveness of the divine to suffering—that specialty of the region, as characteristic as the crossed-swords trademark on the court's much-prized porcelain.

9

A few decades more, and the city was destroyed anew. This time the torment and loss of life was great. Technology had advanced: the explosives unleashed upon Dresden on the night of February fourteenth, 1945 produced sounds and spectacles not familiar before then in mankind's rich experience of siege and war. Much of the city's centre was liquefied by the heat of the explosions rained down on it, and the resultant firestorms. The air itself became a cause of death, for oxygen from the atmosphere was sucked into the flames: men and women fleeing from the destruction fell, asphyxiated, to the burning rubble at their feet, or died huddled in their shelters; the bodies discovered in those havens were cremated by flamethrower, for want of graves or gravediggers after the event. The bombing has been described, and picked over in great detail, from both strategic and moral viewpoints; the testimony of survivors has been printed and used for propaganda; indeed, the city and its fate were a cause, more than a place, all through the post-war decades: its name became a byword not for beauty but for the beauties that had once been there. The accounts of the bombing, though, all fell short of the scenes they related: what style would fit, what authorial presence seem appropriate? Those who wrote from experience were both too close and too far away from their memories; those who imagined themselves into the streets and houses of the city as the bomber fleets approached were too inclined to seek out the higher meanings embedded in the sequence of impacts and consequences.

But by chance there was a well-placed witness, familiar with the task of level, meticulous narration, who survived that fiery night in the city, reached safety and set down at once a detailed relation of all that he had seen. This witness, a professor of romance literature named Viktor Klemperer, who was already sixty-three years old on the night of the firestorm, stood in a strange relationship to the destruction: he was of Jewish descent, and he had endured the unending humiliations heaped upon him by the Third Reich until that time, and recorded them in a series of clandestine diaries. Klemperer had recently learned that he was at last bound for deportation, together with the few remaining members of the local Jewish community, all of whom, like him, had been spared until then only because of their marriages to Aryan partners. Klemperer was still absorbing this news, turning it over in uneasy fashion in his thoughts, still wondering what the exact nature of the ordeal awaiting him in coming days might be, when the sound of the massed engines became audible in the cold dark sky.

There was salvation for him in the flames: 'Whoever of the bearers of the star was spared by this night was delivered—for in the general chaos he could escape the Gestapo.' So Klemperer wrote, in his most portentous fashion, in the book he published early in the next phase of his life: it was a formal academic study of the language of the National Socialist state, and all he permitted himself by way of personal recollection was contained in a brief, snatched preface. His diaries, with their recitation of his experiences in Dresden from the fledgling days of the dictatorship through to its convulsive end—they saw the light only years after Klemperer was dead, and Germany's division at war's end had been undone, and the long inheritance of grief and damage was being smoothed away. They seemed then like tidings from a far-off world, and yet those who read them felt their force at once; their words were like a lash upon the skin: they preserved the texture of the moments Klemperer lived through, and lived purely to record. How unfailingly he paced his sentences to catch the ebb and flow of chance impressions. How closely he gave attention to the way time accelerates, slows down, and circles back in grand repeating cycles to overprint our thoughts.

When he heard the first bombs of the great raid falling, as he relates, Klemperer was sure it was the most terrible attack that he had known, but this conviction quickly vanished: for more explosions came, much stronger ones, in waves, surging, forming into mingled washes of distorted sound. From the men and women in the shelter round him, when silence came to the skies, he heard only whimpers, sobs. At last, an all-clear; Klemperer struggles up: it is deep night-time still, but outside the sky is bright as day, fires burn, a fierce wind blows, broken glass in a thick glinting carpet covers the ground. More sounds of bomber engines, more detonations: Klemperer takes refuge once again, is separated from his wife, 'Then an explosion at the window close to me. Something hard and glowing hot struck the right side of my face.' He puts his hand up: it is covered in blood. He checks for his eye: it is still there. He runs again, and hauls with him his precious bag of manuscripts. Under cover: the vaulting of some half-destroyed cellar: bombs again, but this time he feels only exhaustion, no fear: Klemperer advances. Voices swirl. New shelter: all of them are strangers, thrown together; they are in the hall of the Reichsbank building, surrounded by soaring flames. The heat is too much: they climb, up a pathway, through the gardens; at last the terrace, high above the Elbe—the firestorm wind is blowing hard, sparks in blazing showers fly through the air. To the right and left, buildings are alight—the art academy, the Belvedere. When the showers of sparks grow too intense, Klemperer dodges from one side of the terrace to the other. Standing out like a torch on the near side of the river is a tall building, at Pirnaischer Platz, glowing white, and on the far bank, bright as day, the roof of the finance ministry in flames. Then rain comes: it is heavy—it falls for hours, as if generated by the wind and storm—the ground grows soft and sodden; the ashes on its surface are still smouldering; steam rises from it like a mist, backlit in reddish shades.

By now Klemperer has lost all bearings, all will, and yet he sets even this down, as being of interest: why can he not observe any details; why does he see only the theatrical fires around him, the burning beams and rafters in and above the stone walls of the terrace at his side? At which point, he is struck by the calm figure of a statue on the terrace—some jewel of baroque artifice, gazing out across the river landscape: who is he? In the distance, new buildings are catching alight, they glow and founder in their turn, great palaces turn blue and silver in the flames. The hours pass; dawn comes, though it can barely be seen through the fiery dark. Eventually Klemperer's wife finds him in the huddled crowd; they reunite: she relates to him an incident in her adventures in the burning old town, when she had wanted to light a cigarette but had no matches. Something was glowing before her on the ground; she wanted to use it—she realised it was a burning corpse.

When a city has lived through such things, do they linger? Does their memory stay, somehow, in the air, imprinted? It is not clear that places can endure disaster on this scale, or escape from the shadows the past leaves for our minds to sense—and many visitors to Dresden in the post-war decades, when a socialist regime held sway in Eastern Germany, found the atmospherics of the streets and restored buildings almost unbearable: the air of loss and damage was exacerbated by the official cult of suffering that was imposed upon the town. Through the firebombing, Dresden had become a victim city: it would now serve as a temple, dedicated to the progressive cause of peace.

This message required a symbol, the starker the better. There was one to hand. As the smoke settled and the rainfall died away, those few survivors in the city's ruins with the inclination to survey their surrounds absorbed the view that stretched before them: there were the hulks of broken buildings and half-tumbled towers, as far as the eye could see. Bellotto's painted Dresden had been erased—except for one monument: the Frauenkirche was still standing; the dome still rose high above the old city's shattered façades. For a day, it stood there, its stone flanks veiled by plumes of haze and by the shimmer from hot currents of rising air: it seemed quite intact—but the next morning, at the stroke of ten, it collapsed upon itself. Fire had been carried by sparks through its smashed windows into the interior; the painted wooden pews and the internal cladding had been burned away; the masonry of the giant supporting piers turned molten: they lost their strength. With a grating, fracturing sound, the structure subsided. Dust from the collapse hung above the site for several hours; at last it cleared: nothing remained upright except the high, curved chancel and the outside wall of the north-west stair-turret.

This gaunt ensemble had an elegance. It remained untouched as efforts to remake the city began—within three years, a fresh metropolis had been put together in the wreckage: brick and concrete collective apartments; new avenues, wide, for ease of surveillance; low, bleak office blocks. It was at this point that the Saxon office for the preservation of historical monuments decided the time was right to rebuild the Frauenkirche: the rubble from the ruins was examined, and undamaged blocks of stone that might be used in a reconstruction project were singled out. But higher counsel soon prevailed: as the wounds and scars of wartime were masked across Germany, the church came, once more, into its own. It was a shrine again, a memorial for all those who had felt the sting of man's aggression against his fellow man—and the remains preserved this badge for many years.

It was still the great sight to see in Dresden when I travelled there on a reporting trip, by train, in the company of a Polish peace activist named Berenika. It was late in 1987, a year of tensions, but few resolutions—a year that has now receded to that midpoint in the mind's recollecting landscape when events disclose their freight of meaning, and fall into relief. It was a dull mid-afternoon. We had just passed through Leipzig's main station. The train gathered speed. We were in a crowded carriage full of sad-eyed Kazakh Red Army recruits in their greatcoats and uniforms. Everybody round us in the compartment was smoking with furious concentration.

'I've never cared for Dresden,' said Berenika at this moment, turning to me conspiratorially.

'Why?'

'The sullen people, the cold, the grit in the air, that sense of being in frontier territory but having the borders closed, the enclosed feel you get from the deep valley like a wall around the town—all that would be enough, but it's that ridiculous ruin, that church of nothing, those blackened symbolic stones. You can't enter Dresden without being thrown back constantly into the past, as though time was a trap with no escape.'

'Why go there, then?'

'In my line of things, you have to go to every peace conference,' she said: 'Otherwise, you'd never get visas for the trips that matter—the ones to the West.'

'And what do you put on your visa applications and entry forms? Activist?'

'Philologist—no one knows what it means, so no one asks questions: it always works! Besides, this is a fraternal country— all friends now. Though I must say I find it hard to forgive the Germans for what they did to Poland, even though it was so long ago. Whenever I arrive at Berlin Friedrichstrasse, I feel ill at first, my head starts spinning, I feel like a traitor to my own cause—and then I remember that my cause is internationalist. Even so, these German meetings are difficult: you always have it in your mind that there are spies among the people you come across, reporting everything you say back to the secret police.'

'It's that extreme?'

'You know how harsh the system is here; but that harshness

can also be an ally—there are people here to learn from: people who've looked into the heart of life. People without the usual illusions: writers who talk of tragic things, but without weight; actors for whom acting is release. And there's one man who taught me a great deal about this world and its contorted affairs.'

'A dissident?'

'Of a kind. More a philosopher. I'd have to say he helped me to see very far: he opened up views and perspectives inside my head. Maybe it would help you to talk to him.'

'I'd like that,' I said.

'Perhaps I can look into it, and ask, and see what might be possible.'

And so it was, some hours later, as the chill evening descended, and rain began to fall in the square before the Frauenkirche ruins, their stones deep brown in that half-light, and standing against the sky like giant execution scaffolds, that Berenika and I made our way down a wide, still street, turned into the doorway of a collective apartment building, and climbed the stairway to its top. HAFFNER—the name was printed on the little sign beside the bell. She rang it loudly; the door opened—and though years have passed, I cannot entirely free myself from the spell of that encounter, or shake the conviction that those hours paved the way for much in my life that still lay far ahead. Indeed, the further in time that evening recedes, the more clearly I can summon up Haffner's most striking ideas, his intuitions and his suddenly unveiled paradoxes—they send forward their echoes now, and the suspicion begins to form in me that our lives are shaped by influences we barely sense; that we trace out our paths in the world unknowingly, registering strange, distant resonances in our hearts. I see him as he was then, alert, his being concentrated in his eyes like some caged animal—yet there was also a softness about his manner, a delicacy, a courtliness that was itself a resistance against the surrounding world. His loyalty was to the republic of letters; he lived for words, that was plain at once: his ideal was to send the mind in flight, cutting and weaving through a concept-laden sky.

Such was Stefan Haffner as he seemed that night, in the dark hours of actually existing socialism. He greeted us as if a visit of this kind was quite routine, and led us down the tight, angled corridor into a study, dimly lit, book-lined, shrouded by thick plumes of cigarette smoke: from the double window, through its thick half-drawn curtains, one glimpsed the darkened city stretching off below. I tried to gauge him. He was grand in his manner, tall, with greying hair; at that time he must have been already in his fifties, and there was at first a tone of resignation in his voice, as he touched on politics: the shadow play of the bloc, the regime, its factions—subjects over which he ranged in sharp detail, with an air of sovereign contempt, the corners of his lips downturned as though he were draining to the dregs some bitter medicine—but gradually, as he sketched his picture of the forces and energies that lay masked beneath the surface flash and glimmer of events, he seemed lifted up, his words and way of speaking changed: how deep the contradictions in the system had become, how short its future life would prove to be; how abrupt the West's looming seizure of control; how total the destruction of memories, so that the entire record of the East German state, and all the thoughts and hopes of those who lived under it, would be no more than a footnote in the flow of time, a curiosity, at best, reserved for historians of neglected shadows.

'And so we live on, or we survive,' he said, 'hoping for deliverance, even though that deliverance would prove the fatal blow to the whole world around us—and the pattern is already set, the sentence passed.'

I listened to these ideas of his, which seemed at that time woven from the cloth of fantasy, and made some polite reply.

He leaned forward. 'Naturally, you think I've lost myself—that I'm in a dream,' he said: 'But sometimes the man who lives in his dreams is the only one who sees the truth—and that truth is close at hand. I make you a promise: before you die, you will be able to visit Dresden, and see a perfect western city—the face of freedom, with all its wondrous beauties lovingly restored. The ruins will be rebuilt: they'll sweep all the grime and the rubble aside; or no, better still, the palaces and churches will be recreated, one by one, but incorporating every single stone from the past, to give each of them the bite of authenticity. You'll be able to walk along the river promenade, and see the old palaces reflected in the water, just as they were a hundred years ago; you'll stroll through the market, past great banks and handsome arcades, and above you there will be the stone bell of the Frauenkirche, rising into a perfect, cloudless blue sky.'

'You think we can destroy and remake the past at will—just like that?'

'Of course: haven't you noticed that we love annihilation so much? History has a pulse of its own, it has its rhythm: it's like a piece of music. If you want to read its shape and plot you have to find the key, to tune your mind, to follow closely—follow as if your life hung on it. Only then does the theme give itself away. Places have their music, they have their evolving destinies, just as surely as men and women do. I'm surprised you even want to doubt me: if you stand back, far enough, events and experiences always take on a form. Or you can look on history as a picture, a distanced, panoramic view: look from the days when the city was first ordered into being; it becomes clear; it's as if we were conforming to some great architectural geometry, with positions determined by a far perspective—and we have instincts that compel us to fit into its waiting shape.'

'It's certainly not the standard interpretation of the headlines,' I said.

'Cigarette?'

With this Haffner reached towards me: he held out a pack, blue, with a bright curve of gold Cyrillic letters on the front. I looked at it.

'Belomor. Belomorkanal.'

'The strongest in the world,' said Haffner, rather proudly.

'And why do you smoke them?' I asked: 'It surely can't be the aroma.'

'There is a reason,' he said. 'A deep reason. Would you like to hear the story? It has its detours—but maybe you'll think it worth the ride.'

'Let's see,' I answered.

'I gained the taste for them on the spot,' said Haffner then, and he settled back, and with a minimum of words, impassively, stripping back the successive episodes in his narrative to their purest essence, situated himself as a young man, in the years after the war, under Russian occupation, when Dresden and the cities of the east were piles of stones. Years passed. He studied; his gifts were clear; he went to Berlin, then Moscow, and Leningrad: he had become a specialist in the German links of Dostoyevsky.

'Of course,' I said.

'Why? Do you find me like a character from that author?'

The flashing eyes, the face worn out by hidden passions, the edge of temper, barely held in check—but certainly, I thought, and it dawned on me that we stood at the threshold of some upwelling dramatic narration.

'Perhaps,' was what I said.

'It's normal that we model ourselves on the figures in the novels of our favourite authors,' said Haffner, sharply: 'Normal—how else are we to occupy those works from the inside, knowingly, truly? Beside, Dostoveysky had particular ties to Saxony'—he ran his hands down the spines of a multi-volume edition in the bookcase close beside him. 'Every true student is chosen by his subject—there is no freedom in the decision; and it was my great fortune to be chosen by my teacher as well.'

It was in Leningrad that he found his master, in a lecture hall. This was the academician and scholar of old texts Dmitry Sergeyevich Likhachev, who, by chance, had lived as a child in an apartment with a view of the Vladimir Cathedral—the same view that Dostoyevsky saw from a corner of the last home he occupied before his death. It was a literary descent line! Haffner made himself a devoted apprentice: he absorbed all he could of the restrained, discreet instruction that came his way. He lavished on the older man the feelings one might have for an ideal father: worship, tender respect, unflinching love.

'But it was plain to me,' he said then, with a frown, 'that there were many things my teacher chose to keep private from me. He would speak, but not reveal. He had been made by events he preferred hidden. His way of seeing the world came from elsewhere.'

At last this mystery was resolved. Haffner was seated one evening at the corner table of Likhachev's communal apartment. 'It was one of those haunting white nights that figure in so much of the writing of Petersburg, and it may be that I saw myself then as a character in one of those stories. We had spent long hours talking. I had been telling him about my childhood years—years in the rubble, harsh times: I would never repeat those recollections now. He was moved by what he heard—and surely amused as well: what absurdity! A young man trying to instruct him in life's hardships. He began speaking about the place of suffering in literature, the sadnesses the masters of the Russian tradition had seen, and how they were mere premonitions of the greater troubles of our age. By degrees, his subject shifted, until I realised that he was describing to me his own experiences in his student years, when he himself was arrested, sentenced and transported to penal servitude on the camp island of Solovki, in the Arctic north. He spoke of those times in a soft, even voice, sighing repeatedly. Eventually he got up, and came back with a manuscript, its pages held inside a torn, shabby notebook. I remember very well what he said then: "I would like you to take this, and read it, overnight. This is a story few know. There is little I can teach you beyond what lies here. By giving it to you, I am, in more than one sense, placing my life in your hands." He passed it to me as if he was handing me the entrance ticket to a new world. What he told me was true; much did change for me that night.'

Haffner took the pages, went back to his dormitory accommodation, and plunged in. Rather than a recitation of ordeals, the memoir was a description of the men and women Likachev had found on that isolated prison archipelago, lost in the waters of the White Sea. By the year of his arrest, so the talk on Solovki went, the number of the inmates and jailers on the island was equal to the population of Belgium. Conditions were bleak; diseases were constantly ravaging the prisoners; the tasks of the labour gangs were exhausting: and yet there was little trace of this in the narrative.

'I made my way through, marvelling at the simplicity with which he expressed himself, and at the way his handwriting, which was of the utmost elegance, could convey even in its lettering the distinct states of emotion that were present on the page. But what most struck me was the gentleness and generosity with which he wrote. He presented the characters and thoughts of others: he dwelled on them. As for himself, he was scarcely there—and it was as I was reading him, in that white, pale light of the small hours, that I realised the true task of a writer is to destroy himself, remove himself: be present, but not visible. Each of his descriptions had a focus: it was as if one were staring at them through a clarifying glass. I still see the words he used to paint the portrait of the Solovki Kremlin, that monastic fortress which had become his home—it had thick walls of boulders, covered by a coat of orange lichen, and round those bastions men and women in their hundreds swarmed: people from every far-flung reach of a continent were constantly colliding; it was a place, as he described it, of repeated sad and happy encounters, of constantly exchanged tales and memories; indeed, the world of the imagination, of books and stories from afar that the inmates told each other, seemed more real than the typhus and the mosquitoes all round them. And beyond the prison compounds and the labour sites, there was the realm of Solovki, beckoning, a sparse, lovely realm: pale polar birches, rocks, the shining, ever-changing sea—and the constant variations in the look of the landscape, the advance of the seasons, the rhythm of the days, the long winter nights and sunrises and sunsets, the sudden shifts in the weather: they all seemed to underline how fleeting is the time allotted to us on Earth.'

Haffner paused.

'Those were strange words for me to read. They pointed like an arrow to the world of faith. I sensed the void inside myself. Of course, I believed in nothing. How could I? There was nothing in my past or my traditions in which I could believe. At last I laid the notebook aside, and fell asleep. It was the time of dawn in Leningrad: the whiteness strengthens, shadows like ghosts take form. I dreamed—and I found myself transported to Solovki. In the theatre of my dream, I saw a scene from the pages I had read: it was a moment, a stray line, in which the writer recalls an afternoon when he left the fortress and travelled the length of the island, to the labour colony, on some official business; he often had to take messages of this kind from camp to camp; he would walk the road to Deep Bay, a long stretch, and sometimes on warm, sunny days, as on this day, he would cut down the coastline, though this was strictly forbidden to all prisoners—and there, in a deserted garden of the old monastery, he lay down and closed his eyes. When he opened them he saw, close by, no more than an arm's length from him, a family of hares—a mother, with her offspring, all gazing at him, eyes wide, as if at a miracle. He looked back, unmoving, overcome by a feeling of loving goodwill—and for a long time afterwards a warmth of affection for all living things stayed with him.

'I dreamed, and saw that scene—it was a message for me, a proof of how strongly experiences can pass from heart to heart. In mid-morning, I went back to him to return the manuscript. How full my head was of words to say to him: how much gratitude I felt for what he had shown me—but things were not as I expected. He was cold, and formal: he received the package with his notebook in it into his hands almost in silence, and escorted me down onto the street. I assumed at first he must have been embarrassed by what he had allowed me to see—but then I realised in all likelihood he was afraid, and regretted what he had done: those were still times when it would have been natural for a foreign student to be an informer of some kind, a creature of the state. We were about to part: it was the corner, on the embankment; I looked at him, with all my youthful affection brimming up. I had made a great decision that night: I wanted to tell him. I struggled, and stared into his eyes, but they were cold, with the coldness and glare of open seas. I remember how I flinched, and turned away.'

'And the great decision?'

'I had decided to go to Solovki, to see that prison landscape for myself. I kept to that decision. I made my plans. It wasn't an easy task, in those days, to travel to such places, deep in military zones.'

'But you had no trouble, in the end,' said Berenika at this point, quite smoothly.

'Trouble? Trouble was all I had. I travelled north on a supply train, by stages, to Arkhangelsk. At first I was marooned there. The penal colony and all its outcamps on the archipelago had been shut down: the fort on the main island had been turned into a naval cadet training base—but there was the chaos of reconstruction just then, all through the north, whole towns deserted, others springing up; unusual things became possible. I found a place on an Arctic survey vessel, charting that coastline, searching for wartime remains and wrecks. They spent some while working in the archipelago: I could inspect what I had only been able to imagine—but it was as if I had seen a film, not read through a manuscript; each view seemed like a picture I had seen before. Every colour was familiar, every sound. If ever I had doubted the power of books and words to capture life, those doubts died inside me then. I walked through the old Kremlin, with the naval crews and scientists round me, and I could see the shadows of what had been there before. It was more living to me in those moments than my own past. Then something strange happened.'

Haffner laughed, but his expression was agonised.

'A transformation—it was almost comical. I reached a limit inside myself. I wanted no more. I could go no further. It had been my idea to go down to that garden by the sea, where the family of hares had come to visit my teacher all those years ago. I had wanted to take into myself all the colours of the islands. I stopped. I felt I had come up against that borderline where art and writing sweep you up too far away from yourself, and become a danger to you, more than a friend. It was a relief for me when the time came for us to sail. The survey ship continued on its course, through the islands, headed south. We had been keeping close to shore: now it was unbroken waters—the White Sea of tale and fable. Of course, it wasn't white at all; it was piercing, hard grey-blue: first the wind whipped up wave caps; then there were periods of absolute calm, when it was almost impossible to distinguish the water from the greyness of the sky. All you could hear was the rhythm of the ship's engines, and the cries of the gulls that flew in our wake for hours, then vanished as evening came. We spent days out of sight of land; at last there was a low, level shore: islands, causeways, a harbour, long wooden buildings, rocks. We anchored close by the entrance to the canal.'

'The canal?'

'The White Sea Canal. Belomor Canal. The canal the convicts built. From the Arctic through to the Baltic, with pick and spade. Nineteen locks with their gates: one hundred thousand workers, ten thousand dead. I had no idea then, beyond hints and whispers; now I know: there was a dead man, a spirit, for every step. They might as well have mixed the concrete for the banks from human ash! There it was, the canal basin, wide before us, gleaming in the light. All was still—a wondrous silence. It was as if no one was living any longer, in that settlement—and that was close, in fact, to truth. In the evening I walked out, alone, to the tip of the northern breakwater: from there you looked back, and saw the town stretched out beneath the thin bands of haze and the looming sky. You saw wide bridge spans, powerlines: there were coastal cutters and transport barges, listing, rusting away; empty loading docks, cantilevers, all motionless. Over everything there was that sense of beauty and desolation you come on at old, decaying industrial sites. So it was all for this, I whispered to myself: all for this, those years of effort: for this, that secret, hidden world of pain. I watched the survey ship making its way into the wind. I followed it until it dipped below the horizon—and even then, for what seemed an age, I could make out the smoke from its funnel rising through the air. It was late, by now, in the progress of the night—and the sun, which had been until then no more than a filmy disc of yellow, dropped down beneath the plume of clouds: it glittered, suddenly; its beams lit up the sea—and at once I realised where the name came from. All I could see was white, a pure, blazing white, white like a fire's heart. I had to turn away my eyes—and as I did so, I could picture myself with complete clarity: what I was, the accents of my being, what would become of me. Of all our kind.'

He paused.

'That's quite an epiphany,' I said.

'The epiphany was this.' His face was stern. He moved his hands in such a way as to suggest things just beyond his reach. 'As I was looking, what was before me had vanished. It melted away. It became whiteness—not waves, and beams of light, and sky. It was the whiteness behind the world. I understood that I was staring into the void at the core of things; that what we see is not the final verdict on what exists. Since that day it has been clear to me there are moments in our lives when the world becomes unstable, when our visual field gives way: things break before us; they burst into fragments, disappear.'

'You're discounting mirages, or haloes in the sky?' I said—not so much mockingly as from embarrassment, so intense had the pitch of his words been, for so long—but this faint note of contestation was enough to break the story's spell.

Haffner had been speaking softly, almost whispering, leaning forward. He smiled at me, then, a betrayed smile: he pulled back from his recitation.

'Go on, Professor Haffner,' I said then: 'Please—take your story through.'

'My friend,' he said: 'My foreign friend. Naturally we know we are mere material for you: we are curiosities, trapped here in a world you journey through, and leave; and every story should have its untold edge—or why would you come back again? But perhaps the truth in this tale is different from what you expect. What I saw then, on the shore of the White Sea so long ago, you might well find elsewhere. There's a whisper of unreality about all our lives. That trembling of the light that was in my eyes: have you never seen that? Never felt a single thing beyond the world? Those shafts of insight I was trying to describe to you—they came to me, after such experiences and disillusionments, only after weeks under strange skies, far from the daily world I knew, at the fringe of the Earth. But I had seen them before. I could have told you a very different story—a story from here—and that is what I was telling you by giving you a tale from far away: only if I had described to you the sights I saw in Dresden, in my boyhood days, when the sky turned white and the world disappeared above me, that would have been enough to break and tear your heart.'

He stood up, and went to the tall windows and opened them. Chill air with the bite of coal dust flowed in.

'Professor,' I said, and stood behind him: 'Forgive me'—but he simply gazed out, and, after some moments, waved a hand, in sweeping fashion, to take in the cityscape.

'Fragments,' he then said: 'Shattered fragments; not just ruins. They also have their fate, their hidden order, their own narratives to tell. And we too.'

He turned, and looked at me, as if trying to see beneath my skin, and gave me a wry, crooked smile. 'I used to have the finest ideas, believe me,' he said, 'about the inner meaning of our life: but my ideas and theories are all gone now. I see us more and more as travellers through the rubble: I look on words as tokens, things we have to pick up to shape some structure in the world.'

'And that's the life we lead? Always in the shadow of a cataclysm?'

'If the world is pulverised, isn't it for us to piece together the broken shards? We have to sift, and search, and gather up. To find the scattered pieces that belong together. To make our way through time, searching constantly, seeking for the echoes that come to us, the parallels; and then, maybe, patterns appear:

a sight, a sound sends us back, or we sense, through some facility, that what we live through will come once more—that we can be lifted from the blur and flow of daily things.'

'Not a very materialist account of man's life,' I said.

'Perhaps not,' replied Haffner, suddenly almost swaying: he held the door frame; the look of a pursued, exhausted fugitive had come over his face.

Before us, at the end of the avenue, the two stone piers of the old Frauenkirche stood out in glow cast by the street lights.

'Do you remember it?' I asked: 'The way it was?'

'Self-evidently I do,' he said. 'It has a different kind of beauty now. A destroyed order is finer than the original. That old stone bell was not only beautiful, and imperial, and grandiose—it was oppressive, too, and vulgar, I would almost like to say; even if it was from a world in harmony, and there was sweetness and charm to it as well.'

'There's always sweetness and charm in the past,' I said, but he made no reply. He turned from the view back into his study, and picked up the pack on the desk again, and held it out.

'You're not a smoker? Want to try? The taste of servitude?'

'You make it sound so tempting. You started with that brand up there, when you were at Belomorsk, on the canal?'

'Later—years later. Those experiences only grew to full significance for me as life went on. I wanted to commemorate what I had seen, and all those forgotten builders of the north: take their spirit into me with every inhaled breath of smoke. I felt my visit to Solovki had shaped me: I even made an attempt to go back there, once, long afterwards, when I had gained some eminence in my chosen field. But something in me baulked at the last moment. I knew it would be the wrong thing to do.'

'Because one should never go back to a place of enlightenment, for fear of disillusion?'

'Because the light of the mind is the strongest of all.'

He produced a cigarette from the pack: gently, caressingly, he smoothed its rough cardboard tip into even shape.

'The design,' he said: 'Doesn't it tell you everything? The curve of the lettering; the blue blaze slicing through the landscape; the schema of towns and rivers, in place of a realistic map: it is the cigarette of ideology—and of mourning.'

He struck a match. I got up to go; but, as I did so, something caught my eye.

'What have you there, on your desk, if I may ask?'

There was a single photo, of a picture, but in black and white, and in a modest frame.

'Surely you know the work,' said Haffner, and he turned it towards me: 'The *Sistine Madonna* of Raphael, that hangs here in Dresden, in the gallery—the most admired painting in the eastern half of Europe!'

I looked down more closely: the photograph was a mass of greys, fading into and competing with each other; the folds in the rich curtain across the top of the image could only just be distinguished; the two cherub angels peering upwards were no more than smudgy dots. The expression on the Virgin's face was hard to read—the large Christ child in her arms was a pallid blank.

'It's difficult to make out,' I said, cautiously: 'Usually, we see her in colour.'

'We scarcely her see at all, the museum is so rarely open now,' Haffner shot back, in tones of bitterness: 'Or if it is, the great paintings are under restoration for years on end. But before: all the time, we went always; and to see her there, in the gallery, was to look on history; it was to be in a succession line of thought. Every master of old Europe took her as the emblem of perfection; she brought everyone to us: Winckelmann, Wagner, Nietzsche—Dostoyevsky above all.'

'And why? What was it he would have seen in her? You'd think he had other concerns: murders, devils, hallucinations, blood.'

'I don't know that those concerns are actually very far from the life stories of the figures in this painting,' said Haffner then: 'But it was something else, for him, at that stage in his writing. He was beyond fears and loves and longings. He was trying to reach one point: it was the point where words fail. Where emotions dissolve—they lose their tone, and their direction; they become just depth. You feel not sorrow, but pure feeling—it's the point where there's nothing we describe. That was what he wanted with her. That's what all true artists want. The moment where ideas and thought vanish, and feelings stay. The great artists looked into her eyes—and they saw there only depth: pity, sorrow, the acceptance of fate. Of course, Dostoyevsky always cared for the work of Raphael: when he went abroad he would study all the masterpieces of painting he had read about; he hunted the great Madonnas down in their galleries—he found them, in Florence, in Rome; he stared at them, each in turn for hours. But this one was his single, chosen image: this one—he gave his love for her

33

to all his darkest heroes; he had his sketched copy of her like an icon above his working desk. Certainly he also knew this was the last of Raphael's completed paintings—and every last work has in it the low murmur of what lies ahead. Her eyes see that: and that was what he looked at in her. Perhaps it's why the Russians felt they had to take possession of the painting, after the war—steal her away.'

'Steal her?'

'Don't you know the story? You don't know much, really, about us, do you? And we think so constantly of western things! It's a story with its own characteristic humour: you would blush to write it in a work of fiction. Picture the scene: the drama's last stage is already unfolding; the Red Army is advancing; its divisions on the front line see the firestorm rising high above the city; but when they enter Dresden, there is nothing left for them to find. Nothing! All the paintings and treasures from the court collection had been gathered up and sent to safety as soon as the course of the conflict was clear, and the great bomber raids had begun striking night after night into the heart of Germany. They were stored away in a tunnel, deep in a sandstone mine, near Pirna, in the Erzgebirge—but it was a humid sanctuary: the works in their racks and storage boxes suffered a dreadful fate. Of course, at the close of the last scene there was a liberation— of a kind: there always is. The new masters were on the trail of art: they found the treasure. They behaved just like Bonaparte in Egypt or Italy—they commandeered everything they could: they carried the Madonna away to Pillnitz, to the castle there; then off on a railway flatcar to Moscow. I have heard the story that they even held a secret exhibition of their spoils, in a closed set of galleries at the Pushkin Museum of Art, and all the dignitaries celebrated their final victory over the cultural antiquities of Europe, and drank vodka and champagne. Then Stalin died; there was the uprising in Berlin: the Madonna was sent back as a gesture of fraternal solidarity—to strengthen the friendship between the Soviet and the German peoples. It was the standard rhetoric—that style of language you certainly know very well.'

Haffner shrugged, as if to indicate a still point where thought could go no further.

'And now,' he said, 'we have come at last, through circling ages, through war and peace, to the present time—and the night is late.'

His manner had suddenly become sombre: he rose. Berenika and I edged along the darkened hallway towards the entrance.

'Indeed, professor,' I said—but his mood was now quite changed: there was no response to this, in word, or look.

We made our goodbyes, which were brief, and formal. He shook hands almost dismissively, ushered us out and closed the apartment door.

Berenika and I walked back through the night, in silence, listening to our footsteps.

'A real eccentric,' I said, a touch hesitantly, after several minutes, as the hotel's ill-lit entrance portico loomed out of the murk: 'And a fine tale.'

'Didn't I tell you it would be,' she said, and gave me an ironic, sidelong smile—the same smile that was often on her lips

35

in the years ahead, when revolution came to Central Europe, and she was the spokesman for the Solidarity movement in Warsaw, and all that had seemed fixed and certain in her world began to change.

'That's an ironic look,' I said: 'You can almost decode it: part resignation, part defiance; part acknowledgement of the way things are, part announcement that they're really something else.'

'But I'm the princess of ironies,' she said: 'Ironies are all we have. We have to play the hand we're dealt.'

And such quick-fire comebacks and one-liners, which she held ready and could deploy with dazzling speed and perfect timing, served her well in her new life: they gained her a degree of prominence, even a kind of brief celebrity. Armed with such weapons she ascended smoothly to the realm of international consultations and diplomatic forums; and I would see her often, at round tables in the first years of European reconstruction, discussing detailed points of economics with an air of vast assurance, her mysterious half-smile flickering constantly—until the cascading of events had led me far away, and time had flowed on with such turbulence that nothing in those countries where I had learned so much seemed familiar any more.

*

Then, one autumnal afternoon, after a lengthy absence from that part of Europe, I found myself in transit in Berlin. Tegel Airport, which was for so long the shining gateway to the West, was nearing the end of its commercial lifespan: its sharp-angled terminal now seemed to my eyes cramped and ill-designed. I was searching the departures board for the connecting flight when I heard a voice call out my name: once, twice. I turned. A woman stood before me. I was plunged into a penumbra of half-recognition: I knew the face, I knew it had been familiar to me once. Then she smiled—a deep, irony-laden smile. It was Berenika, changed: immaculately dressed, radiating authority, a handful of aides deployed at a discreet distance around her.

'And what do you remember most, from those days?' she demanded, almost as soon as the first words had been spoken: 'Tell me. What? Those crowded press conferences, every morning, in the Europejski Hotel's corner suite on the first floor, when history was being made each hour, and we had to laugh at the pace of things, and repeat the headlines because they were so impossible to believe? Do you remember all that? I do—vividly—I can still live through those moments as if they were unfolding inside my head. I can even remember the day the new government was formed: do you? We went together to the national museum, and there was the famous Witkacy exhibition, with all the savage portraits and the notations beside the artist's signature, giving the details of the drugs he'd taken, and I can hear myself arguing with you, and telling you it was the greatest cultural event in the modern history of Central Europe. My God—what could I have been thinking? We've all come a long way since then! And just think: we had no real idea, in those times, what would happen, what our future might be.'

'But don't you also remember that trip we made,' I said: 'To Dresden, maybe a year before the changes came. I'd only just met you: we went to visit a dissident you knew, Haffner—and he told us everything; the course of the story still to come, laid out, as if he had an open book to read from, and the laws of history in his hands.'

Berenika looked unsure, and screwed up her nose, as if at some distant, unpleasant smell.

'Listen,' she said: 'It was the strangeness of the time. Back then, anything a dissident said seemed deep and true.'

'And what about his own story,' I persisted: 'That story he told us, about the north: the whiteness of the sea, the white gleam veiling the world—nothing?'

'I don't dwell on the pre-revolutionary times too much,' she said.

'You don't remember any of that? I do. Even when we went to see him I had the sense of being present at a moment when patterns in the world were becoming clear. And he was very clear: it really was as if he understood that a golden year was coming, when all the regimes would fall, one by one.'

'I know who you mean, now,' she said: 'You mean that Stasi man! He was working for them.'

'What makes you think that? I didn't hear his name mentioned after the Wall came down. Did you check? Did you find out from the files?'

'I didn't need to—it was obvious to me, at once, that night, as soon as he began talking about his Russian years. And if he had the idea there were unstable times ahead, and told us, maybe he knew: maybe he'd already heard about some deep security service plot. The whole saga comes back to me now. He vanished from Dresden as soon as the changes came: his old students couldn't find him; you won't find any trace of him there. No sign of his former presence; no hint; no memory. Besides, he was a fantasist—it was clear at once, and you didn't seem that taken with him at the time.'

'Perhaps not—but often one doesn't grasp what matters when it first comes. That night's still very present for me: that entire trip. I've thought about him, and the things he had to say.'

'What kind of things?'

Berenika had been joined by a handsome individual, wearing a cashmere coat of great elegance, who now turned his head attentively, cocked it slightly to one side, and adopted a pleasant, neutral air.

'Not so much the politics,' I said: 'More the ideas that seemed so important to him, about the paths we have to take in life. The way everyone has to find their own order from the rubble. How time's deep current flows, on rare occasions, close to the surface of events—just as it did then; how places give off echoes of other places; how there are secret affinities waiting for us, strewn all through the world...'

I tailed off. Berenika let the silence hang an instant, and stared at me with something like triumph.

'My husband,' she then said: 'Klaus-Emil: he has responsibility for economic progress in the East—among other things'—and with that majestic formulation, she bestowed on me a brief smile that seemed to mirror all life's richest ambiguities, and swept on her way.

*

Some days after this encounter, its after-echoes still at the forefront of my mind, I was driving south on the autobahn from Berlin, headed for Ostrava, when a turn-off sign for Dresden loomed ahead: Dresden, which I had not set eyes on since the Wall came down; Dresden, which had been rebuilt and refashioned in its old image during the intervening years. I was alone for the journey, and in that space of cocooned solitude where even slight decisions take on great weight. Should I turn the wheel, and change my route? Would that be free will; or just another sign that all my actions were conditioned by past events; or would any attempt at free choice prove more deeply the extent of my subjection to circumstance—and what was free thought; what could it ever be, in the mind's crystalline, interconnected realm? The turning rushed towards me: 'World Culture City'—at the last second, I veered right, across the slow lane, almost colliding with a Polish long-distance transport truck.

A side road, thin, straight. Pale landscapes, ploughed fields, wind turbine farms, assembly plants. As I was driving I became conscious of a dullness present in the sky, a greying, a leaching out of colour from the air. An hour passed: the feeling grew in me that I had made a wrong choice, a sentimental choice—then, abruptly, before I could think further, I saw the city, in its valley, spread out, as if in the shelter of a protecting hand: all its buildings, old and new; there were the churches, and the palazzos, and their soft reflections in the curving river. It was Bellotto's view—a view that I had never seen, for at its centre was the stone bell of the rebuilt Frauenkirche, rising where the ruins had once been. I stared at this spectacle, calmly, as though I was staring at a trick of the light, a play of shadows—something atmospheric, worthy of note—but inside myself I felt time's different levels clash: they ground against each other; they ground hard, as if memory itself was being pulverised, and time's forward movement could come only from what pulp it made of us.

I stopped, and began walking towards the city centre, which was still at some distance. The spires and palaces rose up ahead, but pale, the colour of warm, clean sandstone, where in my memory they were stained a dark brownish-black: with such stray ideas and impressions as these in my head, I navigated through the maze of crowded, unfamiliar streets, and through the museum quarter. At last I found my way to the new gallery of paintings, and spent some while in a systematic, dutiful survey of the lower floors, examining an exhibition on the history of court life in old Dresden, and becoming conscious, as I lingered, of crowds of Russian schoolchildren, laughing, speaking loudly, hurrying through. I followed them: up the grand stairs, through the main galleries full of old masters, to a final room. It was the home of the *Sistine Madonna*—there she was. I gazed up at her. How familiar that figure should have been to me—and yet the Madonna seemed to my eyes to float rather disquietingly upon her cloudy platform, raised high above her painted, saintly worshippers. Her eyes looked out in serene and non-committal fashion. The entire canvas was coated by a thick yellow glaze that damped and masked its colours. I must, at some point, have frowned as I took this in.

'She doesn't please you?' said a voice with a faintly Slavic intonation.

I turned. It belonged to a young man, with long hair, and a soulful expression on his face, wearing a brown corduroy suit and a polka-dot cravat.

'She means a great deal to us,' he went on.

'Us?'

'Russians'—he waved, at that point, at a large class of students who were traipsing out of the gallery where we stood. Suddenly it was quiet in the room. 'Young Russians, of today's generation. We come on pilgrimage to see her; she speaks to us; she fills up our thoughts. I find myself set free a little just by being here. All the hatefulness and self-involvement that grips me in life flies away.'

This was said in an easy, confiding fashion, as though it was the most normal thing in the world to strike up such a conversation, with a stranger, in such a place.

'And why are you telling me this?' I asked.

'Don't be defensive,' he said: 'Don't be like the world outside. Everyone who comes here, to this special little room, in this city in eastern Germany, has come for a reason—because they need to. I came all the way from the province of Tver—perhaps you know it? I came because I had reached a point of stillness, where the shadows were gathering around me. I had dreams with dark figures raising their arms against me. I would wake up every night in black fear. And you?'

'If I were to tell you,' I said, 'that this picture has been in my life for many years, but I have never seen it, would that seem too strange to believe?'

'You can tell me whatever you want,' said he: 'What matters is what you feel, and see, in her. What I see is time's stamp. I see all life tangled up: the past, and the present, and what will come. We're bound together, all of us. Long after my little trials and darknesses have gone, and I am nothing, nothing but the dust, men like me will stand here, and seek their peace in turn.'

'You—and Dostoyevsky!'

'And them all. Every author, every artist, every seeking man.'

'What's your name?' I asked him.

'Alexandrov—Sergei Dimitrievich—and I am at your service, if I can be of any help to you at all.'

'Truthfully?'

'Of course.'

'Then—will you do me a favour, Sergei Dimitrievich?' I went on, and I listened to myself speaking: my voice was low. 'Will you walk with me through Dresden for a while: just to take the sting of time away. Time's stamp is different for me, you see. I know the city. Or I knew it before, I should say. With every step I take I come up against the past: the mind's eye and the eye collide.'

'Do you mean that you were here in Soviet times—in the time before I was born?'

He looked at me, with an air of wonderment on his face, and I wondered, in my turn, that such a creature could have grown, been educated and reach adulthood in so short a space of time, a blink of memory, a quick carousel of days and nights, no more— and this creature could be standing before me, now, offering me words of kind advice.

'It was exactly those times that I was thinking of,' I said: 'The student protests, the rallies and the demonstrations, the days when police with batons patrolled the streets. And before that, too: further back. I can still see the dark buildings, and dark skies, and the people who were here before: I remember what they felt, I hear what they said.'

I continued; he listened; we walked out together, into that greyish light, through the pavilions and the gardens, to the riverfront, and back, our conversation drifting: his childhood, his work, and mine—the coincidences and accidents that go into shaping a life. Then we turned, and headed down a stone-paved street. I glanced up. I realised that I was once more where Haffner's eyrie had been, high above, on the top floor of the concrete-fronted apartment block—but in its place a new building, a recreation of a baroque house, with pillared arcades, and an ornamented façade, and projecting windows now stood, commanding the angle of the street, which was lined with boutiques, and neat market stalls, and was full of passers-by. I veered over: there, beside the entrance, was an elaborate video intercom, and the names of the residents. I looked: I ran my fingers up and down the list.

'You knew this address,' asked Sergei Dimitrievich, watching.

'I used to come here, once.'

'Life must be a succession of ironies for you, when you revisit places like this.'

Before us, the piers and spurs of the great church rose at the street's end: the pale blocks of the new structure glowed; the old stones, deep dark brown, retreated from the eye so much they seemed like gaps.

'You would know the story well,' said my companion: 'How they rebuilt it. Why.'

The campaign began almost immediately after the upheavals of 1989, only a few weeks into the new year, while the reverberations from the collapse of the old regimes were still dying away. A 'Call from Dresden', an appeal signed by a list of citizens with unblemished reputations, went out to the world, seeking support for a scheme to rebuild the ruined church, and rebuild it as a Christian centre of peace—a testimony in stone to faith. Was the ruined church not the cradle of the protest movement that had helped dethrone the dark powers of the past? Had the young people of Dresden not ceaselessly persisted with their lighting of candles, and their placing them amid the fallen stones, as signs of hope—hope that peaceful times and justice would one day return? And something in this high-flown text, issued from the silent, frost-ridden East in deep midwinter, seemed to resonate with the established powers of the German state: the appeal was heard, and disseminated. I was sitting in a conference room in Moscow one morning that same month, together with a colleague of mine, leafing through the western papers; he opened the feuilleton section of the *Frankfurter Allgemeine*; there, beneath a fetching photograph of a Bellotto view of Dresden, was the appeal from Saxony: 'Rebuild the bell of stone', proclaimed the headline, above an article rich in grand abstractions. We both smiled quiet, world-weary smiles, and raised our eyebrows gently. How impossible! My colleague said nothing; he turned the page—but, placed as we were, watching the fine detail of events, too close to them, we had no instinct for history's slow, well-masked patterns.

The appeal circulated, the funds flowed in, debates were held, the scheme took shape. It would be not just a rebuilding of the church, but an archaeological recreation—it would use the first structure's scattered stones: the rubble would be undone;

annihilation would be annihilated. Everything would be as it once was: a sandstone bell, bound together by iron ring beams, would once more set its seal on the cityscape.

As I was recounting this story, we walked through the church, gazing upwards, like all who set foot there, our eyes drawn by the frescoes and the high, receding vault above—and perhaps it was a phenomenon of the dull sky that day, but with each passing second my capacity to resolve the painted surfaces that stretched overhead seemed to weaken; the objects before my eyes faded; the light became an obstacle, more than a transmissive field. No such problems plagued the legions of stone carvers and engineers, the gilders and the carpenters who laboured for a decade to remake what had been in fragments. In October 2005 the church was reconsecrated, before large crowds, on a day of piercing sunshine—and its fame has only grown since; it is the symbol of the city, and the remade nation; it speaks, even now, of realised dreams; it looms in grandeur over the sharp roof eaves of the town.

'What a tale,' said Sergei, as we walked out into the market square. 'A tale of will, and triumph. As you were telling it, I realised that fate can be turned back. It is the proof that disaster can be confronted—it is an example for us.'

'Indeed,' I murmured, listening to him—but why, then, did I feel so insubstantial, as though we two were no more than figures in a painting, tiny figures in a panoramic view, with shadows dwarfing us, and the grey sky stretched above us? Why did I feel so caught, in those moments: so trapped in the vice of time?

46

II

MURATTI AMBASSADOR

LATE IN THE YEAR 1895 the art historian Aby Warburg left Europe, the centre until then of all his studies, and embarked upon a short trip to the United States, where he spent some weeks in New York City, and was present at the grand, dynastic wedding of his brother Paul. But the charms Manhattan held for him soon dissipated: Warburg moved on, extending both the scope and the duration of his travels; he went first to Cambridge, and its Peabody Museum, then to Washington, where he visited the newly established Bureau of American Ethnology. This journey coincided with a point of inflection in Warburg's life. He was twenty-nine years old; he was well advanced in his dissertation on the forms of Florentine art and poetry; he was on the verge of committing himself to his lovely, long-suffering companion, Mary Hertz; he was increasingly aware of the manic tendencies that expressed themselves in both his stray thoughts and the texture of his intellectual endeavours; he was eager, above all, to escape the confines of his being and his background: it was his dream to expand his grasp of man's symbolic language—the language he saw inscribed in the artworks of the Renaissance, and which he now began to pursue and seek to read in a new continent.

In later years, Warburg pondered what lay behind this decision, and came to incisive conclusions, which he set out, in a private sketch note, in words of striking violence. Outwardly, his reasoning was clear enough: he was repelled by the emptiness of the civilisation of eastern America. He attempted to flee towards natural objects and science, and it was this impulse that led him to the bureau in the Smithsonian Institution, the 'brain and conscience' of the new world in which he found himself. There he encountered pioneers in research on indigenous peoples: they were men of encyclopaedic learning; they opened his eyes to the universal significance of prehistoric and 'savage' America. 'So much so,' remembered Warburg, with his customary self-capturing precision, 'that I resolved to visit Western America—both as a modern creation and in its Hispano-Indian substrata.' This desire for romantic, indistinct horizons fused in him with a longing for ordeals and 'manly' tests—for shame was already with Warburg, and it would attend him all his life: shame at his own delicacy and frailty, a dark shame whose shadows he countered in his every sentence with the sinuous probe and thrust of unfolding, illuminating words. But words were precisely the problem: they were the limits; they were the chains—one had to see through them; one had to bend and break them and recast them to escape their mesh—they constrained thoughts; they fell far short of the realm of form. And it was this awareness that drove him forward, with a wild, urgent energy—it provoked him to his constant stabs at revolution in the world of ideas: for he had developed, by this stage in his researches, a 'downright disgust' with the established system of art history: the tranquil, formal contemplation of images was nothing any more to him; he wanted action, life, the blood of life.

Indeed, his chosen subject now seemed in his eyes so vapid, such a 'sterile trafficking in words', that on his return to Berlin the following year he tried briefly to go back to his first field of study, medicine—and life would, in its bitter, twisting fashion, in due course, satisfy this longing for deeper acquaintance with the domain of treatment and the healing arts. Why were things so? Why was he so? He would cast his thoughts back constantly through the record of his experiences, as though peering into the lines of some blurred manuscript. How much he knew of himself, and his mind's workings, and how little that knowledge helped or saved him! He felt himself in those days urgently pulled westwards, west—to where the Indians were, to where the world's well-buried symbols would come to life—and doubtless much in that attraction stemmed from an episode in his childhood, his first encounter with Indian landscapes, which had come about in strained circumstances.

The scene was imprinted on him: he saw it in pictures and in deep mood washes that swept through him once more as he gazed back. When Warburg was only six years old, his beloved mother had fallen deathly ill during a family holiday in the Alpine resort of Ischl, at the heart of the Salzkammergut. In her weakness, she seemed to him then both pitiful and uncanny. He sensed her illness 'like a frightened animal': it was on her; he could smell it. In silence he watched as she was carried in her litter to the shrine with twin cupolas on the flank of the Kalvarienberg, high above the town. They all made the pilgrimage: and there he saw for the first time with his own eyes scenes from the passion of Christ, 'whose tragic and naked power' he mutely sensed. He remembered how the children had been obliged to abandon her and return home at the worst moment of her sickness: they were driven away in a mail carriage, drawn by a red postilion. Before their departure, they were taken to visit the patient. An atmosphere of inner despair crept over Warburg: it reached its climax when their grandfather urged them to pray. Pray? To which God? Dutifully, they sat down on some trunks with their Jewish prayer books and, bent over them, muttered out something.

During that holiday, which seemed to stretch out for an eternal length, Warburg was only able to free himself from his surrounds by reading: there was a lending library at Ischl, on the esplanade that faced the lake; it was full of Indian romances, the Leatherstocking Tales of James Fenimore Cooper, which were hugely popular throughout the German-speaking world in those days. He devoured 'entire piles' of these novels; he steeped himself in the highly coloured landscape of the frontier—and when at last he reached the American west, he looked round for traces of that world that had so held and consoled him; but it had vanished. Terrifying battles between the Apache and the invading armies over the preceding decades had resulted in a vast destruction. After some years, as he soon discovered, the Apache survivors had been deported to the regions along the borderline with Canada, and transferred to 'those human zoos called Indian reservations'.

*

It was through the library of the Smithsonian that Warburg found his way in: an image, and a book, opened the door. He was studying the pages of a newly published Swedish monograph, written by a young archaeologist named Gustaf Nordenskiöld. The text described in detail the Mesa Verde region of northern Colorado, where 'the remains of the enigmatic cliff dwellings are found'—and a particular photograph in the volume caught Warburg's eye: a wide view, showing the ruins of a Pueblo village, its half-crumbled towers shadowed by a cliff-face overhang.

Like many photos of the era, when the art of deliberate pictorial composition was still predominant in camerawork, the printed image, spread as it is across two pages of the folio, has a haunting quality: it seems to invite one in; it demands prolonged, reflective scrutiny; it leads the eye through the maze of tumbled bricks in multiple directions, but always to the dark, receding shadows of the engulfing mountain wall. For Warburg, it was a summons. He absorbed the image: he would make the voyage to that landscape, and see that scene. He learned all he could about Nordenskiöld, who had been out in the field only four years previously. In winter there were great difficulties in visiting the cliff dwellings—but this simply attracted Warburg: it was something to be overcome.

He set out by rail for Denver, armed with brief, fulsome letters of recommendation, determined to follow his precursor's path step by step, and by the beginning of December he was deep in the abandoned landscape of the Anasazi, surrounded by remote, inaccessible sites. Finding no guide to these prehistoric fortresses, he made his way south to the centre of the Pueblo region, where the boundaries of the states of Utah, Colorado, Arizona and New Mexico meet, and took up lodgings at the Palace Hotel in Santa Fe. From this base camp he plunged deep into the Indian landscape; he visited a string of pueblos, stretching as far as distant Albuquerque to the south.

In a letter to his family he described his experiences, and his sense of the country: the land was dotted with the outposts of vanished civilisations, but also by the homes of the Pueblo Indians of the present day, who lived in little settlements about the town, and on a more substantial reservation further to the west. What, though, was the connection between the ruins and the Indians? To establish that was Warburg's 'true task' in investigating the primal history of America—and it was a task that was vital, for his own conception of the world as much as for the knowledge he might gain. 'I do not believe I am wrong,' he wrote, 'to consider that gaining a vivid representation of the life and art of a primitive people is a valuable corrective to the study of any art.' In truth, these distinctions were dissolving in Warburg's mind: all his categories were unstable, and this flux served, in turn, to stimulate the scaffold of elaborate schemas and systems for classifying cultures that he was devising in his transit through the west.

On the tenth of January, 1896, in his room at the Palace, Warburg received a visit from two Indians: they were Cleo Jurino, the priest-painter at the nearby Cochiti sanctuary, and his son Anacleto. Father and son executed a set of drawings, using coloured pencils: depictions of their view of the universe. Totemic figures and the potent forces of nature were ordered in those images: they sank deep into Warburg's being. He was careful to take Jurino's photograph as a record of the event, and the image survives: the Indian priest is handsome; his face is open; it has a gentle candour. Behind him are the horse-drawn open carriages and shanty houses of the township, and the surrounding rangeline, beneath a blurred and sombre sky.

This meeting spurred Warburg to a height of field research and frenzied speculation. Jurino had drawn for him the lightning-bolt snake, the celestial serpent, which brings rain to the parched desert, and forms the central axis of the Pueblo fertility cult. The snake, with its flickering tongue, moved between the heavens and the step-gabled house of the world: what was the creature but a messenger of things to come, a guarantor of life, an emblem of time's sinuous, rhythmic path?

Warburg's understanding of his travels in the desert was changed by this meeting: it is hard not to feel that the encounter with Jurino was the key to his life's course and the weavings of his mind in later years. He set out directly afterwards, together with the Catholic priest Pere Juillard, on an inspection tour to the Indian hill settlement of Acoma: 'We travelled through this gorse-strewn wilderness for about six hours, until we could see the village emerging from the sea of rock, like a Heligoland in a sea of sand'—so wrote Warburg, long afterwards, fusing this experience with his memory of the windswept cliff-island of the North Sea where he walked as a child. Immediately on entering the sanctuary Warburg understood that the heart of the Indian cult had been infiltrated into the Christian rite; the church wall of Acoma was covered in pagan symbols: snakes, lightning signs; and there was the stylised world-house, with its stepped gable— the ladder by which one might ascend to the stars. As his eyes adjusted to the dark of the church interior, and the rhythm of the service bore in on him, he even made out the fork-tongued lightning images Jurino and his son had drawn. Theory, at this point, came rushing in: surely these emblems were embodiments of knowledge; surely the mind, here, was depicting itself: the steps even spoke of advances, progress, evolution—the forward march of humanity. It was clear. Man who no longer moves on four limbs can hold his head aloft; standing upright is thus the human act par excellence, the striving of the earthbound towards heaven—and this notion propels Warburg to an unhinging discovery, one that whispers like a secret in his work. Light draws man: but there is a light beyond the light, there is code beyond all codes—the world of the senses, the wide world that exceeds us will simply not submit. Its glare annihilates: 'contemplation of the sky is the grace and curse of humanity.'

As if torn apart by realisations of this nature, Warburg fled the desert: he made his way to California; he dreamed of crossing the Pacific, and pursuing his investigations in Japan—but by the end of March he was back in Arizona, in quest of deeper traces of the pagan past. Years later, in his recreation of his western travels, Warburg sees himself as journeying not just through topography but through history: from the Catholic churches, where hybrid religious rituals were enacted, to the surviving dance sites of the Pueblo—and on, further, beyond the borderline of the Atchison,

Topeka and Santa Fe railroad, into the territory of the Hopi, where the dances were still performed not just as mementoes of lost time, but with active intent. And what journey could make sense without an arc, a looming endpoint in its narrative?

Even at the beginning of his quest, Warburg knew he was in search of a goal that would escape him all his life: self-release. He had spoken, in Washington, just before his departure, to Frank Hamilton Cushing, the pioneering and veteran explorer of the Indian psyche. Cushing, he felt, was filled with grace and splendour, as if the attributes of the men and women he had studied had transferred themselves to him. 'I found his insights personally overwhelming,' remembered Warburg: 'This pockmarked man with sparse reddish hair and of inscrutable age, smoking a cigarette.' And what were those insights? One came first: animals had a special gift, which the Indians recognised. Man could only perform what the animal actually is, and is wholly. Man's mind and words are what help to make him incomplete.

As the discussion advanced, it seemed to Warburg almost an initiation: as he sat in that office at the bureau, he realised he was being told the secrets of man's will to leave his own awareness, to change himself into the form of animals. This would be a running theme, all through the years ahead, of Warburg's researches in the depths of art—and it was already present in his imaginings: he spoke to birds, and to insects; they were signs and messengers for him; beings in the natural world were sincere, and true; they held beliefs, and were free from the dreadful weight of knowledge.

Such ideas had long been with Warburg when he travelled onwards from the railway halt at Holbrook, in a light-wheeled carriage, crossing desert sands during a journey of two days towards the Black Mesa foothills, driven by Frank Allen, his Mormon guide. 'We experienced a very strong sand-storm, which completely obliterated the wagon tracks—the only navigational aid in this roadless steppe.' They made it through—Warburg encountered another in the strange cast of helper figures who punctuated his progress through the Pueblo landscape: 'Mr Keam, a most hospitable Irishman'. From Keams Canyon he could at last reach with ease the three remaining Indian villages where old beliefs, untrammelled, held sway.

At this point in Warburg's attempt to recapture his experiences, though, for all the clarity of the event sequence, words begin to fail. Images take over: the photographs he preserved from his visit to the west are spare, and the austerity is deliberate. Warburg was an image man, for all the force and beauty of his analytic prose: he thrilled to images; his life was poured out worshipping them and deciphering them. Those he made in the desert bore the stamp of his character. They differ greatly from the pictures in the ethnographic surveys of the time, which are detailed, and aim at an objective clarity. Warburg's photos are hazy, impressionistic, fiercely over-exposed: they are emblems, as much as records.

He arrived first at 'the remarkable village of Walpi', perched upon a rock crest, strangely resembling a Tuscan hill town, its step-roofed houses rising 'in stone masses like towers' from the rock. He climbed the narrow pathway between the walls. The view was of nothing: the blazing shimmer of the sky. There was the mesa's edge, and a woman, walking; ladders up to raised first-storey doorways; goats, wandering here and there; stillness. He saw 'the desolation and the severity of this rock and its houses, as they project themselves into the world'. Much like neighbouring Oraibi, where at last he was able to observe the Kachina, the dance ceremony of the growing corn, and even to spend an evening in the cultic temple underground—he watched the young men there, painting their masks for the coming day: green and red, crossed by a white stripe and white dots: raindrops; while the patterns on their helmets showed the heavens and the sources of rain, as did the painted decorations on the bodies of the dancers, and the red-dyed horsehair fringings and the feather ornaments that went snaking round their costumes.

The photos Warburg preserved of the rite are rich in texture, and in the sense of motion they convey: light blurs, but the blur is fixed, rather than bleached away; the images are at the scale of man, not nature, but the bodies of the dancers are not caught neatly in frame; it is the pattern and the play of elements in the composition that are all. Dance allows the imprisoned self to break its bonds—and there is even an image that shows Warburg himself in the attempt. He stands, in his morning coat and tie, wearing a large mask from the Kachina dance: much of his face is shaded by the painted helmet and its leafy fringe, but his eyes, dark-circled, open in a look of amazed vigilance, stare out; behind him, the desert, out of focus, stretches away. Transformation was the order of the rite, and of his visit. At last he was at Oraibi, which scores of books and articles had celebrated: he was at the heart of the Pueblo region. It was here that man's longing for unity with nature through the animal world was at its height.

It was in Oraibi that the dance of the snake handlers survived 'in an intense expressive effort', and could be witnessed in its unadulterated form. Each August, when rain was essential to preserve the crop, the redemptive lightning storms were invoked by dance sequences, nine days in their duration.

Warburg was not on the mesa in August, and he was far too restless a spirit to bide his time, but, in a manner entirely characteristic of him and his style of thought, when it became necessary to draw together his impressions he pressed his narrative far beyond the point where the track of his own experience failed. He writes this section with immediacy: we have his notes; they race across the page. He relies on photographs by others, and old field descriptions, but he is very clear: he sees; he sees how the rattlesnakes and the dancers become one; the dances serve to join their beings; it is the mystery made visible. These events are more patent to him than what he has seen though his own eyes: and this pattern, as he knows well, is typical for him, a temptation, as for all who live beneath the sun—how hard a task it is to be present to oneself, to accept the day's blessings, and not be blown through time, backwards and forwards by the dark horses of the mind. Now Warburg writes the magic down, in sinuous, subtle words: he is with the priests, he is with the animals; the entire ritual, for the snakes, is a 'forced entreaty', captive as they are, caught as soon as the storms are imminent, tended to by clan chiefs in a range of rituals. For days on end, they are purified, as if they themselves are initiates; they are held underground, in a dark temple; they are washed in water, then thrown onto sand paintings on the temple floor that depict lightning serpents, and clouds from which issue lightning bolts: at last, a ceremony unfolds in the open air at the summit of the citadel. A group of dancers approaches the serpent tree, festooned with rattlesnakes: the high priest pulls a snake down from the branches; a second Indian, wearing a fox skin, places the snake's neck in his mouth and holds it there; a third companion distracts the creature by waving a feathered stick. The dance is swift; it is done to the sound of rattles—then, abruptly, the dancers rush out at lightning speed to the surrounding plains; the snakes are freed; they disappear; the rain comes.

For years Warburg turned these rituals over in his mind: he had visited a world where man's first beliefs could still be seen, and grasped—and he felt the resonances: it was a religion of danger, plea and intercession: this was the serpent's part, to speak for man: 'If the rain does not appear in August, the plants wither in the otherwise fertile, alkaline soil.' How could he not recall the prayers of his childhood, the retold pattern of mirage and drought they sought to break, all the Old Testament's familiar anguish: the urgent distress in the desert that only the rain god in his remote grace could alleviate?

*

These scenes concluded, Warburg, in a swift displacement, left the west, and America, returned to Europe, married, moved to Florence and embarked on the series of investigations into art history that secured his academic name. The discoveries of his journey through the Pueblo settlements played no part in his writings of those years. He felt the fierce press of change about him: aeroplanes, the electric telegraph, cars, speed, haste. The shadow of war hung over his world of émigrés and exiles: it can be felt in the extended studies he prepared then, as his children were growing, and the little circle of modernists around him in Florence was contracting. Each of those essays seem to be exclusively devoted to questions of art and the history of culture—but each is in truth a self-portrait, and a sketch of the time, shot through with premonitions of what lay close ahead.

Warburg had an unusual way of writing, well suited to this slow infiltration of mood and tone from outside in. He wrote constantly, and with the greatest difficulty. His archive consists of endless drafts and sketches, fragments repeated over and over with minute variations. Enrst Gombrich, his biographer, an art historian as celebrated in his day as Warburg himself, describes this method in a book, now little known, that is itself a grand Renaissance portrait: man, time and culture—a work quite in the spirit of its original, thought and feeling in perfect step. As his biographer describes, Warburg's way of making up the world was kaleidoscopic: he shook and rearranged the elements before him one by one: he would take up a theme, dart off like a butterfly on the wing, collect a fragment, then come looping back. It was his habit to bring together photographic images from far and wide and build them into collages, the better to isolate and trace motifs and enduring patterns as they evolved in time: 'This dissatisfaction, this need to reshuffle and rearrange the elements of the picture had an almost paralysing effect'—so Gombrich—'The picture refused to set.'

War broke out. It was the Great War: its scale was soon plain. Warburg recorded events; he kept a diary of dark entries; he collected news cuttings; he was sleepless; he had to know the course of things. He was certain that the old world of form and grace was on the way to being lost. He wanted to involve himself: he set up and edited a short-lived publication, the *Rivista*, to advance the German cause in Italy. As the conflict extended, his health became precarious. It was in those years that he drafted the most disquieting and most beautiful of all his studies, *Pagan-Antique Prophecy in Words and Images in the Age of Luther*, which he first presented as lectures in the autumn of 1917, on a series of days when thousands of soldiers were dying on both the Eastern and the Western fronts. His chief focus was Dürer's engraving *Melencolia*, which he interprets as a depiction of the conflict between superstition and enlightenment in the soul of man: it is a constant battle; there is never space for peace; the demons have been fought back, but the seated, reflective figure of Melencolia still fears the onrush of darkness—and the power of fear destroys the realm of reason and reflection. Detailed examination of an ancient printed image gives way: there is a strong kinship between Warburg and his subject. 'We feel,' says Gombrich, 'that for him, too, victory is not yet. He, too, is crowned not with laurel but with nightshade, the remedy against the influence of Saturn.'

The war's outcome, and the defeat and breakdown of Germany, left Warburg prostrate. The chains of order in his mind were now quite rearranged: he saw delusion's gleaming spider web. Late in 1918, a few days after the abdication of Kaiser Wilhelm II, he suffered a definitive collapse. He seized a pistol, and rushed through the house in search of his wife and children, whom he wished to shoot, so as to prevent them from falling into the hands of enemy soldiers and being murdered in dark prison camps. He was restrained, and swiftly transported to a private clinic in his home town of Hamburg. For three years he was held there, sedated, until it was decided that the best place for him would be the famous Heilanstalt Bellevue, the sanatorium in Kreuzlingen, on the Bodensee. Here he came under the care of Ludwig Binswanger, a pioneer of psychoanalytic treatment, and a nuanced follower of Sigmund Freud.

At Bellevue, Warburg was heavily sedated with opium, and placed under a close observation regime. The Binswanger archives record the state of his mind, and his capacity to recall and describe with exactitude the events of the recent past: 'He practices a cult with the moths and butterflies that fly into his room at night. He speaks to them for hours. He calls them his little soul-animals, and tells them about his suffering. He recounts the outbreak of his illness to a moth'—and this narrative, rather disturbingly, is given in full, as if a stenographer had been concealed, somehow, close by all through the night, and had been present as Warburg poured out his heart—the giving over of these confidences was natural for him; the butterfly had always been the emblem of dancing, escaping perfection in his eyes.

'On November 18, 1918,' said Warburg, 'I became very afraid for my family. So I took out a pistol and I wanted to kill myself and my family. You know, it's because Bolshevism was coming. Then my daughter Detta said to me, But, Father, what are you doing? Then my wife struggled with me and tried to take the weapon away from me. And then Frede, my younger daughter, called Max and Alice, my brother and his wife. They came immediately with the car and brought Senator Petersen and Dr Franke with them. Petersen said to me, Warburg, I have never asked anything from you. Now I am asking you please to come to the clinic with me, for you are ill.'

This marriage of awareness and fantasy drew forth a detailed diagnosis from Binswanger. He greatly admired his patient, and lamented both Warburg's condition and his prospects. In a letter to Freud, he sketched out his opinion. Even in childhood, he wrote, 'Professor V' had displayed tell-tale signs of anxiety and obsession; in adulthood there were always fears and delusions in him, which had harmed his literary productivity; his condition in the asylum was subject to extreme fluctuations. 'He has been placed in the locked ward, but in the afternoon he is usually calm enough so that he can receive visitors, have tea with us, go out on excursions.'

Indeed, Warburg's formal logical capacities seemed intact; he was interested in everything; he possessed excellent judgement concerning people and the outside world, and still had full control of his remarkable memory—but fears and defensive manoeuvres were the pattern of his mind. Binswanger did not believe, in short, that Warburg would ever be able to resume the scientific activities that had been the core of his life before the acute psychosis struck. 'Have you read his Luther? It is a terrible pity that he will most likely never be able to draw from his enormous treasure of learning or from his immense library.'

And so years passed, with Warburg in his quarters, speaking to the moths and butterflies, his mind enchained by opium, his dream world full of snakes.

Snakes—their species and their habits, their symbolic resonances and associations—have a hold on a good number of the high-relief figures one meets on life's winding course, and the goal and logic of that journey seem at once more mysterious and decidedly more serpentine with each fresh twist and corrective turn. I see my friend John Dawe, the tall, sardonic park ranger who guided, for many years, the wetland management systems in place across Kakadu. His bearing was much like that of a file snake at rest amid camouflaging branches: watchful, inward, yet benign, full of a primordial innocence. Abrupt enthusiasms would sweep him up repeatedly: he developed a fierce obsession for the late-model Jeep Wrangler, and subjected the vehicle in all its variants to extreme field tests in the jungles and paperbark swamps that stretch from the Mary River wetlands back to Humpty Doo. He threw himself into the task of breeding pig-nosed turtles in captivity; he built a freshwater lake system on his property so large its outline could be clearly seen on satellite photographs—but none of these passing crazes could rival his love of snakes, which was already full-fledged during his childhood in the sparse backblocks of Naracoorte.

Reptiles, in that country, had to be searched for: they were precious rarities. Dawe escaped to regions of richer supply, and became a keeper—first at zoos, in Adelaide and in Melbourne, then at the Australian Reptile Park in Gosford—but despite this decade-long pattern of persistent snake handling, his charges never turned on him: the strange state of harmony that existed between the Pueblo dancers and their totemic rattlesnakes mantled him also; he tended and ministered to vipers, mambas and cobras; on one occasion a bushmaster wrapped its fangs around his index finger, paused, gazed up and withdrew tenderly, without injecting any of its venom into the puncture wounds left on his skin.

Such experiences, much discussed, ensured his fame in the serpent world, and it was only a matter of time before my enquiring colleague Kelvin Cantrill appeared to pay homage and seek instruction at Dawe's property on Darwin's rural edge. What were the possibilities of locating obscure pythons in the savannah country of the North? The consultation began: their friendship blossomed, in the odd, glassy way that snake ties grow—they strengthen into a kind of brotherhood of shared affections, much like the feelings that Tolstoy pictures binding Karenin and Vronsky beside Anna's sickbed: a species of love that vanquishes all rivalry and sense of self. Cantrill was a traveller in quest of pure emotions of this kind: he had pursued them; it was his life's task to describe them. He was a fluent writer: his prose ran richly to metaphor, metaphor piled on metaphor, until it became hard to keep track of the thread of his initial intentions—and the theme of the work as well as its structure was often serpentine, so that a simple-seeming essay on volcanoes, or a treatment of the evolution of stringed instruments, would offer the unsuspecting reader an excursus that touched on various aspects of snake behaviour and taxonomy before returning to the main flow of the narrative. This focus was near constant, in person as much as in written word.

'Elapid Tourism,' Cantrill might well exclaim in greeting, when we met up in some remote roadhouse in the Gulf Country, or made a rendezvous on the straight, oppressive highways of the

Barkly Tableland: 'That's the future for the Northern Territory—a tourism based wholly on the lure of venomous snakes.'

'But aren't they hard to see and find?'

'Of course—that's the whole point!' And then it would be the moment for him to sketch again his beatific vision of the Australian tropics and the monsoonal country, flush with international visitors on reptile safari convoys, travelling deep into the snake-rich rangelands round the Simpson and Great Sandy deserts. Year in, year out, they would come: 'And every visitor would have a special snake passport, with all the details of the most elusive species, and those places where you would have a reasonable chance of spotting them.'

'And you could even have dedicated pages,' I would say, lifted up by his excitement: 'Something like the visa pages on a standard passport, divided up, and each rare snake would imprint its fang marks on the right page in the passport as identifying proof of the encounter.'

'Absolutely. What a wonderful idea! And that level of contact would lead inevitably to a rise in incidents of snakebite, and antivenene sales, so it would improve our understanding of toxicology and increase our expertise in emergency medicine as well: a perfect economic circle!'

Such was Cantrill. His happiest hours were spent at his dark home in Seaforth, on Sydney's North Shore, peering into his elaborate terrarium, and whispering loving words to his indifferent-seeming diamond pythons, whose elegance he would seek constantly to recapture in word portraits—portraits that became baroque, self-sustaining cathedrals of wild imagery and speculative thought. Their tone and style were somehow familiar to me, and for some months I puzzled over this, as I made my way through the lengthy emails Cantrill liked to send off in the small hours of the night, each file containing whole cascades of these majestic compositions, works of beauty and allusive splendour so elaborate they resembled nothing so much as the growth of corals on some tranquil, sun-dappled reef.

And then I remembered: I had come across just such patterns of snake rhetoric before, long before, when I worked in the Americas, and became caught up with the rattlesnake researches of José Díaz Bolio, the celebrated historian and poet of the Yucatán Peninsula. We corresponded for several months, and his letters, handwritten, in the most courtly style, gained in intensity and flourish with each exchange. It seemed essential, in the end, to pay a visit. I took the flight down to Mérida, and began a series of trips to the Mayan snake-cult sites of the inland, and immersed myself in Díaz Bolio's vast outpouring of books and pamphlets: they contained his interpretations of the art and symbolism of the temple complexes, his calendric studies, his ideas about the snake as the axis of the region's enduring traditions—and these works, printed on flimsy paper, available only in the back rooms of obscure provincial bookshops, seemed like hidden, fragmentary texts of revelation. In fact they were mere apéritifs. Díaz Bolio was still working on the definitive statement of his philosophy when at last we came face to face.

It was late in the afternoon of a stifling summer day. At the appointed hour, I rang the bell at the gate of his palazzo. Díaz Bolio received me in a lovely tree-shaded garden. He was wearing a linen suit of fine cut. He shook hands. For a few seconds, he endeavoured to preserve a formality of manner—then the front broke.

'To the study,' he cried: 'At once!'

It was a large room, warm, sun-drenched, with antique maps and deep-shadowed photographs of temple friezes displayed above the bookcases: sheafs of manuscripts and notes were piled on adjoining desks. Behind them, wide-eyed, staring rattlesnakes of various sizes and colorations floated, coiled up in large preserving jars. He described each one: its characteristics, anatomical and mythological. We delved into the latest theories to come to Díaz Bolio's thoughts. Was it not clear that the cosmos itself, as it was being progressively disclosed by modern astrophysics, had a snake-like quality? Had the gods of creation not revealed this cryptic structure in the first hallucinatory visions that were vouchsafed to the rulers of the Mayan realm?

'It is crotalic thinking,' exclaimed Díaz Bolio, stroking a small statue of a serpent deity perched on a table by his side.

'Crotalic?'

'From the classificatory name of the Mesoamerican rattlesnake,' he said, looking a touch offended. 'Crotalus. But of course you, as an enquirer yourself, will see these connections immediately. I have begun to set them out. Here.'

He handed me a thick typescript: upon the cover there was a stylised tracery of snake scales and feather plumes: *Mi Descubrimiento del Culto Crotalico*, announced the title.

'My last work,' he said: 'My synthesis: I draw my thoughts together; and in so doing, I draw myself.'

I began reading from the first chapter: he listened. Even by Díaz Bolio's own standards, the prose was labyrinthine; it was lush in sound; it took delight in its rhythmic unfurling of clause and paragraph.

'It's almost as if the beauty of the structure is what holds the key,' I said.

'You mean the meaning is there is no meaning? It's only the convolutions? How much I fear those ideas. Throughout my life they have tempted me. But all the ideas in the world are our work: nothing more. We are vain interpreters. The thing remains. The longer I live, the more I succeed in thinking like a serpent, and the more I realise that the enemy of truth is man.'

∗

Convictions of such a kind leave snake people exposed to easy detection, and almost as soon as I met the wildlife photographer Deion Palomor I caught the distinctive signs. It was the early dry season in Darwin, a time when spirits lift, sun returns to the sky, the bright colours of the tropics have not yet taken on their sterile, desiccated midyear hues. I found myself in the heart of town, in Smith Street Mall, a pedestrian stretch that runs past arcades and half-empty office blocks, a commercial wasteland, devoid of grace or elegance—but, in those days, at its eastern end there was a haven, a little sanctuary of vivid life: an unusual studio-gallery had just opened there, Monsoon, the brainchild of the North's artist-photographer Peter Eve, an individual with cold contempt for market tastes. Monsoon's glass display windows were very often veiled, the better to communicate this sharp defiance of the outside world—but from time to time its proprietor would put on view a handful of his own more enigmatic images, in large-scale reproduction: bright-green lily pads, shot close-up from directly above; smoke plumes, unfurling at sunset; a tormented flock of wheeling birds.

I called in. A young man was skulking in a corner of the gallery, shuffling photos, hanging work. It was Palomor.

'What do you think?' he asked, and held up two mounted prints.

He wore khaki field clothes, but with a certain poise. He was thin, but with a sapling's taut energy. He blushed as he asked his question, but held the eye. The prints showed a set of faint, blurred, lozenge-like patterns.

'What are they?'

'Can't you tell? Snakes' scales, of course. The undersides of heads of Pilbara death adders—and some from the Top End, too.'

'How do you take them? Isn't it hard to get them to stay still?'

'The art's in that,' he said: 'All the art. You have to think your way in. The photo's just an afterthought.'

Other people came, and went. I moved on. Some days later our paths crossed once more, and then again. I began working with Palomor, and heard his story. It had a delicacy and charm, not just because of his youth, but because he was engaged in a task of conscious self-fashioning. He was in the North to choose and shape his life. Each day he spent there was a day lived in this pursuit; each choice he made had an end in view. The future he was designing would be redemptive: freedom loomed there—but it had to be won, to be earned, through work, and through the

72

force of capital, for Palomor believed fiercely in the power of rent, and compound interest. He longed to own property, to build, to make himself into a man of substance—and this developmental passion sat somewhat uneasily beside his love for untouched country. Only a few weeks earlier, he had begun working as a nature guide; he was soon dispatched on treks across the North Kimberley and Arnhem Land, and over the months of that long, balmy dry he proved himself to be a bushman of special gifts, a man so much in harmony with the order of the tropics that he could lead parties of strangers for weeks on end through swamp and savannah: he could sense the presence close at hand of sacred sites; he already knew each plant and each tree of the Top End; he understood the instincts of the birds and animals—and all this knowledge had come to him purely through walking, and through constant watching: he was an untutored master in the bush.

I was travelling widely through the central deserts then, on research trips. Often Palomor would ride with me, and those journeys were always times of concord: he would read the landscape as I drove; he saw the changes all around, and caught them in his words—words that mirrored with the greatest exactitude the country's look and feel. So it was something of a surprise, one late afternoon, during a long eastward haul, as we made our way in his old, rusting Troop Carrier back from Warburton Ranges towards the Rawlinsons and Ayers Rock, when he turned to me: 'How self-contained the bush is out here! How Randian!'

'What?'

'Randian—you know, as in Ayn Rand. The writer. You must have heard of her, and her books. *The Fountainhead*, or *Atlas Shrugged*—she's an inspiration to me: I've read everything of hers I can find.'

In front of us, beneath a cloud front, bushfire plumes were rising north of the Great Central Road; the low red curve of the ranges was just becoming visible: there was the Giles Weather Station radome, shining in the late sunlight, far away.

'That's probably the first time anyone's spoken that name in this landscape,' I said.

'You don't think the desert's a Randian environment? Remember: John Galt set up his hideout in the remote American far west. You know the plot, don't you? Hold the world to ransom: men of force and genius take their labour, and withhold it—keep it—for themselves.'

'That was only a story. And I can't imagine a less Randian place than here, in fact.'

'Why? Isn't it a place where you have to make your world? Where nothing is, except what you see: what's to hand?'

But for me, it was a place where what lay beneath the surface was ever present, and all the tension in the landscape was hidden from the eye. A place of secrets, and reticence: where one would seek, rather than knowing, and be fearful of what was there to be found.

'Always an answer!' said Palomor. He shook his head: 'See the turn-off? Let's take it. There, that road—to Wingellina—I'd like to: it's a special road for me. When I used to work at the Rock, before, I turned onto that track once: it was an interesting experience. It was at the time when I had a broken arm in a cast, and I was travelling alone. I made a bet with myself that I wouldn't have a flat: it looked like sandy country all the way—and it was. At exactly the halfway point, one of the back tyres shredded: a hundred kilometres from anywhere—too far to walk; no chance of anyone coming by. I had to get the spare out from underneath the truck, and jack it, and change the wheel one-handed. It took eight hours.'

'Death or life on will power. At least that must have been a fairly Randian kind of experience!'

'My point,' he said, with an air of triumph: 'My point exactly!'

*

Months passed. The seasons shifted. One afternoon Palomor and I arranged to drive out to Fogg Dam on the Adelaide River floodplain, a lush, half-forgotten landscape to the east of Darwin, where grand plans for rice-growing export farms came to nothing, long ago, and the surviving dykes and embankments create a wide, enduring wetland, with a world's-end quality, remote from view. We headed out, well prepared for all eventualities. The aim, of course, was snakes, for the dam structure and its surrounding swamps hold large supplies of dusky rats: frail, unhappy creatures, subject to constant ordeal and suffering, since they form the chief prey of the water python, also endemic to the region, and present in greater concentrations than at any other of its surveyed breeding sites. As a result, Fogg Dam, at certain times of year, resembles nothing so much as a gladiatorial arena, where terrifying pursuits and swift executions are constantly underway; and the struggle's pitch is irresistibly attractive to western science:

all through the build-up months herpetologists, wetland experts and population ecologists throng the near reaches of the dam road as night descends.

We passed the Coolalinga lights: there was that sense of release that comes as Darwin falls away and the carpet of the Top End bush unfolds—all burnt screw palms, yellowed scrub and half-dead stringybarks. Soon we saw the croc farm and the circling kite-hawks high above its feeding pens. We turned onto the Arnhem Highway: past the electricity substation, the lagoons, the mango farming belt. Ahead, the masts of the defence radars were gleaming; a storm front loomed; the wind picked up.

'How wonderful,' I said, 'to be here when the first rains come in from Cooinda and Kakadu.'

'They won't reach as far as here,' said Palomor: 'It's too early; it'll be weeks before the rains. It'll just build up the tension, more and more. You can see everything drooping and panting all around us. Look—the kingfishers can barely hold themselves up straight on the powerlines.'

He veered off the bitumen, sharply. We took a series of turns down a muddy track.

'I thought we'd come in by a back way I found. It must have been an old access road, from the construction time. It's narrow; the crest is just below the water level—it's like driving through the sea, or, when the sun sets, through fire.'

'Good for pictures.'

'That's the thing about photography—you always come away with something—or the ghost of it, depending on your point of view.'

We began to slide: he steered back onto the submerged road.

'Don't look like that—we won't get bogged.'

'That's what you said last time, out at Blackmore.'

'But that was completely different. It was obvious from the very start of the day that we were going to come to grief; we both knew it: it was a kind of sacrificial mission; you have to have one every now and then. Anyway, we got out of it in the end. Look—over there, see—that's the old shooting reserve—and here's the dam basin—from the other side.'

Ibises and herons gazed at us suspiciously as we edged along. We pulled up. It was almost sundown; a haze of rainbow spectrum reached across the sky; the clouds changed colour: bright orange, deep red, pale pink, grey.

'It's like Jurassic Park, here,' said Palomor: 'If you know. There's everything. I was up in a helicopter over the dam the other day: all the animals were flushed—buffalo, dingoes, wild pigs, birds by the thousands; you could see the crocodile families basking on the banks.'

By this point we had reached the viewing platform set at the causeway's end. We climbed its steps; the dam was spread out like a fan before us; the water's surface caught the gleam from the horizon, and quivered in the wind.

'And now?'

'We wait—until the snakes come. And they will. It's an ideal night for them; they like to stretch out on the asphalt of the dam wall road; there are hundreds of them, if you wait long enough. What's that you've got there?'

'*Images from the Region of the Pueblo Indians of North America*,'

I said: 'It's a snake lecture—maybe the best one ever delivered. I'll read a bit of it to you—it might tempt them out.'

He checked the book.

'Aby Warburg. Who was he? I know the name. There was a Warburg Bank.'

'There was—the same family—but this one gave himself to art. He's someone who means a great deal to me: he had a life that stays in the mind. I thought you might like to hear how things seemed to him.'

He leaned back. I set the scene: the trip Warburg took; his reputation and his name; what he longed to find, and what confronted him when he reached those far-off desert citadels. I began. Warburg's gentle opening words seemed to hang in the humid air.

'"If I am to show you images, most of which I photographed myself, from a journey undertaken some twenty-seven years in the past..."'

'You didn't say he was a photographer!'

'A very great one—but nothing was enough for him: he needed every way of getting to the heart of life.'

I went on; darkness gathered; soon we were at Oraibi—we reached the climactic story of the dance: the high priest at the serpent-tree, the dancers taking up the rattlesnakes and holding them in their mouths.

'"Here the dancers and the live animal form a magical unity—and the surprising thing is that the Indians have found in these dance ceremonies a way of handling the most dangerous of all animals, the rattlesnake, so that it can be tamed without violence, so that the creature will participate willingly in ceremonies lasting for days." '

I paused. I tried to sketch the background.

'All this led Warburg into strange terrain. He thought he had come to know what lay at the core of the world; he thought there were secrets in the snake cult: that the snake was lightning, power, that it was the sun and all its fire—he even believed our first religion was devotion to the sun. But there were caves of darkness for him, everywhere, caves to trap us, pits into which we might stumble and fall, and lose ourselves. You can hear it in what he says, can't you?'

'That's the most beautiful book I've ever heard,' said Palomor, and looked up through the murk.

'More beautiful than Ayn Rand?'

'Different! But those Indians back then aren't the only ones who handle snakes. Anyone who follows down this path is looking, like them, of course: looking for something.'

'So the snake's not always just an animal.'

'It's never just an animal,' said Palomor, with great firmness.

We walked the causeway's length. At its midpoint, a scientific party had gathered. Torches flashed; there were gruff voices, wry remarks. We reached them. It was a scene of industry. Trap nets had been spread beside the road: a spotlight was turned on them; moths and insects were fluttering and struggling in their mesh. A pair of mud-stained Troop Carriers drove up slowly, and parked alongside each other: lightning flashed, and lit up the faces of the drivers. They knew Palomor; they nodded gently to him. 'That's Canadian Dave,' he said to me, softly, as we walked on:

'A very serious man. He's been doing his doctorate here for eight years, on tropical snake distribution—but it's hard yards, these days, just getting the data. The cane toads are going through this country, you can hear them, later on in the night: they sound like Honda 300 quad bikes revving up. And that's Gina—from the university—she's studying python mating patterns. I used to dream of being a researcher, once.'

'And what happened?'

His voice became vague.

'When I was growing up, on the Sunshine Coast, I was able to find anything, in the bush. We used to go for holidays to Tin Can Bay. It was quiet, and lovely, and full of reptiles: that was when snakes really took hold of me. I look back, now—I think about that time a lot. I used to dream snakes into being: I would see them in my dreams, and then I would see them, in the day, curled up in the gum-tree branches along the coastal adventure walking strip—or I'd feel them close by when I went to the marina harbour to watch the dolphins coming in. I'd climb up into the range behind the bay, and I could tell what was around me. I could sense them: black snakes, little pythons, sand goannas. It was a strange sensation. I stopped talking about it; no one believed what I was saying; but I knew. It lasted for years—it was as though the snakes were guardians, and they were there to look over you, to watch, to help, to warn. They weren't negative forces: not at all. They were everything around me that was quick, and clear, and true. I used to long for them, to close my eyes to see them. I felt that would stay with me forever.'

'And did it?'

'Later, I remember, at school camps, in the bush, I'd go out secretly, every night, all night, snake hunting—and only come back to sleep in the daytime, as if I was leading a vampire existence. I was very good then at finding the rarest creatures in the hinterland; I was even on the trail of elf skinks; you'd find them by tracking the bush turkeys between their nests: that's how you'd see them—but you'd longed for them so much they looked unreal. And that's when I learned a bitter lesson inside myself.'

We were far down the causeway now: his voice had filled with sorrow, step by step. I let him speak on.

'It was a lesson I hadn't expected. That life will give you what you want. That you will find what you're looking for. You will see beyond the surface. You will. The thing is to deal with it. I had another experience like that, once, in Queensland, before I came north. In fact, it was what decided me on coming here. It was in Chinchilla. I was working for an environmental survey firm. One late afternoon, I was out, alone, and I saw the light, at sunset, coming from the flat west. You know how suddenly in that country a chill comes into the air. You know that outback chill. That vacancy. I knew that I had to get out. I felt darkness all around me in that landscape. I felt what had happened there, without knowing. It was a few months after that I left, and came to the Territory. I'd imagine everyone who comes up here has something in their life like that.'

'And things seem different now?'

'This is a lucky place for me. Unknown tracks. Every time you drive down a back road here you've got an eye out for some lovely billabong you didn't know before: sometimes you get rewarded by the bush, and there's a dingo running beside you for kilometres at a stretch…Quiet! Listen. Do you hear? Do you see?'

In front of us, in the blurry light of refracted stars and cloud glow, on the straight roadway, close by, a knot of shadows was twisting: sinuous, shimmering, in a constant subtle arc of motion.

'Water pythons,' said Palomor: 'There they are!'

'They're not afraid?'

'They like human beings.'

He knelt, and with swift, flowing movements picked up a snake, and then another. 'They have a very pleasant presence. They like being looked at, and admired; they like being picked up, and handled.'

'Just like the rattlesnakes.'

Palomor had wrapped one python round his arm; another coiled itself round his waist, and gazed up at him engagingly, its tongue flicking in and out. It is the image of him I preserve in my thoughts: a tall, slender figure, two snakes entwined around his body, laughing, smiling as lightning cascades from the cloud banks on the horizon, and thunder rolls, far away.

*

The new year came: rain, floods, a flurry of art events. I took Palomor to the opening of the first show of the Darwin season, in the upstairs art space at Parap. We climbed the stairs to the exhibition.

'I heard the artist might be here,' I said over my shoulder. 'He's from Arnhem Land.'

'The artist!' he replied, in a hushed voice, which echoed in the narrow stairwell: 'I don't know I've ever met a real artist!'

In the gallery the familiar crowd had gathered: administrators, curators, the enlightened classes of the North. We navigated our way through the throng. The walls were hung with ochre paintings: small, lustrous squares; their grounds were in dark hues that gave the impression of void, more than surface, and against this darkness a variety of plants and animals had been depicted: bats, sugar gliders, sand palms, lilies—all shown in schematic outline, their edges picked out with such finesse they seemed to float. Palomor gazed at them: he stood with his face pressed close up to the panels, as if he was trying to trace the individual brush marks.

I stepped back. They were unusual works: they lacked the appealing, urgent quality one finds in the bark painting styles of our day; they held themselves back. 'Come and find me,' they said to the viewer: 'I'm not looking for you; you might not even exist for me.' I had paused before a large rendition of a snake-like creature, its flanks surrounded by curved lily pads.

'Strange art, isn't it?' said a voice, and laughed: that was a laugh I knew.

'But you're a veteran,' I said: 'An expert. You must have seen all this before.'

It was Tom Elman, a remote community manager, and a man of literary inclinations and descriptive gifts so well developed that only a desire for obscurity could explain his continued presence in the Top End.

'I was just checking this one out,' he said. 'I'd say it's a file snake, wouldn't you? When we lived at Ramingining we saw them all the time: docile creatures—but very odd; they seem to be completely without an instinct for self-protection. Certainly they got eaten quite a lot: the local women were always heading off into the Arafura wetlands to get bush tucker, and their haul always included file snakes.'

'They ate them?' said Palomor, in horror.

'All the time. I remember late one afternoon the ladies came back from one of their trips, and deposited their catch at the women's centre for cooking the next day. My wife had a lot to do with snakes in that country: whip snakes seemed to be particularly attracted to her, mangrove snakes as well. The locals were very conscious of that affinity—in fact, they came to think of her as a semi-formal snake custodian: so she was put in charge of a large plastic rubbish bin full of the file snakes to lock up and keep safe overnight. Next morning, she came in: of course the lid was off, and there were no snakes to be seen. How many snakes were there, she asked. Mmm—maybe twelve, they thought. But even after the most extensive search of the women's centre and its vicinity she only managed to find eleven, hiding under fridges and freezers, behind cupboards, under the sink, everywhere. She could tell from the dubious looks from the ladies there were more—they scoured the whole area again, but it wasn't until lunchtime that they found another four, large ones, in a bad temper, all hiding in the washing machines in the laundromat.'

'Wild,' said Palomor.

'Ramingining had its share of dangerous snakes as well. King browns, taipans: the taipans were always out at the barge landing road at night, and it wasn't a great idea to get out of your car; they were quite aggressive. And there were green tree snakes, too; they came sliding on to the front verandah of our house to eat our beloved frogs. It was a harsh place: everything you loved was always dying in front of you.'

I slipped away. There was Dyson—the man behind the show.

'What are you doing with that dude?' he said, suspiciously, pointing at Palomor.

'Why? Some problem?'

'He's a lunatic. He came out to our bush camp with some walkers not so long ago; and he was going round at night with a torch picking up death adders and bringing them back in to photograph beside the fire: you'd have thought they were fashion models or something.'

I explained. He frowned and glowered for a while, then brightened.

'Come and meet the artist,' he said. 'You wouldn't know him: Don Nakadilinj Namundja.'

'Namundja?'

He nodded, with a look of pride: it was a great name in the art circles of the North.

'Any relation to the famous Namundjas—to Samuel? To Bob?'

'Full brother—it's a creative dynasty. And just look at the way he paints.'

We were back with the others now, in front of the twining snake.

'What is it?' asked Palomor. 'What species?'

'You ought to know,' said Dyson: 'Snake man!'

'Don't hold back,' I said.

'The locals call it Nawaran, in the various dialects of Kunwinjku,' Dyson then said, in a milder voice, becoming slightly professorial: 'But what is it in fact? There are ambiguities. Western experts might well disagree. You can see the head is broad, yet delicate: and that tells us we have a python on our hands. But is it a children's python, or an Oenpelli?'

'An Oenpelli python,' breathed Palomor: 'How much I'd love to see one of them. How much I'd love to go there—see Oenpelli, and that country—over Cahills Crossing, and up in the plateau where the rock-art sites all are!'

'The odd thing,' Dyson went on, 'is that people in West Arnhem Land use the same word for both snakes—even though to our eyes they look very different. The children's python is minuscule, discreet and mid-grey; your Oenpelli is vast, and iridescent—all the colours of the rainbow—I'd say there's no doubt it was the original Rainbow Serpent.'

'And it's exotic, and beautiful, and rare,' finished Palomor, breaking in.

'Not so rare,' said Dyson: 'You can find them, if you put your mind to it, out in the back country of the plateau. In fact there was one just the other day slithering around the Oenpelli community art centre, looking for mice: it met a dreadful fate.'

Dyson began describing the show: its elements, its themes, how it came about—a twisting tale. He was at his base in Jabiru. There was a call one day from a remote outstation camp he knew well, high in the stone country: a painter had arrived, a traditional man; he needed materials. Dyson flew in. Namundja and he met; they worked together: bark paintings poured out, renditions of bush haunts and totemic creatures. They both felt they were on the verge of something new. After a few weeks of this collaboration, it seemed natural to them to make the long trip out to the Namundja clan estate.

'Mankorlod,' said Dyson. 'The name alone was enough to evoke Eden for me! All the paintings I'd seen of it showed a lush, magic-seeming world. Don hadn't been out there himself for more than thirty years. It was two hundred and fifty kilometres down back tracks. We set off: I could hardly wait. All the conversations we'd had in the months we'd known each other, and all their strange metaphysical overtones: they'd had their effect. I was imagining a place with cool streams, a rich monsoonal rainforest, palms, noisy fruit bats and birds, ringtail possums on the rock ledges, yam vines growing, pandanus, lilies on the sacred waters. How wonderful it would have been!'

We were hanging on his words. He shook his head: 'I suppose, after so many years working in the Top End, I should have known. Expect the unexpected. The tracks petered out almost to nothing. When we finally found the outstation, no one was there. It was dry, and hot. The ground was spiked with charred grasses from an old burn-off. There was a scatter of tin huts, a schoolhouse, a water tank, a repeater tower. No sign of any lush forest or magic spring—no running water. You don't get to see what you dream quite that simply in Arnhem Land.'

A slightly built Aboriginal man with keen eyes, short, greying hair and heavy forehead furrows had joined us.

'The painter,' said Namundja, with an air of great formality: 'Me'—and laughed. He had been circling round the room.

He paused. He turned to Palomor. 'You like the Nawaran?' He reached up one hand, and with the tips of its fingers stroked the python's painted head.

'Very much,' said Palomor.

'Come and see. I'll show you him. At Oenpelli, if you want.'

*

The year just then beginning took its course. For much of it I was caught up, working on long-term projects overseas. Time went by before I came back to the North: the storm season had circled round again. The flight I took in was rough all the way, through thick banks of cloud: we were weaving; the descent began. At last I could see the shining turquoise water, and the silt flows being carried by the harbour tide. There were lightning fires on Cox Peninsula; there were rainbows hanging in the air. All was as it should be on the ground: humid, enervating, hot. Then, in the terminal, I heard a voice call my name, and I caught a sadness in its tone. I turned. It was Dyson, smiling an agonised smile.

'You've heard the news, I suppose, from last month? No? I'm just on my way south again: my flight's not leaving for an hour. I can give you the story, if you've got the time. It's about death.'

'Where better, then,' I said, 'than a departure lounge?'

We found a table at the airport coffee shop; I settled back, and, surrounded by a slowly shifting amalgam of travellers, fretful airline staff and blue-uniformed cleaners, Dyson told his tale. It, too, began with a journey; it began fast, then abruptly the pace slowed: he lingered, he fell into reveries, he retold entire episodes from varied perspectives. It was an art story. There had been an exhibition arranged, long before: a year's end event, in Sydney's

Kings Cross—a show to reveal Don Nakadilinj Namundja's work to the wider world, and highlight the bark paintings of his elder brother, Bob Wanur, who was at that time gravely ill. Things diverged from the set plan early on. Instead of flying in a week before to Darwin, Namundja had gone off south, to the furthest reaches of the Arnhem plateau—to Bulman, his mother's country: he had important duties there.

'You don't know that much about ceremony in Arnhem Land, do you?' said Dyson.

'Nothing.'

'It can be an involved affair: things are never what we might think they should be. Look at Don Nakadilinj, for instance: he comes across as low-key, wouldn't you say? Just an average bush man who lives on outstations: friendly, doesn't say much. But that's not all he is. There's another level.'

Dyson leaned over: 'He's a man of law,' he whispered, but with emphasis: 'He's at the centre of things we don't even know—or we're not supposed to know. He's a different man at the ceremonies: he has knowledge, in all its layers. The anthropologists have told me; they've heard him describing the journey paths of the ancestral beings across the stone country in the finest detail: all that country we just fly over and regard as harsh and trackless and inaccessible—that's his world. He's got no house, but he's always got a roof over his head when he arrives anywhere; he's got no car, but he's always travelling long distances; no wife, but scores of sons, daughters, nieces, nephews from his extended families. To our eyes he might seem simple: in that world, he's a master. A master of suspense, as well. He was still out at the business camp in the bush the day before we were due to go south. He knew exactly what he was doing. He drove all the way back across the plateau, pushed through to Manmoyi outstation, caught a light plane from there to Jabiru and then in to Darwin to catch the Qantas flight. We travelled down together. I was as out of place as him. I hadn't been to Sydney for years: I had no clue about all those tunnels and the dual carriageways they've put in between Mascot and Darlinghurst. How lost we were! It was late when at last we reached the gallery, dark: the paintings were hanging there. They looked like jewels, each one beautifully lit. There was a message waiting for us to ring Injalak Art Centre at Oenpelli. We called. They asked Don to come to the phone—and that's how he heard the news that his brother had died. There he was, on his first visit south, in a strange bleached-white gallery cube, surrounded by the sacred paintings he and Wanur had made. He wept; he tried to sing—a mourning song; he broke down again. I remember that moment, very clearly: it began raining right then, outside; strong rain—it came lashing hard against the windows of the gallery.'

Dyson paused: a handful of Arnhem Landers who had been exploring their way through the airport had caught the sense of his story; they settled quietly in the empty chairs at our table; a couple more stood to one side, also listening, saying nothing, nodding gravely from time to time as he spoke.

'Go on,' I said.

'It's hard to capture things like this. I want to tell you, and I can't. I want to give over every precious detail: I want to tell you how beautiful those days were—and I just have pale memory: not the reality, nothing like. I tried to write about it all, immediately afterwards: I even finished off a piece for the *Jabiru Rag*—you know, the little newspaper they print out at Jabiru. That brought some parts of what had happened into focus—but others just slipped from me: I was too close to it all. What I see clearly in my mind's eye now is the opening night—when the crowds were gathered, and the time came for Don to speak. What would he say? What would the reaction be? I was worried for him—he'd been quiet, and full of sorrow, ever since we'd got the news.'

'And what happened?'

'He stepped forward. We had Murray Garde, the great expert on Kunwinjku languages, to translate—and now I think back, it was probably the only time an artist from West Arnhem Land has ever been understood by a southern audience. It was the most extraordinary speech: precise, thoughtful, full of pride and poise. As he was giving it, I realised it was a portrait of himself. Don told them how he'd been living with his brother, for years, in Oenpelli, and they'd been painting together, side by side: painting their identity—the same paintings that were all around us. Those works showed the things that meant the most to him: he belonged to them—they were his clan's emblems, the badges of his being, the foundations of who he was. They were his brother's, and they were a tribute to his brother; they were the sites in his country, and the creatures there: the snakes and possums and black wallaroo; the plants, as well, the sand palms and the lilies and bush plums—all the things that made him happy, even in the sadness that he felt. The audience was quiet. I could hear my breathing. I could hear the pulse of the blood in my ears.

It was one of those moments of intensity: when you're completely present, when you're at one with yourself. That was what he did for us, that night. Then the applause came. He took all the hugs, and handshakes—it was over.'

Dyson stopped. His listeners waited.

'And that's it?'

'Not at all. There were other episodes, in those days: little scenes—and they were pure, and very telling, each in its own way: you know how rare deep experiences are in modern life. It was as if all this was a brief interval lifted out of time's usual flow. We went on an excursion to the art gallery, and looked at all the Kunwinjku paintings there; they asked Don about the themes and elements there might be in the different works; he just ran his hands over their surfaces: you could see him singing the songs for the paintings underneath his breath; in fact, the barks seemed quite different when they were in his presence; it was as if they'd come alive for him.

'We paid a visit to Ian Dunlop, that old film-maker who worked so long in Arnhem Land: he showed us a film of first contact on the Sepik River that he'd made in the 1960s. His house was full of art, and not just Aboriginal: there were Tucksons; there was a Picasso that Don quite liked; there was even a pair of ceremonial boomerangs for him to play.

'We made other visits; and all these cameos seemed very strong events. I didn't realise why at the time: perhaps now I do. Everywhere we went we were meeting men and women who knew Arnhem Land, and knew enough about its depths: they were linguists, art curators and collectors; they were all experts in the study of some aspect of the culture. For them, Don wasn't just a small, quiet Aboriginal man of middle years: he was cloaked in grandeur and authority; he was like a prince, or king—and at each place we called in there was this sense of a formal mission under way. They responded to him. If he was excited, they were excited; if he was grieving, they grieved. He was like an amplifier. It became quite clear to me in those few days just how important he was for each one of them. It was as if they needed him in order to see, to have great thoughts, to speculate about man's place in the world. And how was all that for me, I wondered. What was I doing on the frontier between two worlds? Have we borrowed and adopted traditional Aboriginal people and their culture because we have so little ourselves?'

At this point, the Arnhem Landers listening gave little inscrutable smiles. Dyson saw, and smiled back.

'It's interesting,' he went on, quietly: 'You never know yourself. You don't step back often enough to look. Though we spent long hours all through that week together just thinking, saying nothing. We were staying in a large house, in Glebe: it was the home of a pair of musicologists, Allan and Linda. They also understood the world of the Top End: they'd been working on the song traditions of the North for years. They filled the house with music, from all the cultures of the world: it was wonderful; you had no idea what was coming next. Sounds came floating through—Schubert symphonies, Bach cantatas, Arabic Café, Islamic pop—we were plunged into the flow of it; it was like a trance. We sipped tea all day long, the clean Sydney light poured in through the windows, and all the world's bitter weight began to fall away. And there was one strange thing that happened in that week, too: it happened almost as soon as we reached the house—it was the same evening that we'd spoken to Oenpelli and heard the news. Do you want me to tell you? Do you have much time for meaningful coincidences?

'Go on,' I said: 'Please.'

'Our hosts had already assigned the bedrooms for our stay: they showed us round. They'd arranged things so Don and Murray would share, and sleep in one of the larger rooms, a kind of lounge, covered in lovely carpets from India and Afghanistan. We walked in: there on the window sill was a large mantis.'

'The insect?'

'A praying mantis. Don spotted it, and froze. "Marlindji," he called out: he showed us all. "It's because I'm here," he said: "The Marlindji is showing itself to me here because my brother died last night." I understood at once. The praying mantis is always in his paintings—it's almost his favourite subject: it has a special place in the ceremonies for death in West Arnhem Land.'

'How?'

Dyson glanced up; the listeners around us had gone.

'It's seen as a skeletal being,' he said: 'It's painted very deliberately on all the barks as a disarticulated creature: you can see its limbs and body parts, but they don't fit, one to the next. The Marlindji is the being that oversees the funerals; it shows itself at times of death. And that all makes sense: it's bound up with the burial practices—the hollow log funeral ceremony, when the bones of the deceased have been separated, and are placed in their coffin. The mantis is the guardian being at the threshold: between

94

life and death; between the time of our presence in the body and our passage to another space. For Don, that moment when the Marlindji came to him was the sign—it was the confirmation of the news. He could see his brother lying in Oenpelli, dead.'

'That's a striking story,' I said.

'It was for all of us,' said Dyson: 'We were quiet. We felt the links between the natural kingdom and the world of man—and once you've seen that, once you've felt that tap on the shoulder, it's hard not to feel it with you all the time.'

*

Weeks passed. That airport story, with its tone of mingled joy and sadness, stayed in my mind. The weather broke; the rains came. I resumed my Darwin life, as best I could. I made contact with Palomor: we arranged to meet up that afternoon, on the verandah of the Cool Spot, where one can sit and watch the harbour's reach, the low shore, the red cliffs and the storm clouds stretching away. He appeared: jaunty, smiling, lithe.

'Did you see the Troop Carrier?' he began.

'I saw that strange thing on the front.'

'The high-capacity solar panel with storage cells. I just fitted it. It's a game-changer.'

'In what way?'

'Self-sufficiency, of course. You can run advanced electronics off it straight away, wherever you pull up—no matter how remote.'

He seemed unchanged: but as he spoke on, it was hard to miss an edge in his words, a racing in his thoughts. At last he fell quiet. He turned from the view of the rain clouds and the shifting light.

'I have to tell you,' he said. 'Something's happened. A kind of milestone. You remember that artist we met together, a year ago: Don Namundja, from Oenpelli? I went to see him at his outstation, over Cahills Crossing. I spent weeks out there. We became friends, in a way: he took me out, into the stone country, into the hills behind Injalak. He told me all about the python, and the best ways to look. All year after that I was out walking in Kakadu, and across the southern flood plains—always watching out, of course.'

'And you found the snake?'

'Wait—let me tell the story. Don't you want to hear?'

I made a sign for him to go on. He set the scene. It was the late dry. He'd begun exploring along the edge of the Arnhem Land escarpment, on the borders of the national park. With each trip he pushed further.

'You can climb from the flat quite easily, if you follow where the wet season creeks come down. It's another world up there: discreet, unvisited, calm. There are fresh waterholes with white sand, places you'd think no one's ever been. There are springs coming up from underground, and pink satin bush, and palm doves, and multicoloured butterflies, and green tree snakes everywhere: it's like an earthly paradise. On one trip, just before the first rains came, I'd led a group a long way up the creekline from Jim Jim Falls, and we'd made an early camp. It was the midpoint of the day. The whole world seemed to be fading, on the verge of sleep: but I was alert. It was one of those spells when you feel you can see everything, you see the whole structure of the bush around you, what it holds and what it hides. I went on, alone, deep into the jumbled back country: full of outliers and ridgelines and breakaways. I'd gone along the base of a low cliff of sandstone—it turned into a narrow overhang. There was a stand of evergreens, and a recess in the rock face, almost hidden by the shading of the trees. I bent down; I stepped in—and I saw it: a grey, gleaming python, with the echoes of the rainbow in its scales. It was very drowsy—it had just had a big feed—you could see the outline of some poor mammal in its gut. It gave me an anguished sort of look, and didn't move. I just lay down alongside it.'

'And told it how beautiful it was?'

'That kind of thing. It calmed down, once we'd cleared up that I didn't want to eat it. It had a very gentle presence. Extremely feminine. I stayed as long as I thought was right, and then I tiptoed out, and back, beneath the cliff, along the creekline, and down, to where we'd made camp. I couldn't resist, though. I had to see it again. In the morning I went back: it had gone. There was just a faint track left. That was months ago—but it's still with me. I remember how quiet, how soft those moments were. They balanced up everything life hurls at you. Every sadness, every pain, every harsh look, every stab. Don't you find that if we stay open to life, it just irradiates us with all the wonders that it has?'

I smiled, at this.

'But there's a dark side, too.'

I turned. I looked more carefully at Palomor—but his eyes were fixed on the distance; he was gazing at the sunset, and the light beams piercing through the clouds.

'By which you mean?'

'Don't be too analytic—I mean lots of different, inconsistent things: that I'd been longing for that second of discovery so much, and dreaming of it so much; and once it came it almost seemed as if it hadn't happened; I was just too far forward in my mind. Why is it we can't stay in ourselves, and in the motion of our lives: why are we nothing but hope, and fear? Is that being human? What does it help us, then, to know who we are?'

'That doesn't sound like a Randian set of conclusions to come to—to be regretful when you reach your heart's desire.'

'That's not really what I was saying, or not the only thing. I just had the feeling, very strongly, in that cave, that I'd actually been there, in that moment, already—not imagined it but been in it—and suddenly I had a picture of life, what it really is; just the images that we receive: a cavalcade of images, blurs of light, patterns rushing by—from the future, from our past, from the people round us, from the landscape—and we're trapped by the world's glare, and struggling constantly to make sense of what comes in.'

'And that's the update?'

'In part—there's a new enthusiasm as well. Glare-related!'

'I thought the snake obsession was forever—you're reinventing yourself.'

'I've been inventing myself since I was a child. Isn't that what everyone should be doing? Don't you?'

'So what is it—the latest thing?'

He nodded in the direction of the harbour, with great formality, as if towards the altar of a cult. I followed his look with my eyes. There was a grey-hulled customs vessel heading out, past East Point, and an empty Perkins barge bound in: a cattle boat was riding at anchor off the far shore, by the Mandorah jetty and hotel.

'You're going to sea?'

'No, I mean diving, of course: free diving. I've begun wreck diving in the harbour: you know it's full of reefs, and wrecks, from the bombing in World War II, and even before, from cyclones in the pearling lugger times.'

He told me something of the story, in an involved, staccato fashion, jumping between sequences of experiences, picking up his first forays into this new kingdom, his halting progress, his path towards expertise.

'It sounds almost like bushwalking,' I said when he stopped: 'You're in a strange environment, deep in it—completely dependent on it. It's indifferent to you, but you have to read it; you have to know its signs, know them perfectly; you have to win it over, and make it your ally and friend.'

Palomor gave a little, pitying smile at this, as though to suggest at once how creditable this attempt at insight had been, and how far from the crystal truths he knew.

'I'll tell you how it started,' he said then: 'While you were gone, I was off in Far North Queensland: trying to buy, trying to build. I was looking for ideal spots: for a place far from the power grid, where there's water flowing, and the sun shines all the time. I went everywhere I'd heard of that was wild, with strange people; behind Ayton and Cow Bay; up and down the scrubland edges of the Tableland as well: Almaden, Dimbulah, Chillagoe. But after all that searching, and never finding, you get

ground down. I'd been looking in the hills round Greenvale and
Lynd Junction, just going down bush tracks, coming on camps
of squatters living rough; I'd travelled into the deserted mine
sites of the cape. I had a sense of ghosts around me all the time
in that country; ghosts without names, collective ghosts: it was a
whole landscape full of unfulfilled and disappointed souls. I had
to break away from it. So I began driving north, up the spine of
the cape. I'd got into a Dice Man mood. You know that book?
No? When the hero decides to live his whole life on the throw
of a dice. You give yourself alternatives: and then you roll, and
follow chance, and trust it. I was at the Archer River Roadhouse,
fuelling up. I waited. I gave myself the options: follow the next
car south, turn back—or keep on going till the road runs out.
I made the throw: it was north—behind a supply truck; pretty
soon it took the Weipa turn-off. All day long I sat behind it, in
its dust: it kept on, up the peninsula, right through to Mapoon.
That was the destination. I stopped there, and found myself a
place to stay: there were teachers I fell in with; they didn't have
anyone much to teach. We went on their boat the next day,
out into the gulf: I'd never seen sea waters like that before—so
still, so ominous. It turned out they were serious divers, and I
went down with them. They had a favourite spot—beside an old
jetty that had decayed away: there was nothing of it left except
the line of wood posts and cross-ties stretching out beneath the
waterline. They gave me a speargun. It took me a few dives to
get used to things: there was a weight to the water, and a gleam,
from all the flow of sediment. So many fish, great schools of
them everywhere—and round the jetty there were bait fish, all

together, a vast ball: hundreds and thousands of them, touching each other, bunched up along the line of wooden posts. I was down below, looking up at them; and then a shark of some kind came racing in: they scattered—behind them, above us, there was the sun streaming through the water: blazing, molten light, so bright it turned the world to nothing. I was staring up at it; I could see right through it. I could see beyond.'

He laughed. 'That was an experience: I almost forgot I had to come up to the surface to breathe.'

'No scuba?'

'Free diving. That's why it's called free—that's the point.'

'And when you're down there, holding your breath, there's danger every second: you're on the edge, you're between life and death, the risk is the thing?'

'More that it just doesn't matter, in that world, in that filtered light, away from words, at one with everything around you. It doesn't seem to matter if you live or die. You're on the same level as everything—nothing is superior, nothing less than you. Everything is just the light.'

He said this in a half-enraptured voice, his hands tracing out a faint arabesque on the table between us as he spoke.

'Do you remember when we were down at Lake Newell, in the desert, on that long trip you took me on? The lake you said looked like a question mark on the map, and in the landscape as well?'

'I do.'

'Where it was so bright that even opening one's eyes and looking at the white salt surface of the lake in full sun was enough to make you feel you'd gone too far—you were about to pass out and lose your senses—something very much like that.'

He stopped, and glanced up; but this time there was the beginning of a new, fear-laden expression on his face—and though I had known him for several years by then, though we had travelled together in each other's company so much, that moment was the first time that I grasped how frail he was, for all his certainties, how faint and vulnerable. I had the impulse to reach across to him: I said nothing, and stared, in fascination.

'What are you staring at?' he said: 'What? You're almost smiling.'

And it may be that I was: I saw him again for a second as he was when he first came north; when he was driving with me down desert roads; out by the dam causeway, too, on the snake hunt as darkness fell; and I saw others like him I had known before. We sense, after some while, the shape and pitch of the lives we know; we begin to make out the destinies of the swirling cast around us; their course through life no longer surprises us; their weaving path announces and contains their fate. And so it was with Palomor: in those instants, as the light from the clouds before the late sun changed, I gazed at him, and shuddered, despite myself.

'What are you thinking of?' he asked.

'About people I knew, before. Friends I had, people you remind me of. And how there's a point in life where memories stop being disconnected things: they form themselves into a pattern. You realise your experiences came in the way they did, in their exact sequence, for a reason—to help you learn, to give you pointers to the depths of life.'

'What are you talking about?'

'There are some people who stay with me—very strongly—even though I haven't had anything to do with them for years: and as I come to understand them more, their stories and they way they tried to live and steer their course make me feel how hazardous the paths we go down can be; how narrow the right way; how full of cracks and dangers. How easy it is for us to lose our bearings, to stumble and fall—and we should always be on the watch, always on guard.'

'And watch out for each other.'

'Precisely.'

'But I'm not in any danger.'

'Of course not,' I said: 'One never thinks one is.'

We said our goodbyes. He was heading off: a long trek, this time, through the North Kimberley; it would take him from Wyndham across the Cambridge Gulf, first to the old mission settlement at Oombulgurri, where the red gorgeline rises high above the huddle of the houses on the bank—then he meant to cross the rough tableland, down to the Berkeley, a straight, fast-flowing river which gives all the landscape it runs through a sharp, dynamic tone. Palomor had already gone through that country: its ranges were choked with rock art, incised and painted, ancient and new. He wanted to record everything he found, and record it in wet season conditions: he believed the most elusive features of the art panels could only be seen in conditions of moisture and extreme humidity.

'And then what?'

'I know what I'm doing; there's a plan: come out at Carson River, through the gap in the ranges, and down to Moonlight Camp; you can see the path down marked very clearly on the charts—and on, then, to Kalumburu. I've heard so many stories from there, such stories—I've been longing to go and see for myself.'

'Soon there won't be anywhere left on the surface of the Earth for you to discover.'

'That's the idea,' he said: 'But there's always the underwater world: you could never run out of wonders there, as long as you lived—and I'll be diving this weekend, on the harbour wrecks.'

*

I travelled down to Sydney the next day, on a short trip, and each morning I made sure to read the northern headlines. I went through them mechanically, going over every little article with the utmost attention. It was as if I knew what I would find. My tasks had brought me to the city's centre early one day: I was sitting close by the waterfront at Circular Quay. The sky was an Elysian blue; the cries of gulls and sounds of churning engines from the ferries filled the air. Then my eyes lit on a story: 'Territory Tragedy', a few lines, hackneyed words, no more. Brief, sharp sentences; sentences like any others: the death sentence of my friend, whose youth, and clear eyes, and longing for life's depths had brought him no protection. He had made his pattern. It was done. I stared out, at the light, the skyline, the bridge's ironwork, the clouds. The conversation was flowing smoothly at the table one along from me: its phrases seemed, at that instant, precise beyond belief: 'At Mount Maragen, the sound of the riflebirds was always clear,' said a voice, with slow, grave emphasis, before the talk swirled on. I looked again at the words before me: A diving accident in Darwin. A thirty-year-old man. 'His companions made repeated attempts to locate the victim's body and revive him…'

And so, with soft, swift movements, those we know depart from us, and leave us in this world, and leave behind them memories to disperse like plumes of smoke haze in the air. I took the flight back north a few days later. We drew near the airport; we passed over the Mary River wetlands; we approached. Soon I could see the outline of the harbour, with its twining currents and its gleams and the light shafts falling on its surface that seem to sink through to the reefs and channels lying below. We touched down. It was close to sunset. I drove out, slowly, following familiar roads—along the highway, left at Humpty Doo, and on, to Fogg Dam, stray notions running in chains through my head. There were rainstorms. I had the radio switched to the news channel: the bulletins came cycling round: more details on the harbour episode. The dead man had been found lying face up, speargun in his hand, resting like an effigy upon the upturned hull of the wreck.

I edged my way in along the half-submerged back road. I stopped at the viewing platform, as before. All was quiet. The downpour had swept the causeway clean; it shone in the last light's glow, the cries of night birds began, and I sent my thoughts back: back to my previous visit there with Palomor, when I read him, at that spot, a part of Warburg's lecture on the serpent handlers, and told him something of its author's fate. And I could still hear his voice, in the humid darkness, just as I can hear it now, asking: 'What then? What happened to Warburg then?'

The story is simple enough to tell. Confined in Bellevue, kept in the clinic's closed wing, isolated, with little prospect of release, Warburg had the freedom only of his eyes: at certain hours he was permitted to stroll through the parklands of the sanatorium, amid the larch trees and the chestnuts, and gaze out across the waters of Lake Konstanz, where the reflections from the peaks above the far shore shimmered and played. Each day he was subject to the healing attentions of Dr Binswanger, and the clinic's nurses and psychologists; their diagnosis was broad-brush: schizophrenia, but also a manic-depressive mixed condition. What were his thoughts, then, and his fears? Given the regime of close supervision the patient was subjected to, they are documented very well. At the onset of his troubles, Warburg had wished to kill his wife and his children, the better to safeguard them from their enemies. Now, he was persuaded that he himself was the chief target of these pursuing foes—they were behind his footsteps, they were round the corner, they were closing on him with every second, there was nowhere safe. In addition, he had come to believe that a group of well-organised conspirators was at large, and plotting to eliminate the most prominent of Germany's Jewish leaders, in the realms of finance, the academy, the stage and the arts—and this was a fear that had its seeds in the world beyond the clinic's walls. Warburg's brother Max, who was at the helm of the family bank, kept guards in those years to watch his house, and his name did figure on the assassination list of a right-wing terror band; Walter Rathenau, the foreign minister of the Weimar Republic, and an intimate of the Warburg circle, was, after many threats, gunned down by extremists near his villa in Grünewald. Warburg had built his anguish on the secret currents in the air—and, as was fitting for an art historian and iconographer, his imaginings were gruesome and baroque. He was convinced that his entire family had been locked up in the clinic and were to be executed in its cellars; when he heard cries echoing in the hallway, he was sure he knew the voice: it was his wife's, and she was being tortured by the Bellevue doctors; the meat set before him at the dinner table was surely the flesh of his own slain children, victims of Binswanger; Binswanger himself was the chief pursuing murderer on Warburg's trail, coming closer, ever closer—he was trapped.

But these delusions, wild though they were, were not only wild. One of his family had been brought to Bellevue, the clinic of choice, in those days, for members of the European elite. Warburg's son, Max Adolf, whose nervous breakdown had been triggered by his father's collapse, was being cared for there, in a ward close by: and during his treatments, which took the form of long, calming lukewarm baths, the son could hear the father's tormented shrieks as they rang repeatedly down the corridors. Indeed, the dividing line between Warburg's darkest intimations and the unfolding fate of Europe is quite hard to trace. The wider one's perspective, the more precise his madness seems. He could sense murdering armies on the march, seeking out his people, seeking to take them away, to torture them, to kill them all. He sensed them; and in due course they came.

How not to feel that foresight, as much as lunacy, lay at his derangement's heart? He had made himself into the man who sees; since childhood he had trained his eyes to look through the surface code, the symptom, to the cause, the hidden pattern, the final, all-deciding force. He scorned knowledge that was fixed, received, accepted: he wanted to be certain, not merely to share the world's beliefs. If there was violence at the core of religion, and ecstasy, it was for him to seek it out and find it, just as he had in the Pueblo region once: if antiquity's pagan strength was to live on in the new Europe of electric telegraph and telephone, then he would be the prophet of that ambiguous future and its winding patterns; it was for him to trace its coming's tell-tale signs.

By chance, a description exists of Warburg during those days in Kreuzlingen, shortly after his arrival and first treatment there, when his initial mania was beginning to subside, and he was waging his great duel with the demons inside his head. A young Swiss scholar of art history, Werner Kaegi, who would later study under Warburg, was passing through the region in the autumn of 1921 on his way home from courses in Florence: he came to the Kreuzlingen clinic to pay a visit to a friend of his who was working there. One morning, he was out walking in the sanatorium gardens when he happened to pass by a slight figure on the path beneath the Bellevue. It was Warburg. Kaegi was struck by the encounter, and set down his impressions years later: 'He was surprisingly small, of a robust and healthy constitution, with the features of his face giving a mixed impression of suffering, struggle, violent constraint and a magical will to power precipitated in marble.'

So Warburg seemed: an image of emotions, of human depths made visible, more than a man. But after some months in those surrounds, the morphine calmed him, his mind was still, his delusions lulled: there was a space within him for the chains of ordered thought to be linked together and the ramparts of his ideas to rise once more. He knew his condition: he could see himself with great clarity; he knew where he was—but should he be there? Could he free himself? A notion came to him. He was not a Warburg for nothing: deals were his stock in trade—the giving, and the getting; giving himself away. In the wake of prolonged treatments, feeling that the full measure of his capacities had at last been restored to him, he made an offer to Binswanger: the quid pro quo was stark.

He would attempt to deliver an hour-long lecture on aspects of art history to an invited audience within the asylum walls—and if he succeeded in this task, which the experts, at the time of his admission, had regarded as forever beyond him, it would be taken as a proof of his restored sanity and equilibrium: his doctors would set him free. Warburg had proposed a similar deal of life-changing resonance once, long before, when he was only thirteen years old: it is part of the legend that clusters round him. He offered his rights as the first-born of the dynasty to his brother, Max, who was a year younger than him. In return, Max was to guarantee that for the remainder of Aby's life the Warburg Bank would buy him the books he wanted—every single one. Max, in the memorial address he delivered at his brother's funeral, told the tale—Aby had put the proposal forward: 'After a very brief pause for reflection, I consented. I told myself that when I was in the business I could, after all, always find the money to pay for the works of Schiller, Goethe, Lessing and perhaps also Klopstock, and so, unsuspecting, I gave him what I must now admit was a very large blank cheque.' It was just such a well-sprung deal that was before the doctors at the Bellevue. They turned it over, and agreed. Mastery of art must betoken a degree of mental order. They set a date, the twenty-first of April 1923, and announced the forthcoming attraction to the more settled of the clinic's inmates— men and women, after all, of a high cultural level: their number included, at that time, the expressionist painter Ernst Ludwig Kirchner, the dancer Nijinsky and the writer Leonhard Frank.

In his quarters, Warburg drew his notes together. His doctors were expecting a treatment of some familiar theme from the north Italian Renaissance, in keeping with their patient's most recent studies: fresco cycles in Ferrara, the *Primavera* of Botticelli, Leonardo's figure drawings. But Warburg's thoughts reached much further back—he returned to the scenes he had witnessed twenty-seven years earlier on the Indian reservations, during his visit to the Pueblo region and the settlements round Santa Fe. He would describe to his audience the successive dances of the snake cult, but beyond this ethnographic narrative he would trace the birth of the rational, scientific picture of the world from its origins in pagan superstition—and in so doing he would show what he had gone through: he would face his own fears, and master them. The lecture text, which he wove between an array of photographic images, survives, as do the first drafts Warburg wrote—'sketches that should never be printed, begun March 16, while still on opium'. He went through them, over and over: 'Help,' he scrawled across the title page. He annotated them, dismissively: they were fragments; they were nothing more than 'dusty documents'. He had dredged up all the memories he could from the Pueblo: and how slight they were, how faint, how much they were confined to the surface of the life there he had wished to know—they reflected only the appearances of things. The problems they brought to mind were insoluble; they weighed on his soul: had he been healthy he would not have dared make any scientific statements about them—but there was no choice, now, none. And with that he turned the spotlight on himself: 'In Kreuzlingen, in a closed institution, where I have the sensation of being a seismograph assembled from the wooden pieces of a growth that has been transplanted from the east into the fertile north German plains and onto which an Italian branch was grafted, I allow the signals that I have received to come out of me.' This was Warburg's picture of himself: he was a creature caught on the frontier between worlds; he was an instrument through which light could pass; he was where thought and instinct met. There were serpent forces, deep within him; there was the gleam of art, and beauty, with its healing grace, as well.

He began: he laid out his themes. His argument had a clear, rapid flow. He recounted his experiences: he had been down in the murk of magic, in the Indian world, in the midst of a remote, primal culture, one that still held the secrets of mankind's first beliefs in its grasp. On that journey, what had he been shown? What images, what mysteries—and why was the serpent so much at the heart of things, snaking its way through men's hearts? Was it the pure lightning symbol? Was it the poison emblem: danger? Was it truth and death conjoined?

All these ideas emerged smoothly from his narrative: he held the details of his travels through that far-off landscape in precise order in his mind. It was a Wild West story, and illustrated: forty-seven images, artfully selected, carefully slide-mounted, gleaming in the projected flicker of the light. There were the Indian strongholds in the sun, and the ceremonial dancers in their snaking lines; there was Warburg himself, against the desert mesas, bandana at his neck, a solemn Hopi chieftain standing by his side.

But gradually, in mid-lecture, the tale fragments: it becomes a succession of images, word portraits, evocations of snake forms in art, matched by free passages of speculation. Might the serpent that could so smoothly shed its skin be sending its devotees a message: for the snake was not only the fatal foe, the assassin, in readiness or fulfilment, destroying without mercy—it also showed how a body could go through a death and yet continue to live. The tone shifts again: now the scholar joins forces with the asylum patient. Warburg finds the serpent spirit where all begins, in the Bible's Eden tree; in the marble coils of ancient statues; in the heavens, too: in the constellation of the great winding snake, where the stars are given focus by an earthly image, in order to make comprehensible an infinity of distance we cannot frame. The creature is answer as much as it is question: its ceremonies among the Pueblo are nature coming into culture; they are the birth of reason given form in dance.

At which point, with these grand notions widening, the dilemma facing Warburg's doctors as they listened and tried to gauge the extent of his recovery loomed large. But their patient was a step ahead. It had been necessary to lead them down that path of fantasies, fears and speculations. There was a way forward, beckoning, for all those gathered in Bellevue. There was the mind's light. Thought was vanquished fear; cult was mastered superstition; art was religious feeling given structure by the mind of man. That was the balance that the snake dance found. But in the days they were all living through then, in that strange present, with the states of Europe pulverised and ruined, the shadows had closed in again; they pressed down: new shadows, gifts of modernity. Not only for the Indians but for all old cultures and religions, an end was close. Their beliefs would vanish: new forms of knowledge would prevail. It was the triumph of science: the snake was no longer needed to control storms and lightning: 'It is an animal that must succumb, if humanity wills it to.' All man's history had been lived in the task of mastering and refining fear: now fear itself had been trampled underground. The consequences were in the future, still taking shape.

Warburg had a last slide to show the inmates. He had met the conquering hero, the figure who destroyed the serpent cult and the fear of lightning: he had seen this victor, who inherited all the lands of the indigenous people of America. Warburg even had his photograph, taken on a street in San Francisco early in 1896. The image shows a burly man in black three-piece suit, thick-bearded, wearing a tall top hat, face set in a scowl as he strides along a wide, light-drenched street beneath powerlines. 'He is Uncle Sam in a stove-pipe hat, strolling in his pride past a neoclassical rotunda. Above his top hat runs an electric wire. In this copper serpent of Edison's, he has wrested lightning from nature.' The machine age had destroyed what man so painfully made in the temples of his thought—the space for devotion, which in turn became the space for reflection. Distance had gone forever. All was instant now. And Warburg was done. He had succeeded, in formal terms. He had strung his arguments together, he had been able to speak freely, for an hour and a half, without losing his train of thought.

The doctors saw, in this performance, 'a very encouraging sign' that his capacity for communication had been restored—and it was precisely such outward signs of rationality that they required. For the patient, the triumph was more qualified. The vision he had presented was of a world in nightmare colours: that view had called forth the wild fears he felt within him. It had not been a question of mere illness in his mind; it was not a simple case of cure. He knew how things stood with him. He knew the praise Binswanger lavished on his performance was misplaced. 'I do not want my presentation of images from the life of the Pueblo Indians to be taken in any way as results of a supposedly superior knowledge or science—but rather as the desperate confession of an incurable schizoid, deposited into the archives of the doctors of the soul.' There was talk of publishing the lecture. Warburg was firm. He realised very well he was a subject for a story: a majestic story; it was a story he wanted to stay untold. He pleaded with his academic assistant, Fritz Saxl, not to show the text to anyone: 'This gruesome twitching of a decapitated frog should absolutely not find its way to print.'

He was released. By this stage his course in life was almost run. He resumed his researches into the Quattrocento in Florence. They became increasingly ornate: his writing style came to match the new scope of his thought; in his lectures and his essays competing concepts were held in suspension, and stayed unresolved for pages on end. He moved back to Hamburg, where his labyrinthine library had been installed, and opened as a centre for scholarship in art: its holdings were an imprint of his life's linked, deeply excavated enthusiasms; there were elaborately mounted displays of his research prints and photographs, and Warburg was constantly engaged in reordering them, or moving the books and papers into new categories to keep up with his shifting ideas on the cultural evolution of man. The main reading room had a magic air about it: it was like an arena for ritual, a stage—nor was this resemblance accidental. The book cabinets curved round the research desks like the enclosures guarding an altar: the library ensemble had been directly modelled on the subterranean chambers carved out by the Pueblo Indians for reflection and prayer.

It was to this darkened space that Warburg went after his release from Kreuzlingen. He had the feeling that he had come back home at the end of a dreadful battle, a battle for life against the forces of darkness and hell, and he transmitted this conviction to his associates, who became the members of his cult. Saxl felt Warburg was a man for whom life in its normality existed no longer: 'An almost awe-inspiring power emanated from him, and he lived and worked convinced that the scholar does not choose his vocation but that in all he does is obeying a higher command.'

This sense's of life's grand, all-shaping patterns was encouraged by the headlines of the day. Systems of belief were breaking around them, new empires were rising. The dawns seemed stronger than the sunsets. In early 1929, Warburg made a return visit to Italy, together with a group of his disciples. By chance, they were in Rome on February eleventh, when Mussolini signed the Concordat that destroyed the last worldly powers of the Catholic Church. Warburg's biographers glide past this trivial-seeming episode in the last year of the master's life, but it is recorded by another intellectual magus, the Piedmontese historian Arnaldo Momigliano, who, in his golden prose and jewelled thought, was fully Warburg's equal, and whose awareness of the shadows in the spectacle unfolding that day remained undimmed when he set down a record of the event, long afterwards, in the eighth volume of his contributions to the story of classical studies and the antique world. 'There were in Rome tremendous popular demonstrations, whether orchestrated from above or from below. Mussolini became overnight the man of providence, and in such an inconvenient position he remained for many years.'

It was hard to move freely on the streets of Rome that day: Warburg was swept up in the crowd and lost from the sight of his companions. They waited for him anxiously back in the Hotel Eden, close by the Spanish Steps, but there was still no sign of him when evening fell. The group consulted. They even telephoned the police. Nothing. Shortly before midnight, Warburg reappeared in the hotel, flushed, his face full of excitement, and when his friends reproached him, he replied, in his convoluted German: 'You know that throughout my life I have been interested in the revival of paganism and pagan festivals. Today I had the chance of my life to be present at the repaganization of Rome—and you complain that I remained to watch it!' The shape of the time had become clear that night. The demons he had pictured in his mind were on the march.

III

WINFIELD BLUE

IT WAS MORE THAN a decade ago that I first encountered the artist Tony Oliver, a captivating, drama-courting figure with a talent for both feud and friendship, and though our paths in life ran close together in the ensuing years, only now, as I cast my thoughts back, do I begin to understand the dreams and ideals that drove him to set up a painting studio in the remote Kimberley, then flee his creation at the height of its success.

The story of his northern life is well known: it is the tale of the Jirrawun art studio he brought into being; the rise to fame of its great painter, Paddy Bedford; and the creation of the grand, mysterious works the old man poured out in his final years. It begins with the chance meeting that led to Jirrawun's foundation: a tale that was circulating across the North well before I came to know its protagonists. You could hear it everywhere; it was told and retold in roadhouses and community art centres; it seemed to radiate outwards from Jirrawun's back-country outstation like a spell; and, like all the best tales, it could be heard in several conflicting variants.

Each one was set in Melbourne, where Tony, blessed with a keen eye and strong enthusiasms, had been a young high-flyer on the contemporary art scene. At the heart of that milieu, one evening, at an exhibition opening in a gallery on Flinders Lane, he came face to face with a visitor from the North: the Gija artist Freddie Timms, a man of few words and great silences, a man whose sombre style and grave look conveyed a forbidding first impression. The two spoke for hours; they found they had much in common: a belief in art's redemptive force, and a longing to make visible the masked structure of the world. Tony saw the work on the walls; he felt its strength; he felt the depths lurking in the lines drawn on the canvas—he looked with care— he was caught.

Freddie Timms was just as struck: he knew their talk was something different from the standard weightless talks he was subjected to each time he ventured to an art opening in a southern capital. He knew white men well enough: he had been a stockman on the East Kimberley cattle stations for years. He took Tony Oliver into his confidence; he described in detail the life he and his fellow artists led, how they worked, what they made. Why not come up to the north-west, he said: come up and see?

There was another version of this account, a touch more fanciful, in which the two met by pure chance as the sun was setting on the concourse at Federation Square, and began talking, impelled by some obscure sense of affinity. But the most evocative variant I came across was the one I heard at Timber Creek, at the service station, from an old Mirriuwong man I once met there, travelling west. In this rendition, Tony Oliver was a figure of vast wealth and unbounded influence, and his journey to the Kimberley had a quite different origin: it was the direct result of a dream that came to him one night, and troubled him so deeply he had been compelled to throw over the settled pattern of his life.

Such stories, so far removed from the usual hardscrabble sagas of the North! And doubtless they were lodged in my mind on the hot day at the height of the build-up when I set off for Jirrawun, and drove the deserted road out from Katherine, at speed, with bushfire plumes spreading thick smoke across the sky. The Victoria River was still, at the crossing, and low. The bloodwood trees were drooping. The rangelines shimmered in the haze. Around the dams, the Brahman cattle gazed out despairingly: I hurtled on, over the grids and floodways, past the border quarantine, through landscapes free from any trace of man. The sun was already close to setting when I reached the Kununurra turn-off. I made a reconnoitre through the town: card games by the lakeside, a Greyhound idling at the BP truck stop, drinkers lying stretched out on the concourse grass—the rhythm of the Kimberley, repeating, loud and strong. A young Gija girl, thin, of utmost elegance, was standing by the shopping centre driveway.

'Where's the famous Jirrawun art centre?' I called out.

'You mean Uncle Tony?' she said: 'I can take you.'

She jumped in, and made a turn sign, with a quick, slight wrist movement; then another, right away.

'Who you?' she said, as we wound through the warren of the streets: 'His brother? Got any silver?'

'What?'

'Just asking. Stop now—we're right here, brother—turn the wheel.'

We had pulled up outside a low-slung, unremarkable house, fenced, with a wide verandah, on a side road facing a dramatic rock peak flanked by eucalypts and boabs. A tall man with dark, slicked-back hair was standing by the driveway, smoking, frowning, gazing at the sky.

I walked up to him.

'I want to bring it to an end,' he said: 'Die—cease to be—right here, right now. End it; no evasions.'

He took a drag on his cigarette, held it up and stared at the glowing tip as if it was a thing of transcendent beauty.

'So young,' I said: 'Before we've had any chance to know each other?'

Nothing.

'Is this the way you usually greet your visitors after they've driven all the way across from Katherine?'

Nothing, again. He looked up once more, accusingly, at the last glimmers of the light on the blood-red rocks.

'Have you considered a method?' I asked.

'A .303,' he replied. 'No question about it. I've seen what they do to the human body. There wouldn't be any ambiguity at all about your passage from here to another world. And the results are always visually striking: you'd be leaving an artwork behind you. In that sense, it's not just wanton destruction: it's a resurrection of the self. A .303. There's one here, right next door, in Freddie's house: the kangaroo rifle. That's what we use to put wounded animals out of their misery: we shot a bush turkey with it on the Argyle Road the other day.'

He turned a pair of soft eyes on me, and put a hand on my shoulder.

'Would you do it for me—as a favour?'

'Hello, Uncle Tony,' said the young woman beside us at this point, a certain anxiety in her voice.

'Misery?' I said: 'Has something bad happened?'

'No: that's just it. There's nothing bad. It's the turmoil of happiness that's tearing me apart. Misery itself: that we know, that we can handle, of course—we're always dealing with it. You're here at an unusual time. We're at the shining summit, right now. What we've worked to build up, for years on end: it's all coming to fruition. Everything we've struggled for, and longed for, and in our secret hearts most feared. Defeat, failure, those are easy enough to bear: you adapt to them quite quickly. Acceptance, though, success: that's a different story. The success that implies disaster; the breakthrough that holds sadness in its hands. I can't bear to see what comes next: what always comes next, in this world.'

'What's that?'

'People die, dreams fail, plans break, grief descends, the white man leaves, things fall to pieces; until there's nothing left. What we've built is like a fragile castle, waiting for the whirlwind to sweep past. Let's go up; sit with the old men; talk—you'll see; they'll tell you everything.'

There, on the verandah, were the artists of Jirrawun, like figures in a portrait, silent, gathered: Freddie Timms, staring his formidable stare; alongside him, sitting on a half-broken plastic seat, Rusty Peters, his legs crossed and folded beneath him. In the next chair, Hector Jandany, wearing a bright yellow checked shirt, head cocked to one side, a wry, measuring expression on his face; far off, at the end of the decking, cross-legged in front of an unfinished canvas, Paddy Bedford himself, looking off into the dark. Dogs scuffled on the edge of the light; a television indoors blared.

'I know how it goes, you see,' said Tony, over his shoulder, almost in disdain: 'I know it all. The high-profile exhibitions are just beginning, the sales are coming. The phone rings constantly. Eager voices, friendly voices: recognition, warmth—and sales, always, sales. It only took five years: five years in the wilderness. Five years to persuade people to look and see what was right in front of their eyes. See infinity; find a new way to look at paint. But there's further to go. More moves to play out in the art bazaar.'

'So that would mean death's off the agenda for now?'

'For now—but you have to be open to it, always. That's the way with the Ngarringgarni.'

'The what?'

'Rusty, what's the Ngarringgarni? You're the intellectual here!'

Rusty lifted the brim of the wide black hat that shadowed his eyes. He peered up.

'You call it the Dreamtime,' he said to me, in a low voice, very slowly: 'But we just don't know why.'

A mazy conversation followed, in which different definitions of this elusive Gija concept were aired, examined from multiple aspects and, one by one, found wanting. It was the past, and it was the future, and the way the two time phases fit together in the present. It was the ancestral beings of the country, and their overarching powers; it was the nocturnal hierarchy of owls and nightjars, and the secret signals they transmitted; it was the perpetuation of life; it was the force that gave man's existence shape, and tension; it was freedom, and it was all-controlling fate.

'Best, perhaps, under those circumstances,' I said, 'to keep things simple; not project.'

'But you have to know your path, up here,' said Tony, sternly: 'You have to be what you must be, not what you want to be. Leave your will behind; leave caprice behind; understand the place the world's made for you. Conform, rather than rebelling against the order of the system. Don't look like that, with such horror on your face! Rebellion's overrated. Think of art: what seems revolutionary always turns out to be conformist; tradition's always changing, and it always holds the clues to new ways of seeing form.'

'That's the lesson of the Kimberley? Did you have to come all this way to find that out?'

'I did, it's true,' he said, in a stricken voice: 'I could learn nothing elsewhere. Nothing at all, in that world I left. For a long time I thought I could never go back there.'

'Now, though?'

'Now: we have to. All of us together. We have a task. Enough fencing and sparring! Who's got time for that? There's something you have to see.'

He led the way indoors, into a ramshackle studio room. There were trestle tables piled with canvases; there were rolls of canvas on the floor, and half-finished works in various states of completion hanging on the colour-spattered walls. He drew the painting on the top of the pile towards us, and pinned it up. It was a rectangle of darkness; large colour fields, with white fringing dot lines bisecting them: blood-red, jet black, a heavy, haunting lilac-blue.

'Look,' he said. 'Take it into you; see what's hidden; look at it until your eyes hurt. It's the story of the Kimberley, the story of Bedford Downs: can you tell what it says?'

It was a still, hard work. There was no easy point of entry; the lines were cold, and strong. How to read them? They showed the landscape, and the landscape's tones, but the marks also had the air of codes and symbols; it was a painting of control.

'The Emu Dreaming place,' said Tony. 'But you know that already, don't you?'

'I do?'

'From the iconography! It's the kind of thing art-world types like to be familiar with these days, isn't it? Reading the image. Knowing the vocabulary of the symbols; going past the surface. It's easy to see there'll be a time, and very soon, when all the Gija knowledge and tradition has gone out, and outsiders have taken everything. When everything's been excavated and become known. You can read the canvas, I'm sure. You'd even know the way a work like this has different levels. It has its metaphysics.'

'Its metaphysics?'

'Absolutely. It's not just the journey story of the bush turkey and the emu: it's the origins of fate. The emu wants to stay in a never-ending daytime. The bush turkey sleeps at sunset. So it is for us, too: so it was the moment we entered this world. We follow the rule of night: we sleep; we have balance in our lives; light, and dark; we know time.'

'Indeed,' I said, and stared obediently at the painting's grid of interlocking fields and lines.

'Or you can read it as a mapping: that's the way they explain works like this these days on the information placards in the public galleries. That mark there—that's the break in the range: that's where the emu's journey came to its end.'

'And?'

'And its presence stays in the country, always: the emu sings over the country, and laments. But there's something further. Something dark. You see the red circle, there?'

His voice had dropped down low.

'See it?'

'Of course.'

'It's a scene of massacre. That's why the painting feels so still; that's why it feels like a block of marble before your eyes. The people of that country were all killed there. Up on the side of the hill, that slight incurving is a cave: it's where the spirits of the dead sang and danced.'

He pulled out a second painting: the companion piece; he told me its narrative—and then the next. All the stories were detailed, and all were drenched in blood.

I felt movement behind us: the artists had edged into the

room. They watched silently, and listened, and moved their hands across the canvases. The country seemed to pass before us, with its folds, and valleys, and hidden tales—Mistake Creek, and Lissadell, and the ranges round Bow River: the gold rush, the coming of the cattle, the time of fear. Tony went on speaking. His words rushed past me; the paintings seemed to throb and pulse before my eyes.

'How did you first come to hear about all these things?' I asked him quietly, much later, as the night drew on. We were sitting on the verandah steps, alone, by this stage, with dogs stretched out before us: the artists were fast asleep on their mattresses and swags.

'I'm sorry I did that to you,' he said. 'Blindsided you like that. But I find maximum impact's always best. That's how it was for me. When I first came up here, and I was living with the artists, out at Crocodile Hole, or when we spent time camped out on country, night was always the time for talk. There were months of testing, to start with: they were waiting, all of them, watching, gauging me, dropping clues. Then, one night, the deeper stories began to come. How hard it was, back then, for them to even think of trusting an outsider with what they knew, and held so hidden away inside themselves! I can hear those talks beside the fire as if they were unfolding right here in front of us. The nights were always dark, moonless, when the tales of the killing times came out. There was just the Milky Way, stretched high above us, and the campfire glow, and with each crackle and burst of flame the faces of the old people sitting round me would appear for a second, then sink back into the night. They'd be sitting on old flour drums: I was on the ground, looking up, listening to the wind blowing through the grasses and the gum-tree leaves, hearing the constant rhythm of the frogs down by the waterhole. For the most part, it was old Gamarliny who told me; he would put his hand on my knee, and lean towards me, and he'd say: "I have a hard story," or, "A bad story now"—and the others would sigh, and shake their heads and stare into the flames of the fire. "That's true," they'd say: "A true one." Each new story was hard to listen through: hard to comprehend. I'd keep quiet, and look up, and watch the stars turning above me in the darkness, and I'd try to keep pace in my heart with everything they said. Those dark tales, with no exit, ever. The end always the same.'

He took a last drag of his cigarette, in dramatic style, and stubbed it out. 'We've been asked to take them down to Melbourne—that set of paintings I showed you. For an exhibition, at the university. Can you imagine? God knows what they're going to think. They don't exactly know yet what's coming at them. I've told them the title, though: "Blood on the Spinifex".'

'Succinct.'

'Why not come down? Come with us? It'll be the first time city people get to learn about the story of the North, the Kimberley saga—I mean the real one, seen through Aboriginal eyes. They think they know, from all the soft-focus histories and well-intentioned studies, but that's just play, compared to what we'll bring: what we'll tell—in words, and in paint. We're all going to go. Come down too!'

He looked around. Behind us, on the verandah, we could hear the gentle sound of rhythmic breathing from the line of swags and mattresses where the artists were all asleep. He smiled, and shook his head: 'Poor things,' he said: 'They're pretty anxious.'

'Why?'

Tony drew himself back, with a sudden, violent movement; he turned his head to me; his eyes flashed: 'They're afraid, of course! Afraid they might be killed for telling all this: sharing it, bringing the secrets out. Haven't you understood a single word I've been telling you? Don't you get any of it? This isn't some culture game, some art project for the natives! Don't you have any heart? Any capacity to take things into your soul? Any intuition? Instinctual understanding? And I was beginning to think you were a kindred spirit. I got you so wrong!'

He jumped up from the verandah steps, and glared at me. He paced its length; back he came, leaned down, and grasped my forearm. I stood up. He brought his face close to me, eyes blazing like a wild animal's.

'Go on,' he snarled: 'Do something real: don't just look, and listen, with that wide-open stare. Go on—push back. Fight, contend, don't give in and break!'

I began to make some answer—but as soon as he had spoken, he slumped down once more, on the steps, shoulders fallen, head bowed.

'Strange,' he said at last, in a low voice: 'It always goes this way, here, in Kununurra, at this time of the night, when the evening star's gone down. It's as if the place was under some kind of a curse. Things begin with kindness, harmony—then, suddenly, breakdown, that black conviction that one's alone: lost in the world.'

He laughed. Through his thin shirt I could see a trembling along his backbone: it was laugh and sobbing all at once.

'That's true,' I said. 'We were cruising along. Let's go back to that. Tell me something?'

'Anything you want.'

'How is it you came here, and stayed here? What made you? What brought you and then kept you?'

'You've heard all the stories, haven't you?'

'How you and Freddie met up: at the gallery?'

'That's all true, as far it goes. All correct. It's the outside story, the simple, unvarnished tale—the one you see recycled in every story and exhibition catalogue. But there's more. Much more. Isn't life always chains of causes, binding us, until we have no choices left? It was painting that brought me here, that led me. I'd like to tell you: the deeper version. I'd like to talk through the night.'

The dark humidity was all around us. We both felt that exhaustion the build-up season breeds, when rest becomes impossible, and one has to chase one's thoughts down without end. We leaned back together, shoulders touching; after a while we began talking, the words in whispers, with long stretches of looking out into the dark, and listening to the sounds on the verandah and in the night-time air: breath, engine noises from the highway traffic in the distance, the dogs whimpering in their dreams, the wind picking up. He told me how, when he was young, he used to stare at the map of Australia, and see the names of the Turkey Creek and Kalumburu missions on the map, and dream of going there. How drift and desperation had been with him all through the years of his first success; how he had yearned constantly to flee the limelight; and that escape had come only after a hinge point in his experience of life.

It was close to the time when he and Freddie Timms first met. Everything was sudden: his father fell ill. The summons came: he travelled home. All the family had gathered. The death approached, in the small hours: it entered the room of the dying man; it claimed him. Tony looked on; he marvelled at the event's simplicity. He sat with the dead body for hours, on his own, quietly, until the sun came up: the room seemed to him to be full of particles of energy, coming into being in pairs and then vanishing. This epiphany had a strong effect on him: he lost the conviction that our familiar ways of seeing mirror anything profound about the world.

'Experiences of that kind seemed to be multiplying in my life just then,' he said: 'I was coming to mistrust everything around me. The world of art, my own ideas about the world and what it was, my judgements about what was beautiful and true. And it was at that time that I first went up to the Kimberley. I was plunged into this landscape: redness, haze, heat, lightning, rain. Suddenly everything I'd known was being assaulted; my senses were under attack. Freddie and I travelled together; we went into deep bush, by ourselves; he took me far into his own country, on Lissadell; he told me a great deal, in a concentrated way. It was like a seminar: a more wondrous tutorial than any other I ever had. He tried to show me what was hiding in the landscape, the past that was there, our place in it. I looked back on my own life, in those days, but with a stranger's eyes: the pattern was very clear. All through that time I could see that I'd been wrestling with myself: painting, writing plays, looking for a language to catch the way we fit with the world. I'd already removed myself from the art scene: it had become repellent to me. I tried to start afresh. I went to Wollongong.'

'The logical choice,' I murmured, but he ignored this, and swept ahead, as if he was speaking into the darkness, on his own.

'There was something about that sombre rangeline rising from the coast that always moved me: and the steelworks, the coal terminal, all those industrial installations that loomed like a fortress guarding the town; the curve of the shore, too, the gleam of the light; that sense of a place on notice, its time running out. I had a dear friend who lived there: he was a mathematician; his special field was cryptography; he was working on code breaking. He knew the struggles I was having with my path in art: maybe he thought we were engaged in the same kind of endeavour. I went to visit him; I stayed. I found an old house, in an old, half-deserted street: I made my studio there. And I wonder if those days set the pattern for my life now—though when I look back I find my old self always seems like a hurtful stranger, full of ill will, driven only by the most baffling, destructive impulses. I can hardly breathe when I give in to memory for any length of time. And you?'

'I wonder how much we really remember, and how much we make up, or build from stray fragments to suit our current selves.'

'I know we invent,' he said, an edge in his voice: 'Of course! But we invent ourselves forwards, just as much as back. We can see what's coming. Time folds on itself: the world gives us its clues. Don't you believe there are symbols that guide us? Portents? When I was in Wollongong, I was very much attuned to nature, and its messages—the way I'd been when I was a child. I felt the presence of the landscape there, surrounding me, brooding, bearing down. I used to drive up to Thirroul, up the coast, often.'

'On the trail of D. H. Lawrence?'

'Who else? I'd just discovered *Kangaroo*, which he wrote during his stay there: I worshipped Lawrence, then, for what he saw about the bush. Australians didn't see it: he could. He heard the land: its rhythms were like music for him, a clear, constant music. I used to go walking on the rocks along the shore, down below the Lawrence house—for hours on end, for days, imagining his thoughts when writing, letting the landscape sink in to me. I was trying to remake myself, to rid myself of every trace of what I'd known. I wanted the opposite of artistry, and connections, and expertise: I wanted their antidote. I'd go down to the wharves and loading docks at night, and listen to the hoists and winches working, to the grind of the machines and the hum of the conveyor belts: I'd breathe in the fumes and dust. Who would ever capture those things! There was so much I wanted to show in paint: sights, sounds, worlds of feeling, things far past words.

'I stayed in that studio house for two years. I painted; I destroyed my paintings. I had bonfires outside in the garden at 3 am: I'd watch, and see my work burn, and think as it went up in flames how much more beautiful it was at the moment when it caught fire. That cycle had caught me. I became completely dejected. I'd tried every way out of the maze. It was night, once more: the hours wore on. I paced around. There was a book on the shelf in my studio, which my mother had given me: it was about Yirawala, that old artist from Arnhem Land. I'd picked it up before, and gone through it: but it was his face, not his art, that spoke to me. On my work desk there was a container of red ochre a friend of mine had brought back from Central Australia: deep-red ochre pigment, lipstick-red. I began to sketch out a portrait of Yirawala: Yirawala as I imagined him, in that ochre—rough, raw. I was lying back, sketching, on the studio bed. My hands were barely moving: I was done in, finished; I had the sensation of drowning as I fell asleep. The strands of my consciousness frayed, and broke, one by one; I slipped away, into a stupor: darkness, more than rest. It seemed to last forever. Then a dream came: suddenly I could hear a bird singing—the sweetest song. I was in that half-awake state, when you can't tell where the border between dream and real lies. The singing kept on. I opened up my eyes—and there it was: a tiny green and red bird, in the studio room, flitting about from here to there. It landed on my shoulder. I saw it; I felt its wings against my face; then it flew out and perched on the table of the glassed-in verandah. The point of daybreak had come: the light was just touching the highest part of the range above the town. I opened the verandah window, and picked up the bird. I cradled it in my hands, held it up and let it fly out—and at that moment something broke in me: I knew then that I was on the right path: that I needed only to be patient, and quiet inside myself—to sit and wait.'

He smiled at me in the half-light, as if both of us had gone through that experience together. He leaned his forehead on the palms of his hands, then ran his fingers slowly through his hair.

'And what then?'

'Shall we drive?' he said.

I felt a deep indifference: it was as if the force of his memories had drained all my will and energy away. I nodded.

'If you like: where to?'

'It's almost dawn. Towards the west. To the open country. It's always good to be out there when the sun's rising, and watch that soft light moving when you're on the road.'

We climbed into an antique trayback, white, dust-coated, dilapidated, with bent bullbars and an array of cracked and broken spotlights. Tony leaned down and jump-started it; he gripped the wheel.

'Music?' he asked.

'I think not, on balance.'

'A wise choice, since there is none.'

'Why ask, then?'

'It's useful to have a picture of the tastes of one's fellow travellers, don't you think? There are quite divergent views, up here, on soundtracks. I always ride in silence. I can still hear the sounds I've heard before in the landscape; it's like hearing shadows: I hear the old chants, and songs, and voices. Even when he's not with me, I hear Paddy's voice, like the far-off sound of rustling paper, and the whispers and the echoes of the old people who used to drive this road with me, who've all gone. But when you travel with people from Doon Doon and Turkey Creek, many of them want country music: nothing else. They were stockmen; they still are in their hearts: they like good sad country music, Australian by preference—and there's a gospel crowd as well, among the older Gija. With the young ones, though, it's different: they always bring their own music with them—strange choices. It took me a while to figure it out. They all go for Motown; for soul, and crossover: Beyonce, Tina Turner, Diana Ross—any star with a strong look, so they can recognise the face on the cover, and work out which CDs to steal from the truck stop.'

'By which you mean they can't read yet?'

'By which I mean they never will.'

He pulled out from the driveway to the road: the verandah dogs all jumped smoothly up onto the back, and took their positions in neat formation alongside each other, staring out. We headed off: through town, over the diversion dam, on to the highway unfurling straight ahead. Dawn broke: the low peaks gleamed as though fire was burning on their crests; the trees cast long shadows across the ground. In front of us, like curved battlements, the shoulders of the Carr Boyd Range stretched away.

'Sombre!' he said: 'See them? Dark: dark, dark, dark—all full of secrets.'

'That back country, in there, behind the range?' I said: 'I've flown over it, and looked down at the ravines and the hidden valleys, and the creek beds.'

'But it's still secret: secret in plain view. Secret, like every deep truth. Of course you can get out to the rock holes and the lagoons along the rivers. It's not what it was before, though: in fact, the landscape round here's been changed completely.'

'You mean Lake Argyle, and the dam?'

'Have you ever been up there, on that road, to the caravan park, and the dam wall? It's just a tourist attraction, these days. All that lovely country's underneath the water: sure, you can see the old Argyle homestead; you can even walk through it. They reconstructed the original station house, stone by stone, like the Abu Simbel temples on the Nile—but people of tradition don't go there any more—it's a place of grief for them—and when I see the lake, even now, so many years after it was filled, it seems artificial to me: false, sterile, with the tops of dead gum trees protruding above the surface of the water like the stones on graves. Even the peaks around the shoreline look wrong—they're out of proportion: the light's wrong; so is the look of the water, so are the waves of its swell.'

He increased speed. The massif ahead of us had caught the sun's rays. It gleamed, and flashed like ice. I flinched; I smiled, and shielded my eyes.

'What are you thinking of?'

'What tricks the light can play!' I said: 'It looks like a range of snowy peaks, reflecting back the sun.'

'Is that something from childhood?' he said: 'From your well-buried, well-mastered past?'

'But isn't all life just a long betrayal of our first, childhood self—and then the realisation dawns.'

'The realisation?'

'We see how far we've drifted from our true being, how hard the journey back has grown. Isn't that it? Isn't that what all the signals life sends really mean? That there is a path for us to follow, and if we lose it we betray ourselves—ourselves first of all? You don't think that was what the messenger in your studio was telling you, all that time ago?'

He laughed. The south-west turn-off loomed up ahead.

'We're not going that way? Towards Turkey Creek, and Lissadell?'

'I tend to avoid that road, these days,' he said.

'Why? Bad associations? A crash?'

'Everybody's got a crash story in the Kimberley. It was two years ago, or three: when we were all still living at the outstation, at Crocodile Hole. Strange times!'

'Go on.'

'And it happened on a strange morning—but the mornings were often unusual out there. I remember waking with a start, peering out of the door of my tiny room. It was just before the dawn: there were shots, raised voices. That's when I heard someone calling my name: there'd been a fight, a stabbing. I tried to ring the police post at Argyle: no answer. We were all awake by then: all the artists. We decided the best thing would be to head for Kununurra, straight away: get out of there, not come back until things had quietened down. Rusty and the others went first. I had a brand-new Toyota; Hector was riding with me in the passenger seat. It was that time of day when everything looks pale and indistinct—just like now. See: distance, mass, volume—you can't be sure of any of them. We were travelling in convoy, but the first car kept speeding up, then going slow. That made it hard to keep formation—and you know that stretch of highway, with all the river bridges that turn into a single lane—it's dangerous, at the best of times. We were coming into Kingstons Rest: that low, narrow bridge—halfway, with the tree canopy on both sides, and the first car sped up to get across. They'd already opened up a gap; suddenly they were far ahead. At that point I saw the gleam of a road train in the distance, coming in our direction: it was one of those explosives carriers heading for the Argyle project; it looked like a mirage in the morning light. And maybe that was it: nothing seemed quite real. Usually I was very careful on those roads: I knew that any drive on that stretch of highway was courting death. I used to always slow down, whenever I saw an oncoming vehicle. That morning, though, it was the other way— I was accelerating, as if I was anxious to keep up.

'We reached the bridge: the road train was almost on us. I braked. Too late. I tried to reverse—but we were still going forward: the gears ground; they wouldn't bite. The truck came rushing closer: it was high above us. I could see the driver's face. And then everything stopped. Time disappeared. There was that slow motion, and clarity: knowing death had come. No sound. I looked across at Hector: how graceful and how frail and thin he was! He put up his hand, as if to stop the road train, and his hand looked like a magic wand—and at that instant, the impact came. I saw his body moving, riding the blow, like some dancer on the air. Then the sound came: glass breaking, a terrible twisting of metal; my head hitting something hard behind me. I could feel my blood on my body; I heard the motor winding up to screaming pitch, then dying. No more noise. Hector was quite untouched: he slipped out of the passenger-side door. I was barely able to pull myself out of the car; I lay down on the bitumen. There was blood pouring down my face. I could tell my ribs were shattered: my body had been torn apart. I struggled up on one shoulder, and lit a cigarette. Hector was leaning against a gum-tree trunk, close by, moving his hands above me; his lips were moving too, and he was staring down at me, and calling out my name. The sun's heat grew stronger; the cicadas were screeching in the trees.

'Cars drove up. The police, the ambulance. There were white clouds in the sky above, floating: they were the very same white clouds I saw as a five-year-old one day on the dairy farm. My eyes began to close. There was a beautiful feeling of peace, deeper and deeper; I was happy, happy to leave the world. I could barely hear the nurse yelling at me: Don't go to sleep, don't go to sleep, stay with us, she was shouting, and then the siren of the ambulance started up.'

'And that's all you remember?'

'Weeks afterwards, the nurse came to see me. I was out of hospital by then: she told me no one understood what they'd seen that day. I had no blood pressure for several minutes in the ambulance on the drive in. They radioed ahead that I'd be dead on arrival at the hospital. The doctors went to work: it was touch and go. I had twenty-eight stitches for the wound in the back of my head—but when they laid me out on the operating table they found no damage to my ribs or side. They could see the blood all over me: but there was no break in the skin, no bruising, nothing. I knew something had happened to me. I found I was almost a stranger to myself: it took me three months to get back into my body; in the first few weeks I felt as if I was a ghost.'

He fell quiet. We took the bend that leads up into the Cockburn Range. Throughout this recitation his voice had been hypnotic, rhythmic, low, as if he was recalling events from an impossibly distant time—I had been straining to hear his words, clinging to them, with the sense I was in danger of losing some vital thread—and each turn in the highway had seemed to mark a subtle shifting of the story's mood and tone.

'A good tale for the road—no?' said Tony.

'More carnage,' I said.

'In a sense—but life, as much as death. The two lie very close together here: that's what shapes the country. I've always had the sense that things are stronger in the Kimberley than elsewhere: everything—colours, feelings, thoughts, regrets. It's like a pressure chamber, this landscape—where the nature of the deal's too clear to miss.

'The deal?'

'Consciousness. Life. Life—that evil burden!'

He was driving quite fast, by this stage. The safety barriers went flashing by. The dogs on the trayback were crouching down. Before us, the winding road to Wyndham stretched away.

'See! The river estuaries and the salt flats, and the town. Wyndham. My perfect Wyndham! The Bastion lookout. The end of the line: where every dream fades to nothing.'

He changed up, with a fluid movement. The shacks and houses of the Six Mile settlement drew near.

'Are we in a hurry?'

'Once I'm on the road, and I can see it up ahead, I long to get to Wyndham,' he said: 'I've always loved it. I even thought I might settle here.'

'Wyndham! What's the appeal? The clouds of malarial mosquitoes? The extremity of the heat? The past everywhere, pressing down?'

'All those things—but above all, peace. It's an even kind of a place.'

'Everyone's on the same level?'

'Everyone's scraping along happily on the bottom rung. Every time I drive this road, and I pass the airstrip, and the little camps and tin sheds, and I see the racetrack shimmering away, and I start trying to make out where the river starts and the mirage ends, I feel like I'm coming into an odd back-door paradise.'

His voice had gone soft; he repeated these last words as if they had cast a spell on him: once, twice. I gazed up. We were right beneath the Bastion peak. Abruptly, he turned off, and took the series of curves and switchbacks leading upwards: higher, higher; the road levelled—we reached the summit: he jumped out, and strode over to the edge. Before us, the panorama stretched away: the wide estuary, the winding rivers and their mud flats, the red cliffs and mesas, all softened by the cloud banks and the humid haze.

'Come this way,' he said. 'Look down.'

There, directly below, was the old port and its huddled, rundown houses; there were the fuel tanks, and the meatworks ruins and the scrapyards.

'You can see it all, can't you?' he said: 'Spread out before you! And what's it saying? How weak and frail we all are. It's the poetry of desolation. The whole town: the Durack store, the old Chinese shops on the main street, the shacks, the jetties. And see over there—that looming bluff, beyond the water: that's the gorge that looks over Forrest River, where the old mission was, where the changes in this country began; and there, in that direction, where the fires are burning—keep going, along those hills: you reach Truscott Airbase, and Kalumburu. This is the real Kimberley. And look at that! Look now!'

The sun had cleared the rangeline: its beams were filtering through dark build-up clouds. Thick light shafts were striking the surface of the water beneath us: they picked out the swirling current; they swept across the cliffs and mesas; the whole landscape seemed to shake and quiver; the texture of the light shifted and pulsed. Rain veils began falling in front of us. On the water below, a dredging boat was pushing slowly against the tide. There was a distant roar, from across the ranges, faint, almost like an echo.

'Thunder,' I said. 'Far away. An early storm.'

'But it's not really thunder,' said Tony, then. 'Or not only. It's a presence. The noise of the country, talking. And it's not far away at all: it's very close. It's here: it's right with us, listening. When I come up here, and see this country, I realise we haven't even begun to look at it, be lifted up by it—respond to it. Here it is. It's showing itself to us: opening itself up. And all we do is hide away and fear it and flee from it. Do you know what I want to do here—here in lost, broken Wyndham, Wyndham at the end of the line?'

'No idea.'

'You can't guess? It was last night that I decided—the idea came to me, while we were talking, on the verandah: it came in an instant; suddenly I could see it, there, in every detail, in my mind's eye. I'm going to build a gallery! A majestic, beautiful gallery of modern art: the most perfect building in all the North. Can't you picture it, set in this landscape?'

'You could call it the Fitzcarraldo Gallery.'

'You don't believe me?

'Well,' I said, 'it's certainly a dream.'

'It's not a dream,' he said: 'It's a promise. A pledge. I promise you. You'll see. Come back, next wet season: come back, and you'll find me. I'll be here—and I'll have built a palace. A palace fit for kings: the gallery at the end of the world.'

*

But it was years later when at last, in the wake of protracted travels, I drove the long road out to Wyndham once again. Tony's celebrity, and Jirrawun's prestige, were then at their height; he had fulfilled his pledge: he had built the gallery. It stood, white-walled, angular, shimmering in the Wyndham landscape; it was his emblem: it took pride of place in all the films and photographic essays devoted to his project and its mounting success. More than anyone in the art archipelago of the North, he had found the key to worldly triumph—and this made the dark communiqués that issued from his bush retreat all the more captivating to their recipients, and all the more disquieting in their jewelled despair. It was clear to me the time had come to see him on his new stage: I set off. Again it was the peak of the build-up, the time of dry thunder: that brief spell, a week or two, no more, when lightning strikes constantly inside the massed cloud banks of the evening sky; thunder rolls, the storms strengthen, the flickers of the lightning sheets flash all through the night. The air is thick, and damp, and seems almost to possess a residual electric charge;

one breathes with effort; one's thoughts and associations become disjointed and rearrange themselves.

Such was the backdrop: I sped through the silent landscapes west of Katherine as the sun sank down: parched country; green savannah turning to pale yellow, leached out—much like the pale backgrounds of the medieval altarpieces I used to hunt down and pour myself into in earlier years, when knowledge of a painted landscape and painted religion were the height, for me, of what a well-formed mind should seek out: those fine, receding vistas, which seemed to hide in them all the secrets that life held. They were opened up to me by one man, a man whose ideas and example made a strong impression on me, and whose memory still floats up to the surface of my thoughts, at strange moments, as on that drive—unbidden, brought back by chance impressions, by fleeting sights or words: Panofsky, the Princeton magus, who brought his rigour and his taste for structure from the old world to the new.

He was born in Hanover, and trained in the great intellectual forcing houses of imperial Germany; he secured appointment at a young age as the foundation professor of art history at Hamburg; and it was there that he joined the circle of thinkers associated with the newly established Warburg Library. By character and cast of mind he was ideally suited to the furtherance of Warburg's lifelong obsession: the pursuit of symbols and their shifting meanings, blown about as they are by the storm winds of our world. In his conversation Erwin Panofsky was all fluency and charm; at the podium he was the image of authority; on the page his writings combine a descriptive finesse and energy that still work their mesmerising effect today—his words bring alive each work of art he touches on; he lays bare not just their coded language but their moods, their tones—and it may be that this urgency and this need for precision stemmed from his perspective; from his yearning, distanced view, his exile.

In 1933, while he was teaching in America, he received a telegram: 'Cordial Easter Greetings, Western Union,' declared the letters on the seal of the envelope; inside was an edict advising him that, in conformity with the newly enacted racial laws, he had been dismissed from all his German posts. There was nothing else for it: he decided to become an American. His fame in his adopted country grew; at the war's end he was invited to deliver the Charles Eliot Norton lectures at Harvard: he chose as his subject the world of early Netherlandish art and the influences of the school's master painters on each other—and it was these lectures that taught me the intricacies of that world, but in delayed fashion, long after I first read my way through them, struck purely by the elegance and beauty of the author's thought and the freedom of its flow.

Gradually, as years passed, I realised that my loves and enthusiasms were Panofsky's; that what struck him struck me; what he saw was what I was striving to see—and this was a kinship of affinities, nowhere more strongly apparent to me than in my feelings on looking at the Portinari Altarpiece, a triptych, painted in the late fifteenth century by the mystic friar Hugo van der Goes: it hangs in the Uffizi, in Florence, surrounded by masterworks of the Italian Renaissance, its austere figures out of place, its landscape backgrounds seeming, in that lush company, like views onto country blasted by biblical curse and plague: pale hills and valleys, tall, gaunt trees—trees much like the gums and boabs that draw one's eye all through the North.

For Panofsky, this artist possessed a strong appeal: indeed, he is the hero of the age, the doomed genius of that world, the creator whose genius transcends the time. Melancholy presides over him and shapes his art; he is at once exalted and oppressed by the influence of Saturn; he is subject to alternate states of creative insight and black despair, 'walking on dizzy heights above the abyss of insanity, and tumbling into it as soon as he loses his precarious balance'—and the work he makes bears this stamp. It is not still, and calm, and bathed in the certainty of a harmonious faith; it is not an art that communicates and shares itself with its onlooker: it is something new. Panofsky frames a theory for it—the human beings depicted in these altarpieces are not stable; they are radioactive; they give themselves up to the surrounding world; they lose themselves through art; they are in a process of continual decay.

It is an idea that was plainly inspired by the dawn of the nuclear age, and by the detonation of atomic bombs above Hiroshima and Nagasaki, which took place only two years before the Harvard lectures were delivered; and the glow of those radiative clouds casts a strange, haunting light on the Portinari landscapes as he describes them—austere, bare, yet criss-crossed by networks of secret symbols; burned, scorched almost to nothing by firestorm flames. The fear Panofsky feels in the face of such deranged forces, the sense that grips him of art as an enterprise constantly endangered by unreason—all this comes through repeatedly in his words: to paint, to look, can bring too much clarity, too much intensity, until it threatens the very defences that keep reason supreme and stable in the world, just as that clarity of sight overwhelmed Hugo van der Goes, sunk as he was in depressions, afflicted by suicidal manias, despairing of the salvation of his soul.

And those parched ranges and burnt trees round me as I drove—what would their words be to man: words of consolation? Judgement? Indifference?

Night fell. How well I had come to know the rhythm of the road: the Kununurra turning; the shadow of the powerhouse; the lakeside lagoon; the diversion dam, its lights surrounded by wildly circling moths and insects; and ahead again, the highway, stretching straight, and pairs of light beams far away, advancing— the road trains, in procession. They drew nearer, their beams dazzling, and I would grip the wheel, my eyes blinded by the glare, and wait for the collision that seemed inevitable as each one swept past; then darkness once more, pitch black, my heart racing, the next road train on the hill crest ahead beginning to bear down. At last the ranges loomed; lightning storms stretched away across the Cambridge Gulf; the gleam of Wyndham shone below. There was the Six Mile, and the town.

I consulted the note; the directions were impressively precise: 'Turn onto a faint track once past Deadman Creek: you've gone too far if you reach the sign for the rubbish dump.' I found the track. It forked. There was the gate, with wheel-spoke decorations and a bleached-white cattle skull on each post. In, down, across a gully: I pulled up. The moon had just cleared the Bastion's crest.

It was almost full—in its gleam I made out my surroundings: a lush, tree-filled garden, arbours and avenues of young fruit trees and acacias, vines and creeper tendrils intertwining overhead. I climbed down from the Land Cruiser.

Facing me, staring at me, its head quite still, was a dingo, caught in the silver light. I stayed motionless; it advanced, came close, circled me, once, twice, touched its muzzle to my legs and stepped back into the dark. I followed, and through the trees I caught sight of a low-slung house in the distance—more shack, though, than house: its verandah lights were on, but they were dim paraffin lamps; there was an outbuilding with a buckled roof of corrugated iron. A set of winding pathways ran off in its direction, before twisting, dividing, and doubling back upon themselves. I tried several of them: the dingo followed me down each one, padding silently, watching keenly. 'What is this place?' I murmured to myself.

There was a sudden movement: rhythmic, loud, behind me. I wheeled about. A sprinkler had come on: water jets were playing at sharp angles all through the garden, striking against the leaves and branches of the trees. Close by me was a large fountain, spurting in every direction: its central spout was made of welded iron, fringed by bulbs of metal, curved, serrated blades and twisted lengths of sawn-off pipe. 'It's like the Villa d'Este—or Marienbad,' I said, quite loudly, this time, into the night, half-expecting Tony to appear at any moment, so great was the noise from the waterworks, so abrupt, too, the variation in the sound: for one set of jets and fountains would shut off, only to be followed almost instantly by a fresh outpouring elsewhere in the garden.

150

I made straight for the verandah, through scrub and undergrowth; past a creek bed, with large boulders, and a still pool; along a fenceline, its barbed-wire strands rusted and broken. The front door was ajar. A note, neatly folded, had been inserted into the fly-screen frame. I opened it. 'Do not under any circumstances walk in the garden in the dark. Death adders very plentiful at this time of year!'

I stepped inside. It was a large room, almost bare: plastic seats drawn up around a metal folding table, mattresses and swags piled up in the far corner, bookshelves overloaded with piles of dog-eared paperbacks; a kitchen, an old stove; two armchairs covered in bright red upholstery—and sprawled in one of them, asleep, Tony Oliver, a book propped open on one armrest, a serrated knife held against his heart. I shook him by the shoulder, gently, then more firmly. Nothing. I gazed down at him. How tranquil he seemed, in that soft light, as if care or anguish had never cast a shadow over him.

I sank into the empty armchair, and closed my eyes, and heard the whine of mosquitoes on their first approach; and soon I had entered that despairing half-slumber old Kimberley hands know well: a state of exhaustion intensified, more than rest; one is prey to every doubt and every fear from waking hours, but dreams never come; the night's hours revolve, and each of them takes its toll in turn, until the victim returns to awareness more broken than before the darkness fell.

'Get up—you've got an appointment: a date with destiny!'

I heard the voice; I opened my eyes. Tony was standing over me, smiling a demonic smile.

'I do?'

'Isn't all life an approach to destiny? Lift up those tired limbs! Rise and shine!'

He handed me a metal cup full of black coffee. I sipped it, and stared at him: he was in Western gear, his long hair slicked back, unkempt. I grimaced.

'It's got a strange taste,' I said: 'What's in it?'

'A little something! Don't make a face like that. It's the best espresso coffee, vacuum-packed, mail-ordered, flown in by courier from Melbourne, made in a professional machine: it's the real thing. You couldn't find better anywhere in all the North.'

'So why does it taste so strange? It's almost as if there was aniseed in it.'

'Yes, well, it could just be the metallic edge you get from the bore water, round this time of year—but I did actually put a little shot of absinthe in as well, just to get things going.'

'Absinthe? Where on Earth can you find absinthe in Wyndham? And isn't it illegal—not to mention very out of fashion?'

'You can get anything if you want it badly enough,' said Tony, reflectively.

'It's not as if we're in late-nineteenth-century Paris,' I said.

'Actually,' said Tony, 'in a sense, we are.'

I glanced out. Green filtered light was all around us; on the shadecloth screening the verandah, an array of stick insects and dark-winged butterflies were perched, bathing in the spray from a fountain close by.

'Where's the dog?' I asked.

'What dog?'

'That beautiful tame dingo that was outside last night.'

'Truthfully?' said Tony: 'You must have seen the ghost dog—the pale dingo from the Dreaming. It only manifests itself to three categories of people: those about to die, those with heightened insight, and those in spiritual distress.'

'I see,' I said, and let this piece of information sink in: 'And how do you know so much about it?'

'It's with me all the time,' said Tony: 'It stalks me constantly—it's ever present, pacing after me, tracking down the pathways of my mind. What do you think of this place? The house isn't much, but the gardens—they're like an ornamental parkland—it could be Dessau, or Versailles. I bought it from a wonderful man: he was dying when he sold it to me; he'd been in the meatworks here—and when the place was demolished, all the old hands who wanted to stay in Wyndham sorted through the scrap metal that was left, and carted off whatever they could use. There's plenty of houses in old Wyndham town that were put together from the meatworks ruins: when you know what to look for, you start to see bits and pieces everywhere. Here, for instance: all the fountain decorations and the little curlicues and the metal trellis arches come from the equipment in the boning chamber and the processing rooms.'

He glanced back at me.

'You look shocking,' he said: 'Where have you just come back from?'

'Afghanistan.'

'That might explain it. I'm still pretty jet-lagged, myself. I've been on a journey of my own. One I wanted to make all my life. I've just got back from St Petersburg. Do you know it?'

'I knew Leningrad, once.'

'I was visiting the Hermitage,' said Tony, proudly, sweeping on: 'We'll be having an exhibition there. I'm choosing the paintings right now. Have a cigarette? A Russian souvenir. They're quite strong!'

He held out a pack: it was squarish, blue and gold, with white lettering arranged in a striking arc on its front, and a map of the Russian north emblazoned below.

'Belomor,' I said, and listened to the tone in my voice. 'I've come across that brand.'

'I didn't realise you were such a connoisseur.'

'It had associations, for me, long ago.'

'Sometimes a cigarette is more than just a cigarette?'

'That kind of thing. So: your journey?'

He launched into his narrative: it was a bravura tale, with multiple perspectives, time shifts, interruptions for sudden reveries—the artists he most admired, the ecstatic moments that had come to him in front of paintings he loved, the nights full of snow and days of frost. We walked in the garden, weaving through the maze of the trees; along the creekline; back.

'The strangest part of it all, though,' he said, 'is how little of that time there has stayed in focus for me, now I'm here again. I just have fragments left: fragments—then great swathes of experience come flooding back, and stay for a moment, and vanish almost at once. The memories drift inside me like clouds, and emerge as images. I can be looking at the dry canegrass stretching out towards the peaks, and there's an angle in the light, a gleam: something in my mind will catch—and then suddenly I'm walking on the slippery sidewalks of Petersburg, and watching the shadows shifting in the light and the canals flowing—or I can picture myself again the way I was as a young man, when I was just starting out in the art world, discovering paintings, making my first trips to Europe, seeing with my own eyes what I'd only seen in books. That's when I decided to spend a few months living by myself in France—that's how I met Dubuffet.'

'Truly?'

'He was a hero to me in those days: he is still. I had an exhibition of his work, at that gallery I used to run, in Melbourne—and he must have found out about it, somehow, though he was always remote from those events: I was in Paris when the call came. I was in my hotel room—I'd been there for several days; the lights were off, the curtains drawn. I was plunged in the most paralysing depression—and I was so young then I imagined the mood was permanent, and things would never shift. The phone rang; it was early—it woke me. It was Dubuffet's dealer: the artist wanted to invite me to lunch; he was very struck that someone like me was showing an exhibition of his work at the other end of the world.'

'A dream come true!' I said.

'It was the worst thing imaginable, then. I said no. I was darkness. I was silence. I was gloom. I couldn't do it. I made an excuse. I apologised, profusely; the dealer on the other end of the phone was quite shocked. The chance slipped by. Some days later I managed to summon up the energy and self-possession to leave the hotel. It was snowing, I remember making my way down the Rue Saint-Denis, with all its butchers' shops and Roman arches, towards the Pompidou.'

'To see the paintings, if not the man?'

'Wait,' he said: 'Don't spoil it: let me tell the story. You've got that awful urge to see ahead: to control. Just let life come to you. Take it as it comes—it's the tropics; it's the build-up!'

'Sorry—it just seemed the way things were going.'

'No—you're right—of course: and that's the sign a speaker and a listener are in harmony, when they're together telling the tale. You're right. I always used to go to the Cubist galleries at the Beaubourg; I spent hours there, every morning: I was memorising every Picasso, every Braque. I wanted to know them so well they'd be with me in my mind wherever I was, wherever life brought me—but that day I varied my routine. I found the Dubuffet room, and sat on one of the benches at the centre of the gallery, and set myself to absorbing everything, but in a different way: I tried to open myself, to be open to each work in turn, and the way they spoke to each other, what they said to me—and after some while in that state, sitting there, I felt someone's presence, at a bench beside me. I looked over: and he was there, holding a walking stick, looking straight at me.'

'It was him?'

'It was Jean Dubuffet, watching as I gazed at his work. His look wasn't a smile—but it was full of compassion, grace. No words. I glanced back towards the paintings, and lost myself in them again: and he stayed there, sitting, watching, by my side.'

'Strange encounter!'

'Of all my experiences with artists, that was the one that meant the most to me. I think back on it now, often. He was the last of the line for me: the last bright star at the end of the tradition, who breathed the same breath as those other masters I loved so much—and I felt him looking at me there, as if he was saying to me: It's for you, now, the burden. I must leave the light; the sun, and sky. The time's here for you. For you to look for yourself, and make some balance of your own with the world. Study's nothing. Knowledge is nothing. Only painting. Only art.'

'And that's what you've been doing ever since: with your artists—with Jirrawun?'

'Of course.'

'And where are they all: Paddy, Freddie, Rusty? I thought they'd all be with you out here.'

'At a funeral—that's where they spend their lives, these days. Don't you want to see the new studio? It's not far. My temple: my folly! Haven't you heard about it? Isn't that why you came?'

'Word had reached me,' I said: 'How could I not have heard? It's a triumph: everybody talks about it. I've seen all the photos. When you told me about it, so long ago, I thought it was just one of those mad build-up dreams!'

'The Fitzcarraldo Gallery. I remember—that morning, after we'd driven through the night—don't worry! The strange thing is that the dream's been fulfilled in life—in every detail; it looks just the way I first saw it in my mind's eye: white-walled, with clean lines, high windows, a panoramic view across the ranges. It's beautiful—and full of sadness, like every beautiful thing.'

'Sadness?'

'I'm sure you know exactly what I mean! In those first months, when the painting at the outstation had just started, when the artists were bringing out their stories one by one, and finding ways to show their world on canvas, I told myself that it was something forever: that those works were eternal things—they would hang in museums of art and outsiders would understand them; feel what was in them; feel the landscape, and what lies in it. But slowly, once I couldn't hide any longer from the Kimberley, and the way the lives around me were being lived, I came to realise that permanence has gone from here. Transience is all there is: things fading, things vanishing. And I began to look at the paintings in a new way. Something shifted in my understanding of them—it felt as if they were becoming less solid, less self-contained: I had the impression that the fields of colour in them were changing before my eyes. I remembered what you used to say to me, about paintings radiating away their strength, being worn down in the world, being looked at too much—and I started to wonder if I really was a saviour in the North, if what I'd done meant anything at all. You know I'd always been afraid of what lay before us: you remember.'

'Of course I do.'

'That fear came to a head when we moved out here, from Kununurra to Wyndham, and we'd built the new studio: there was room to think: everything was calm and still. I used to go up to the gallery space, alone, after sunset, as darkness fell; I'd sit with the paintings, and watch the stars, and the clouds drifting; and there were all the noises of the night to hear: you could hear the owls calling, and the nightjars, and the dogs from far across the valley would howl—and I'd lie there, thinking how I'd done what I wanted to. I'd made a gallery, and filled it full of art, and that art was like a doorway: into what?'

I turned to him.

'Don't,' he said: 'Don't speak. The words aren't there. They aren't in the universe, even to begin to say. If they were, if there were words to express that, why would you paint? Why would anyone?'

'There are some people,' I said, 'who only have words.'

'But you know words are just traps: mirages, nothing else. You know that as well as anyone: you're always running, looking, moving—trying to see past the surface of the world. Isn't that why people like you always come out here? Why everyone goes out into the deep bush—always further, further, as if they could reach places where the landscape's still strong enough to unravel everything they are. To unmake themselves: and only when we get to that point do we believe we might begin to see. Isn't that the truth?'

His voice was harsh. He gave me an assessing, almost vindictive look.

'Shall we go out?' I said, 'And take a look through the studio together? After all, I came a long way to see it.'

'You did,' he murmured: 'And I should show you, I know: go with you—give you the tour—occupy my dream. But I can't. I can't anymore. It's all played out, now. There's an art movement; there are paintings, exhibitions, collections—everything we longed for: but I can see the way things will be. That I can see with perfect vision.'

'How will they be?'

'One by one, the old artists will die. Hector's dead. Paddy's already halfway into another world: he's leaving; very soon he'll be gone. We'll bury his heart at Bow River—there'll be a funeral, the dignitaries from down south will fly up, and make speeches. I'll write a eulogy, we'll have the usual grief and ceremonial, and the grave will be left—left for the heat and storms—the world here will continue its dissolution, and all the children we see around us will grow up to lead dark, short lives. You go up—you go, and walk through it—I can't: it gives me no joy any more. I realise now that I wasn't building a temple—I built a mausoleum instead.'

*

All went as he saw it would. I spent some hours with him; our talk flowed on—Wyndham: its shifting atmospherics, his diversions there, his sense of what lay in wait: for him; for all his friends. I made my visit to the studio, alone. I gazed up at the paintings; I had the sense of being on a pilgrimage: I knew they were the last great works from Jirrawun. Late that evening, I drove back to Darwin. Within the month, the news reached me of Paddy Bedford's death. A funeral was held; the obituaries appeared; Tony dropped from sight.

It was the next dry season before I began to hear word of his doings: the stories, as always, were baroque—he had fled Australia, and reappeared in Vienna, or Petersburg; he was in Manhattan, plunged once more among the modernists; he had returned to the haunts of his childhood, and was deep in the Yarra Ranges, living alone. These tales swirled around his name for some while, then subsided; the trail went dead; and it was only when I collided with the Melbourne gallery owner William Mora one day several months later, on a trip south, that the picture clarified: I learned the truth; it was more exotic still.

'Tony? Yes,' he said, and gave me his most quizzical look: 'Yes. I can fill you in, if you like. It's an unusual narrative. You might even want to go and visit him: it's worth the trip.'

'Where to?'

'He's in Vietnam,' said William, and paused for effect.

'Go on,' I said.

The story tumbled out: the two of them, after the funeral, overwhelmed by their unbroken sense of grief, had decided to travel. They opted for a tranquil, little-visited stretch of the Vietnamese coastline, and found rooms at a small hideaway beside a fishing village, directly on the shore of the South China Sea.

'The effect of that beach was peculiar,' said William, and he cradled his chin on one hand, and assumed a reflective air: 'The pressure of the tide seemed never to stop; you had the sense of being in a constant, unavailing battle; it was like being slowly pulverised, torn apart and remade: the light was so strong, and the sound of the waves so metronomic and intense.'

Tony made it his habit, on that trip, to stroll from the small retreat where the two of them were staying into the village close by, and there, one evening, as the sun was setting, he met a young woman of great reticence and charm of character. Something shifted, at that point, in his way of seeing the world. He came back to Vietnam: he rejoined her; they married; they had a child. He forged contacts in Hanoi: they were tentative; they deepened.

He met the artists of the capital; he moved in their circles for some months. Soon he found himself giving advice to the Central Committee of the Vietnamese communist party on cultural relations with the wider world.

'What a reinvention!' I broke in.

'Are you surprised? Really? I go up there to see him, from time to time. You could almost say he was happy—or at least on the edge of happiness. You should make contact with him again. The moment's right. Although you still have to treat him slightly as you would a wounded, high-bred animal: you can tell he's still recovering from a dreadful blow.'

'You mean the death of the artists he knew? Or the end of his northern life?'

'I mean the end of the dream that beauty can save the world. That's what drove him away. That's what he was running from. And he spent the first years of his Indochinese life travelling, constantly: up and down to Hanoi and Ho Chi Minh City, steeping himself in that milieu. But I think now he's come to rest—in fact, he's building a house. It's an intriguing design: French tropical meets antebellum South. It even incorporates a studio.'

'Everything he builds incorporates a studio.'

'Check it out,' said William: 'Go and see. Why not? It could be just what you need—a break beside the pounding, rhythmic ocean.'

'I'd like that. There's so much left open from our earlier talks. So much unsaid.'

'That's always the way. Probably what real friendships rely on. Here, then: take this—his details.'

With that he handed me a card, and vanished into the crowds of Federation Square. I glanced at it. On one side was a bright yellow five-pointed star set against a vivid blood-red ground; on the reverse, a sea of Vietnamese sentences, a set of numbers, and a name: 'Mr Oliver—Cultural expert.' Undeniably, I thought, and laughed to myself: from Fitzcarraldo to Colonel Kurtz's apocalypse in one swift step!

*

And so, a few weeks later, almost by natural progression, I found myself crouched in my seat on a Vietnam Air jet bound for Ho Chi Minh City, staring down into the darkness, tracking our progress as we soared high above the lightning storms and thunderclouds. At last we dipped down towards the city's lights and sprawl. Long before, in the days of Soviet influence, I had known it well.

I lingered there for some days, lost in memory and nostalgia—I immersed myself in its sounds and rhythms: by morning I roamed the avenues, and inspected the galleries of the fine-art museum; when evening came I read my way through histories of the guerrilla campaign and studies of the impressionist movement, which had flourished there in the last days of French rule. After this series of acclimatisations and forays, on the appointed morning for my rendezvous with Tony I drove the coastal highway north, through quiet towns and tourist precincts, past military camps and training centres, past schools and factories. It was a winding, twisting journey: more than half the day was gone by the time I reached my destination. There he was, waiting, smiling his wry, sad smile.

'You thought you would never see me again!'

'I was sure I wouldn't,' I said: 'Life's in chapters. Sometimes people turn the page on you.'

'But lives have their themes, and those themes keep on coming back. Some people you never know at all; some you can never leave behind. Look!'

He waved his hand towards the beach, which was veiled by drifts of spray: it stretched to a promontory, a mountain, a cape. Tall dunes, rough shacks and houses, fishing boats at sheltered anchor: 'My new world! Let me show you, before anything. It's the softest, gentlest part of the day—see how beautiful it is!'

'A good subject,' I said, 'for a painter with an eye for light.'

'What was it,' he said then, in an abrupt voice, and turned to me, and stared at me as if the stare's strength would bring forth some vital clue: 'What? What was I looking for, chasing after, all through those years when we were spending time together? What was that gleam in the North? I see you, and I send my mind back now—to the Kimberley, and the world of the old painters, and Jirrawun.'

'And?'

'And that was it: light. That's what it was; that's all it was— the gleam: the flame inside the light. It was that glow in the country they were trying to put down in paint—and that was the secret strength that pulled me there, and held me there.'

We walked: he was full of words, and tales, and there was a force and drive in what he was saying to me; he watched my face to see my reaction to every sentence that he spoke. How much he told me, in those hours, as dusk drew near: the artists, their strengths, all that they had given him, the decisions that he made, and failed to make; the ties he still felt to the Kimberley—the pressures that drove him to his drastic flight. Our steps had fallen into a rhythm, slow, dreamlike, as if we were trying to keep time with the sound of the waves and tide.

'I'm glad you came here,' he said: 'To my exile. I wanted to show you this. All this: not just the sight itself, but what it seems to tell me at different times. Each time of day is completely distinct. There's dawn, and the first glare: it's hard, sharp light then, avenging light, that damages the viewer as much as the viewed. There's the effect that comes when the tide's pushing in, in the lush, soft mid-morning: everything seems part of a single creative act—everything is joined together by shafts of burning sun. And there's the late afternoon: that's a clean, documentary light; it picks out the colours of the painted wooden fishing boats, each shading of red, and blue, and grey and black; the tide's out, then, the sand's hard and flat, and all the boys from the village are playing on the beach, and the families of fishermen sit on the seawalls of their houses and feel the breezes blowing in. That's the cycle. It's a meditative cycle, for me: a conversation with the landscape.'

'A talking cure.'

'Every day; and each day seems to send those hard Kimberley times further into the past: I forget more and more of what I was.'

'And that's the aim?'

He smiled, as if absorbing this idea, admitting it gradually to the confines of his thought.

'It doesn't work completely, of course. I try. I aim at oblivion:

release from what I saw, and what became of me in my northern life. I watch the sea, sometimes all night long; I listen to the pulse of the ocean pounding on the beach, and see the clouds in their movement, and the stars, when the breaks in the cloud cover come—the stars shining down in their patchwork fields of Prussian blue. The winds, the clouds, the ocean—they're like a language to me: continually speaking, continually forming, and dissolving, like thought itself.'

'And saying what?'

'How can you think of making anything literal from that? Not every language has to have words.'

'It can be an abstract language?'

'Of course! Moods, tones. It's like a dance, where the meaning is just the dance, and nothing more—there's no hidden code. Painting's like dance for me: it always was; a kind of ritual, where you want to end everything and become one with what surrounds you.'

'Become one,' I echoed: 'End it all. Remember? That's where our friendship began: with you leaning on the driveway gate in Kununurra, at that Jirrawun house, all those years ago—turning over in your mind the best way to die.'

'Death,' he said, melodramatically: 'The harshest critic! The only index of our life that really counts. It seems less abstract with each passing day. That beloved limit: that frontier where every single road runs out.'

'But you don't think there's only death waiting for us, a full stop, do you? Your life's full of presences and spirits—at least, it used to be.'

'There's nothing,' he said, in a hard voice: 'Nothing. That's what being here helps me to sense: to know, and accept. All the spirits of the Kimberley: they have their energy, and force. How persuasive they were, how seductive. But they're not for us.'

'Then what's left?'

'Why question life like that? When I was much younger, I came across a lovely story: it taught me something. It was a novella, by Camus: you could see his thinking very plainly in it. It was short—from start to end no more than a hundred pages—and there was a passage that's been etched into me ever since I read it, more than thirty years ago. I hardly ever remember anything I see in print—the words and thoughts just slip by and leave no residue: but it wasn't like that this time. It's the story of a young man, Meursault. He's on his deathbed as we come to the last pages of the book. Camus frames the scene like a cinematographer: his central character looking through the open shutters of his window from his bed onto a blue ocean with a red fishing boat—and his lover, Lucienne, looking over him. Meursault thinks to himself just before his death about the fullness of her lips, and how after he's died another man will kiss and enjoy them.'

'Fairly bleak!' I said.

'No! Not at all. There's such overwhelming acceptance of reality, in that sentence: and truth. Such love of life, such delight in being in the world. That's the heart of life for him. Sight, breath—just that; he remembers the acrobats somersaulting on the hot pavement in Algiers; he leans back; he thinks of Lucienne's sun-tanned body, the salt spray on the wind, the red fishing boat through the window.'

'And you're building that room here: with the shutters, and the view of the ocean, and the red boat.'

'Perhaps I am. I know now that our path in life is to live not by program, not by idea and manifesto, but through the senses and the heart—and it took me the lion's share of my time on Earth to find that out.'

'Who from?'

'We go through the world, and from time to time we meet people who fill us up with grace, and hope. Nature throws them up, and gives them to us—people who are more at one than we are with the rhythm of the world: rice-farming peasants from the country round here, old Aboriginal painters from the Kimberley. People who live without dark hesitation. That's what I've come to believe in. This life, here; not life after death, not salvation far ahead, but life itself: what we live now.'

'And for so long you dreamed of permanence, and worshipped art.'

He looked at me. The noise from the breaking waves was getting louder as we walked on: I could barely hear his words.

'And I still do,' he said: 'Only now I see permanence in dreams.'

'It does feel like a dream, walking here, with this constant crashing of the sea, and the spray in the air all round us.'

'It is one. Don't you have that dream sense, that the living and the dead are all part of consciousness? That both find their way through time and space? I see life as a dream, more and more, and I think the old men I knew in the Kimberley lived that way: that was their life; all time was running at the same time for them, and death somehow forms completeness, and time and history stop running, and come into phase—in the same way a piece of music can end but the notes still play on in the mind: the way old songs from Crocodile Hole are still echoing inside me now.'

I looked across at him.

'Why are you staring at me? Back to staring? It's not just the North that made me think this way: it was childhood, it was travels, it was everything. We see so much in life, too much—and then there's a dreadful weariness just from what we know. It's natural to want to renounce knowledge, and go back to a world of simple things: rhythms, colours, patterns, tides. We only ever needed ideas to mask what lies ahead.'

All this was said in a calm, tranquil way, as if exchanges of this kind were common on that hazy beachfront, with the late sun pouring down its dazzling light.

'What lies ahead?' I echoed.

'You always pretend not to know what I mean, and you always do, of course. Why else do you want to talk to me, and seek me out, if not because you think I've seen things: found something out. And I have. Deep things: in the Kimberley; here, too. Some people dive pretty deep, in their art—and then they find a very simple thing. The world joins up. The patterns become one. The light on the waves when you look down from the Wyndham Bastion as the tide's just turning; the brushstrokes on Leonardo's paintings in the Hermitage when you inspect them through a magnifying glass; the markings on an old Hanoi sketch work from the wartime years with the pigments drawn on hessian ground. They're the same: the same pattern. Things cohere. Every sadness finds its place; even the darkest griefs fade away. There's just life—that's all we have to worship.'

'And at the close of it we're extinct: we're nothingness.'

'I feel increasingly that it's more as if we're turned inside out, we're set free from a container that's holding us: we leave its confines; we achieve an end. And we recognise the brutal truth: that life's just the colour of the light hitting the water, or the red sail on the blue ocean, or the salt on one's skin. Enough. Let's go on up!'

'Up where?'

'Don't you see the house—almost hidden—surrounded by the palm trees?'

There, among the lines of low, rough shacks and concrete dwellings on the sand dunes was a white structure, with a pediment and columned façade, and a separate pavilion alongside, its square bulk softened by overhanging eaves, much like a temple, or a tomb.

'There? I noticed it before, when we were walking. I wanted to ask you about it; it's extraordinary: it looks like a palace from another world.'

'That was rather the effect that I was striving for, actually— so come: we'll talk more; there are whole realms we haven't even touched on. Come, and leave all your regrets and cares behind.'

I paused a moment.

'I know they're all you've got, but leave them! Come with me—come with me, after so many years of only knowing me marooned and lost—come up, and see my home.'

IV

MINGKURLPA

IT WAS NEAR THE year's end; the build-up heat was pressing down. It was dark; there was a young moon in the sky. We were on the beach, at the waveline, I with a torch in my hand, my friend Jared with a shotgun in his. We advanced. The spray hung in the air; lightning from far-off storms flashed.

'You really feel you're at the edge of things, don't you,' said he, 'down here on this shore? You feel the nothing close at hand.'

I listened. What I felt was that trapped sense that comes in the Australian tropics—the immediacy—everything depends on the next breath; life to that point has been nothing; hope, memory, they mean nothing: the only choice is to endure. How wonderful it would be to have some passage out, some way of breaking free, some tale to while away the heat of the night; what was the point of living if not to live through tales, and then retell them, and be consoled by their words as they flowed through time: words that give us the surest sense of knowing who and where we are.

'What are those lights?' I asked him, 'Out so late?'

'Patrol boats, maybe. Or tankers, and supply vessels, headed for the rigs in the Arafura Sea. Have you ever been out that far, or made a flight over them? What structures: they rise up like cathedrals, towers looming from the waves—and they're all blazing with light by darkness too. Still, they're just specks in the seascape—I can't set eyes on them without thinking how fragile everything human is on Earth.'

'You? A soldier like you?'

'I was more of a strategic operative, actually: the point was never to go to war.'

'You mean the threat of war guarantees peace? That kind of thing? Like now, when your presence guarantees we won't see a single crocodile all night?'

I flicked the light beam over the swell: it frothed, and tossed, and seethed with menace.

'Haven't you grasped the basics yet?' he said: 'Quests are fulfilled by the act of questing, not the goal. These islands are the wrong place for you if you're looking for something solid and real.'

'We aren't on a real survey?'

'We'll come back out later,' he said, in a long-suffering voice: 'It's real enough. We'll make another transect, maybe, when the moon's gone down. We'll stop for a spell, there, at the Dingo Camp—just ahead. After too long keeping a lookout in this humidity, just staring at the torch beam picking out the waves in their rhythm, I find you start seeing things.'

'Imagining things?'

'And the languor this weather breeds: the hopelessness, the sense of being at the end of your tether, being half-dead, so close that dying wouldn't even be a change of state, and there'd be nothing interesting about it at all.'

I made no reply.

'I thought you'd appreciate that last one, at least,' said Jared. 'I give you my best, always, in my reflections on the trap of consciousness.'

'I did appreciate it,' I said: 'It was remarkable. I know exactly what you're talking about. Isn't it the same for everyone? Sometimes, when you hear things like that, so perfect in their phrasing, it seems right just to be quiet, and let the words go, let them flash by, and give them silence for their flight. Why's it called Dingo Camp?'

'Who knows? Does it matter? Maybe Ernie Dingo did a live broadcast here. Maybe an ancestral dingo lived here. That's the name. It's just this way, sheltered, in between those dunes—and there's someone you might want to meet.'

We came up. There was a circle of figures sitting round the fire. A young woman with angular features was speaking, telling a story, gesturing, her gestures picked out by the glow of the flames.

'Who's that?' I whispered to Jared.

'That's the film-maker I was telling you about,' he hissed back. 'They've just been out to Seagull Island, north of here, out past the reefline, the last island, in the open waters.'

And it became clear that trip was being retold. I listened. Her voice was rhythmic, and soft. She had a slight accent; there was an elegance about her manner; she chose her words with great precision, correcting herself, frowning, leaning forward as though her life depended on catching the perfect phrase for each tiny detail of her recitation: the boat's movements on the swell, the look of the island, which was in truth no more than a low sandbar, its surface covered by the nests of thousands of black-capped, fork-tailed terns.

'Even from far away we could hear them,' she was saying: 'Their calls, the calls from those hundreds of seabirds, thousands, they blended together, into a single noise, a note constantly held—horrible at first hearing, terrifying, like a curse, a curse being rained down—but after some minutes it shifted; the birds began flying close above us, swooping low, and circling, or hovering against the wind, and then the noise seemed different, quite different, and beautiful, more like a song, or a prayer. We were close, almost aground: the boat's hull was scraping against the sand. We went ashore. We knew we were short of time. There was a storm on the way: even as we set foot on the island the clouds in the distance were building up.

'We'd only been filming a few minutes when the boat crew started signalling to us: they were getting desperate; we were taking too long; they were on the verge of leaving us behind. They'd already told us how dangerous those shallow waters were when the waves picked up, and how quickly the winds could turn. The light had changed completely: thick sunbeams were falling through the clouds. I left the cameraman, and walked up to the very tip of the island. I had to see it: the point where the sandbar comes to nothing, where it narrows to the point of a sword—that little island marks the place on the continental shelf where the swell from the Indian Ocean and the currents from eastern waters meet; they collide there; the waves come from both directions, and in those moments they were crashing against that strip of sand, and making a wall of spray: screens of spray on both sides, hanging in the air, and you could walk between those drifting curtains, and it was still where you were; you could walk, and your shadow seemed to be beside you, on your left and on your right at once; there were rainbow arcs, ahead, above; the terns were in the air, crying out, calling. I stretched out my arms. It felt as if some revelation was very close by.'

'It sounds,' said one of the listeners, 'just like one of those out-of-body experiences that saints and mystics have.'

'And even as I tell you I wonder,' she said then, 'if we truly made it back—that was days ago: I still feel as if I'm there. We hurried: we went into the waves, waded out, clambered on to the boat; all the gear was drenched—half-wrecked—we had nothing we could use from that whole day. It was a tense trip back— pitching constantly, being tossed here and there, watching the corals gleaming just beneath the surface of the water all the way, until at last we reached the shelter of the strait, and we were in the channel: we could see the outline of the wharf and Garden Point ahead.'

'That was quite a story,' I said to her later, after the talk around the fire had died down. We spoke more: we fell into conversation. She looked at me, carefully, appraisingly: she shielded her eyes from the glow of the flames.

'And who are you?' she said: 'Where are you from? How do you fit in?'

'Does one have to fit in?'

'It was compulsory, once, where I came from.'

'Where's that?'

'A place that's no longer what it was.'

'In Germany?'

'In Eastern Germany. A town whose name no one here would ever have heard.'

I glanced across.

'Try,' I said.

'Halberstadt,' she said, then solemnly: 'Halberstadt, the damaged jewel of Sachsen-Anhalt—the town of rebuilt spires, the broken gateway to the Harz.'

'And how was it, growing up there? When you had to fit in?'

'What? You want me to tell you the story of my childhood? Here—now—in the darkness; it's almost midnight; everyone on the crew's exhausted: we've been working all day long.'

'Why not?' I said: 'Reminisce. Bring back the past. You're at a beach camp on the Tiwi Islands: probably you'll never come here again; you won't cross paths with anyone here again. Just talk, for no reason: don't you find it sinister the way everything in our life has to lead somewhere? Tell a story—just for the darkness—for the night and for the heat. Anything—at random.'

This challenge issued, I leaned back.

'No,' she said. She frowned again, and looked at me. 'I won't do that. But I will tell you something that matters to me: about a friend of mine, a friend from those times. Someone I was very close to: who was a part of me; who still is. I never bring him to my thoughts, and yet he's always in my mind. I carry him with me.

When I see something beautiful, or something strange, like those mists and rainbows on Seagull Island, it's as if I want him to see them too. And do you know why I'm going to tell you about him?'

'Of course not: how could I?'

She stared over.

'It's strange: it's very striking. I thought it at once. You're like him: you remind me of things about him. Not in the look, so much: no—it's something in the tone. I've always thought there were ties between people far apart, people without links or bonds of any natural kind: you can sense them, sometimes; an intuition reminds you of something you've caught onto elsewhere, with someone else. Don't you think so? Haven't you ever had that idea?'

I let the thought run through me for a moment.

'I used to work in the East, the Eastern Bloc, in Soviet days: I still feel caught up in that world. I think there are ties to places: maybe that's what you're picking up on—maybe that's why I came to talk to you.'

'Ties to places! And what are people, but places crystallised— the world's mirrored in them. There's a way people can have the same being—be alike at some deep, hidden level that we never see. I feel that, more and more with time. And with you, it's as though that friend of mine has come back to life—that friend from whom I learned so much, who I grew with, who I would have wanted to protect: who was swept away by all the changes we experienced in our world.'

All this was said in a low voice, swiftly, in the most straightforward manner.

'You don't need to reply,' she went on: 'Don't say anything.'

'What was his name?' I asked, and looked around. Everybody else in the camp had moved away. Sleep had taken hold.

'His name was Armin,' she said: 'That was him.' She stared into the embers of the fire, and clasped her hands. 'We went to university together: in Jena.'

'This was still in the communist times?'

'The last years, yes—there was a small group of us, studying literature, and he was the one who knew everything: he was a scholar, he specialised in Greek and Latin. He'd been to school at the famous Graues Kloster, in Berlin: it was an elite academy; it was for insiders of the party—they still taught those subjects there. His father was very prominent: a prosecutor in the military court, and there was a dreadful, oppressive atmosphere in the family— he was in flight from it—but we were all in a kind of exile from the world in which we found ourselves. We stuck together: we had something rare in common.'

'Dissent?'

'Not dissent, or not precisely: we could feel the system pressing down on us, its rules and its constrictions—we knew we didn't belong there; we existed in it almost as if by chance; we made our own quiet, internal rebellion against it. We had a kind of special standing, in those days, as students in that university, studying those subjects—but there was anxiety and fear all around. There was the façade: acceptance, conformity—and there was another way of seeing, thinking; and in that shadow world, if you understood the way things were, if you knew, then quickly you recognised others of the same cast of mind. We acknowledged each other. We spent our lives together, in a small circle: he and I shared an apartment together—in Jena—Schottstrasse, number twenty-nine—near the Westbahnhof. It was in an old rundown workers' house—to get there you had to climb up a steep hill. Living right underneath us there was an alcoholic couple who used to scream at each other constantly. What a time that was, coming to awareness of the landscape stretching ahead of us in life.'

'But surely you had some sense that the end was coming for the East?'

'Not at all. That world was all we knew: that was our reality. We could barely imagine such a change. We couldn't see that future until it came. They were days when the regime was under stress, we felt that—of course. We talked about it: but most of all we talked about books, and art, and how they were linked to life, and that was nothing at all theoretical. We relied on art, then, for lessons, and clues: how to exist, how to be true to oneself. We'd travel up to Berlin for performances of classical pieces, old Greek dramas at the national theatre—all that was vital for us: you could translate those plays into your own little situation; there was some hope from their example that you could survive, and make sense of things; you saw that the tragic was nothing new. Knowing what there was ahead for us, we had few hopes, we couldn't take ourselves too seriously— we learned quickly during those years of study. Maybe we might have wanted to be of some use in the world—but you could see that was quite impossible in the East.'

'And then the change came?'

'The radiative change: the change that changed us all as well. We were there, that night: we saw the guards on the Wall; they fell back; we saw it breached; we saw it come down. We crossed: we passed into the West, that other world. It was as though we'd been in silence until then, or in black and white. Suddenly, there was wild, rich, technicolour life around us, and all its frictions and its forces to bear. I found a path ahead: I began to make my way. I travelled. How strong the drive was to see the world we'd been kept from—to come to know it all: its countries, its peoples, everything we'd only been able to imagine. For us, the furthest journey we'd been able to make was to the Bulgarian Black Sea youth resorts for a week or two. The borders opened: we flew like birds. I made a journey with a friend of mine who'd found some work in West Germany; she'd already got hold of an American car: it was old, and deep wine-red, and in good enough shape to take us on our pilgrimage.'

'Where to?'

'Not to a place. After a man. Remember, for us literature had been everything: we were lost in books—they were the best place to be, in that secret world. We would always hunt down works by western writers, as though they held life's blood in them; we passed them from hand to hand: the words on the pages of those authors shaped us—they sank into our hearts. Above all in those days we loved the critic Walter Benjamin, and the story of his flight from the Nazis—and his death. And so as soon as we could we drove off, into France, down the valley of the Rhône, to the coast, towards Spain, following him: we traced the route he took through the Pyrenees; we went to Portbou, where the trail goes dead—where he took his life. We ended up there, on the hillside overlooking the Mediterranean, gazing down. We wanted to feel for ourselves the truth of his experiences, which we already knew in words so well—see what he had seen, be where he had gone before. We were caught up in a longing to witness things. That was the pattern, all through that first summer: see something real. Get away from books, away from faded, bad-quality photographs on cheap paper stock.'

'And then you found your way out into the world for good—with a camera—making films.'

'And I left my old life behind: I was working, filming by day, editing all night long; I was completely consumed—it was a dance that never stopped. I tried to stay in touch with my friends, of course: we'd been so close; I felt those bonds couldn't be undone. But things didn't go so smoothly for all of them. Some of them became writers; a few became teachers, in the West. Armin had managed to find a position: he was at the university in Greifswald; he was not fulfilled. There'd always been an edge to him: too much acuity; and there was a thread of depression, as well, running in the family, in the blood. He had an x-ray vision of himself: he always said he could see the shape of the life path ahead of him, he could read off the experiences that would come to him simply by consulting his character: when he went into a new romance he knew at its beginning how it would end. He abandoned all his teaching tasks, one by one. He was looking for a pathway, a means to give shape to everything he knew—and I believe he came close to finding something very like that path: I almost believe it. But it was around then that I began spending long periods abroad, away with crews, on documentary projects: I made my first trip to the southern hemisphere—I came to Australia.'

'Here—to the islands?'

I gestured into the dark: low clouds were gathering, and blocking the gleam of the stars; there was that heavy moisture that forms in the depths of the build-up night.

'First, in fact, to the north-west, to the Pilbara,' she said: 'That was our big project. We were making films about iron ore and the mining industry: the open-cuts, the trains that reached for kilometres on end, the great cantilevers and the causeways and the ports. I was wide-eyed. I'd never seen such landscape—I'd never seen anything made on such a scale, where man's presence was so dwarfed by the horizon. We drove out. We broke our journey down that long straight highway that runs from Broome to Port Hedland: we stopped at Eighty Mile Beach—you know that coastline?'

I nodded.

'When I was a child,' she went on, 'every summer we went to the Baltic, to those cold, windswept beaches, with their hard sunshine and pale light—and they were the peak of beauty and nature's perfection for me; that was heaven, just to walk along by myself, and scour the sand, and look for washed-up shells, or for the strange, half-eroded stones you could find there with holes worn through them: they were precious—you'd hang them on a string like pendants, and put them round your neck, for luck, because they were so rare. But when I saw Eighty Mile I realised the beaches from those times meant nothing—they were just narrow strips of crowded sand: the Indian Ocean's waves were different, and the water—I never knew water could be clear like that. There were trochus shells lying on the high-tide mark that looked like abstract sculptures from a master's hand! But I'd already been prepared for vastness: for silence. Our first tasks on that trip had been in the Centre, between Coober Pedy and Alice Springs.'

'And what were they?'

She laughed.

'You wouldn't believe it. You'd have to think yourself back into that time. In those days the memory of East Germany was still very much alive: we were searching for eastern subjects, and we managed to find one in the deserts: the writer from Dessau, Joachim Specht—our communistic king of the outback.'

'It's not a name I know,' I said.

'I'm shocked! You don't know his majestic *Australian Cowboy*, or *The Lady in the Bush*, or *Pearl Diver in Frances Bay*?'

'I'm afraid not.'

'Specht was a refugee of wartime: he was still a boy when the fighting began; he lived through the bombing of Dresden. In the aftermath, he fled the East: he managed to make his way to Hamburg, and from there to Australia, to Adelaide. He didn't speak that much English, but he'd been trained as a metalworker. That helped: he found work on the railways, at Peterborough, in the wheat country, near the foothills of the Flinders Ranges. He only stayed three years or so—but in that time he made a number of trips out into desert South Australia: he went to Woomera, to Ooldea siding on the transcontinental line—the new surrounds and new life didn't suit him. He went back—to Germany, and then home, to the East. He set himself up as a writer there: he began writing frontier stories, adventure tales, and since the East German literary establishment was based on a strict doctrine of separate development, free from outside influences, and there was no one much left inside the country who knew anything about Australia, they needed just such an expert, someone with personal experience—and so there was a place for him: his brief, unhappy days in the bush became the core of his life. He was well known; he invented his own fantasy of the desert outback, and it was quite popular: he was a member of the regime's own circle of approved writers—there was even a special publishing house that specialised in international-flavoured books of the kind that he turned out.'

'Were they any good?'

'I've tried a few of them: they're not easy to forget. There's *Capricorn*, and *Coral Joe*, and *The Camp on the Burdekin*. It's strange writing—the bush, only with a faint socialist tint. Action, tension, but everything insubstantial, arid and unreal. That was Specht. He was still alive when we came to make our documentary: no one knew much about him anymore; he seemed quite untouched by time's passage; he was still living in the East, in Dessau—probably he's still there today. Someone in the production company I was working for had a bright idea: we should interview him, and take him back—back to the scene of his former glories, to the adventure landscape of his youthful days. We tracked him down: he didn't need much persuading to go. But he turned out to be a hard case: we arrived, expecting him to be our guide and host; it became clear at once that he remembered next to nothing about his Australian years. He was quite withdrawn, not much inclined to talk or share in things. We travelled with him: to Peterborough, to Woomera, hoping for some grand series of recollections—out, too, into the protected area where the atomic bombs were detonated all those years ago. And that journey was what mattered. Specht and his ambiguities and memories and all his made-up stories just fell away: we scarcely paid any attention to him.

'I was overwhelmed. All my life I'd been hemmed in by lines and borders: what you could say; where you could go. I'd never had an experience until then of freedom—total freedom—freedom as the absence of any force acting on you. It was the first time I'd been in a landscape as simple seeming as that sandhill country, or as subtle in its complications. We went out into the deep desert: west, beyond Glendambo and the restricted zone; beyond Tarcoola; we made our way round Lake Labyrinth—we drove down dirt roads for days on end. That emptiness, full of questions! I felt opened up. Of course, for the first few days I could only register the surface things—the sweat, the heat, the colours of the sunset—then, slowly, my impressions deepened. I found I was sleeping heavily, dreaming with great intensity. People I'd known and loved came back to me; scenes from my life, scenes I'd long forgotten. I was living them again, and picturing whole episodes from my course in life: real experiences, and variations on them, too, things that never came to pass—I saw my yearnings, my longings—they came, unsummoned, in the most elaborate order, beginning, breaking off, interweaving, making new connections in what I'd already experienced and given shape and logic in my mind. It was like that all through the journey: my ideas were changed—my ideas about what we are, about what we carry in us, in potential; how we stand in the world.'

'Meaning?'

'That there's no limit. That's what those days showed me—the limits we see and agree on are the ones to break: there isn't any boundary to what we can conceive, and make inside ourselves; or there doesn't have to be—if only we can escape the gridlines of our thought, all the patterns that bear down on us and trap us every day. I had the sense that I was being shown something: it was a breakthrough. Ever since those days in the desert I've tried to keep the feeling I had then of unending dimensions in life—tried to look out, and see widely, not to zero in with the defining eye. Make films that explore, not fix; hide from rigid plot and fact and form: they're death to me. Death—like everything set and still.'

She fell silent. The fire was down to embers. We had travelled almost through the night on words.

'And that was it, for Specht?' I asked: 'Or did he have a late-career renaissance?'

'In a sense, he did. We came back to Berlin and made our documentary, and it was shown, and it presented his impressions and adventures in the most constructive kind of light. There was a good response: mild interest, some sympathy, even. We never heard from him again—but some years afterwards I was passing through Leipzig station and I noticed that he had a new book published. The title stood out on the newsstand shelves. *G'Day*, it was called: *Return to Australia*—so the trip must have sparked off something in his thoughts.'

'And in yours?'

'I was lifted up by those experiences: troubled, too; divided. Things were running well for me—work, new connections, success: but for my old band of fellow students, the way ahead was much less straightforward or clear. They'd spent their youth struggling to make contact with the outside world through books, films, through any means they could—suddenly it was there, all round them: they were in it, they were part of it; but their backgrounds and their temperaments were quite different from those of their western counterparts; they were much more serious, and more jagged; they had the minds of crusaders; they'd equipped themselves for a life of despairing, secret rebellion, not for competition, and cut-and-thrust. There was nothing they could do but think, and analyse: they saw their circumstances without sentiment; they saw themselves with ruthless eyes. There was a real harshness to them, my friends from the Eastern days: they were radicals—so radical as to destroy themselves in reflection of their times.'

She stopped.

'It upsets me still, and ten years have gone by, and more. Armin had made a long journey of his own, as I found out: it was his quest. His search for something that could serve him as a holy grail. It led him deep into a world of thought: it led him to other places, other cities, as if there might be clues and fragments lying there for him along the way. It began in a backwater. He went north, up the river Elbe, to a little town on its bank: Stendal. Have you been there? You'd remember—everything's always closed there: every kiosk, every store. You haven't? Then you have to go.'

She said this with fierce, abrupt insistence, and I smiled.

'There's nothing to smile at,' she shot back. 'There's an affinity. That's why I've been talking to you. Don't you understand? I'm giving you something. There's a path to follow. Don't you see life works like that?'

She levelled her eyes, and looked straight at me: a look that was harsh and pleading at once.

'Well?' she said: 'I think you do—I think you see very clearly: this isn't just a story for the darkness, just a story to be thrown away. Some people have to seek, and hunt, seek out even to the borders of our world—and chase their intuitions down—like him.'

'And why there?' I asked.

'If you make that pilgrimage, maybe you'd see what drew him there: good reasons. He was lifted up, at least for a while: he had grand plans; there would be some synthetic masterpiece he'd make, critical, explaining—but everything withered; the whole journey just seemed to bind him more deeply into his darkness; perhaps that was even its secret aim. What could a creature as made from words and highly wrought as him ever find out from searching? What was there that could free him from what he had inside himself; from the sadness that trapped him, that stopped him from feeling any other thing? I wanted to tell him all about Australia and what I'd seen when I came back: I looked for him; I found out where he was. He'd had a breakdown; he'd been hospitalised, at a clinic at Weissensee. Eventually they discharged him: he was full of medication. I went to see him: we talked through the night.'

'Much like now.'

'Night brings things out. He told me many stories I hadn't known before: he told me he didn't want to be a burden to people; he didn't want to suffer through the next twenty years of life. And I listened, but I wonder if I really heard. It was quite soon afterwards that he went to a high-rise apartment block, and jumped from a window on the tenth floor: he chose a bleak landscape to die in, on a bleak day. I would have loved to show him other places—other sights—and perhaps all the films I make and I dream of making now I make for him, and everyone else I've lost.'

She said this simply, quietly. Dawn was breaking now: light began to edge into the sky.

'Many months later,' she went on, after a pause, 'I had to go back, to the East—as chance would have it, back to Halberstadt, on some kind of documentary business, a profile of the great poets of the past and their travels in the region, something like that— and I was caught up, also, in a project to describe the rebuilding of the cathedral, which had been gravely damaged, like the whole medieval town centre, by a series of bombing raids in the last month of the war.

'It was a homecoming!'

'If you like: it was the scene of my early childhood, but I hadn't been back for years. I wandered through the streets, odd memories surfacing in my thoughts. I decided to visit the cathedral, and take a look: how cold and austere it was—the afternoon had worn on; it was wintertime. I went into the cloister. There was no one else that I could see: I walked round, checking shots, and camera angles, busy with all my setting up and planning—but with every step I took I could feel someone's presence, close to me, keeping pace with me, right by my side.'

'It was him?'

'And if it was,' said she, turning at last to face me, eyes full of anger, full of tears, 'if it was—then what's your part in this: who are you?'

*

That question, and her low voice as she asked it, stayed with me during the unsettled weeks I spent after that encounter—weeks that stretched into months, while I made my slow way through the social archipelagoes of Darwin, the city I had chosen long before as my home, and to which I was just then returning after a prolonged absence—only to realise how little I knew of its changed face: its fabric, its people, the temper of the life. I made several trips to the other northern islands; I travelled in the Kimberley, and Arnhem Land: I traced out long journeys, alone and in company—but none of these displacements dimmed the memory of the Tiwi campsite and that night-time talk. On the contrary, the film-maker's words took on greater depth. The exchange played continually inside me—the sweep of her story and its details; each distinct episode, their echoes and their joins—and though I never saw her again, it was as if her will was being slowly realised; I felt myself dwelling more and more on my own days in the East: days long gone. I would dream, and find myself back in some cold, distant capital; I would be driving through the deep bush, alone, on corrugations, and picture myself once more on cobbled streets, at dusk, in some rainy city on the brink of curfew.

Gradually, the idea began to form in me that I should take a trip back to that world I once knew—changed though it was, utterly, from those times when I was there, and party-states held sway. That idea turned, almost against my intent, from a notion into a plan; it gained definition, it became convenient, it fitted easily in with other projects—and by the year's end I was setting off, bound for Europe. All, at first, went well enough: I spent long days on the trail of my particular interests, in the towns of Weimar and Wittenberg; but how hard the past's shadows fell; in my mind's eye I could see my younger self in the castle square, or walking, half-lost, down the alleys of the Ilmpark; impressions and odd thoughts from long ago surfaced in me: how much more I knew, about life's patterns, and fate's grip, and how little what I knew now brought by way of benefit. A glance, a stare, a touch— they were still the same—it was still a mystery to leap from breath to breath, to survive a second, let alone a lifetime—to endure, and be aware that one endures—for what?

The trip unfolded: it was archives, it was hotels—but throughout its course I could feel a tension, an expectation building in me; I could tell how it would end: I would give in to the film-maker's wish—I would follow her script. It was an unfamiliar pleasure: the acceptance of a bond; the surrender of one's will. I decided: the obscure town of Stendal it would be. I made my plans: one morning, in the murk of the clouded sunrise, I set out, on back roads, bound north from Magdeburg, following the bank of the wide, slow-moving Elbe. On both sides, water meadows: sky, land and river channel interweaving. Towns, villages—neat, well-ordered—factories, rail crossings, church towers, lights. There was Tangermünde; there, ahead, Stendal: the pedestrian zone. So easily from thought to life.

I clambered from the car; the streets were quiet. The clouds darkened: they came lower. It began to rain, gently at first, then more insistently, angling down, until standing or walking in the open were impossible. I took shelter: beneath awnings, or in the arcades of shopping streets, making quick feints out into the rain; then retreating, until an interval between the showers, or a slackening, and then I would go darting here and there, looking up from moment to moment, trying to track my progress, to take the measure of the town, its landmarks, and how they hung together: the cathedral spires, the main gate, the station, the theatre square. Soon the rain became a downpour: I was in a byway off one of the main avenues, running, staying close to the walls of the buildings; there was a long, half-timbered house front; I found a doorway, with steps up; I pushed against it: it opened.

Inside all was warm, and calm: no sound of driving rainfall. I was in a large hallway: it had the feel of the entrance to an academy, or institution. At the centre of the open space, dominant, stood the marble bust of an individual with anguished features; there was an archway, columns, a small stage with lectern, chairs in precise rows. To one side there were faces: a gathering. Eyes turned to stare at me.

'What is this place?' I asked, and there was the sound of gentle laughter.

Standing nearest to me was a young woman, half-turned, smiling.

'Please—come inside,' she said: 'Are you looking for somewhere?'

'I was on a search, of a kind,' I said. Water dripped off my coat: I took in the scene, and its absurdity. 'A quest, as a matter of fact.'

'A quest—in Stendal! Then you must have been looking for us: there's nowhere else here anyone would want to search for.'

'What is this place?' I asked.

'But it's the Winckelmann Association,' she said, smiling and looking round.

'Winckelmann,' I echoed, and she took the echo as a sign of bafflement.

'Surely you know of him? The founder of classical archaeology. A man who saw very far.'

'I imagine, then, this is the place I was looking for,' I answered, a little hazily, still glancing round.

A group of men and women, both young and middle-aged, all of them immaculately dressed, all with subtle, open faces, looked back at me.

'It's a small enterprise, of course,' the woman went on, 'our association—but in the tapestry of art and learning, it has its part to play: we publish; we hold symposia.'

'And are you all always here, like this?' I asked.

'No, no!' She laughed: 'Normally there's only a handful of us: two or three, the staff. It just happens that today is the day that Winckelmann was born, in 1717—here in this town.'

'You celebrate his birthday?'

'It's a little custom, with us: a tradition. We feel close to him: we admire him—and in his life, there wasn't a great deal in the way of kindness or love. Maybe it might interest you to look through the exhibits we have here, in the set of rooms behind you: they offer a brief account of the externals of his life. And then, perhaps, you might want to join us—we stand at your disposal.'

And with that she made a brief gesture of courtly elegance, as if to escort me on my way.

*

Johann Joachim Winckelmann was of simple background, and for all the elusive, airy glamour that surrounds his name in our time, he lived a simple, emblematic life, enslaved to beauty and to his love for it. This love gnawed at him: it drove him on. He studied it; it was his subject and the centre of his thoughts and theories— those theories that are emotions frozen into structure and form. At first, Winckelmann took the familiar path available to a young man of his station and multiplicity of gifts: public schools, where his adoration of Greek and Latin literature was first kindled; then higher studies, but of strictly practical stamp, and in provincial centres—theology at Halle, medicine at Jena. He was an instructor in languages: he became a teacher in a small school in the Altmark; he took a tutorial post near Magdeburg, with a landed household, and there fell deeply in love. This affection, like the great passions of his later life, was for a young man, unattainable, of noble birth. It hovered in his mind, gaining ever greater resonances and depth: longing, unrequited longing for the perfect, youthful body became his religion—to love was to want; art's purest, truest form and wellspring was love; to see beauty and know it was to worship nature and its finest emblem, man.

Such thoughts as these pulsing through him, Winckelmann, who was even in his early writing years a stylist of chill perfection, turned to anatomising his own sense of incompleteness and grief. The pain he felt needed form; the longing needed words, to damp it down; ideas, to veil it, to staunch the heart's blood. Love, above all else, must seek the far horizon, he believed, and know that it is a horizon dweller: it must adopt the logic of distance, of abstinence; hold itself aloof from its desires, and, like a storm that feeds on its sheer intensity, gain, from its self-denial, strength.

He turned thirty: his life underwent a change. The literary-minded Count Heinrich von Bünau, with whom he had been in correspondence, appointed him as secretary of the castle library at Nöthnitz, close by Dresden with its royal gallery and collection of antiquities. There, for the first time, Winckelmann came into the company of artists and scholars. He was engaged in helping Bünau compile a history of the Holy Roman Empire—but what could such a history be if it was not based on its deepest origins: on the art of ancient times that still survived and could be seen, far away, in the citadel of beauty, Rome itself. Winckelmann had been taken up by the court painter at Dresden, Adam Friedrich Oeser: they shared ideas; the first book Winckelmann published was dedicated to Oeser; it was a dream in print, an evocation of the beauties of classical sculpture, based wholly on the casts in the royal collection and the bound engravings of Greek works that Winckelmann had discovered on the Nöthnitz shelves— how sensuous the statues he described in its pages were, how self-contained in their poise and grace; they exhibited an inner quality—a 'noble simplicity and calm grandeur' of the soul.

This love song to works of art that Winckelmann had never seen he set, entirely characteristically, within a complex frame. 'Thoughts on the Imitation of Greek Works in Painting and Sculpture' was presented as an essay, tentative, uncertain: it was followed by a sharp text of rebuttal, anonymous, though written by Winckelmann himself, and a further coda, also from his pen, but offered as the last word of a third, impartial critic surveying the scene. The sole means for modern man to become great, and even inimitable, wrote Winckelmann, was precisely by imitating the ancients, developing an intimacy with them—and so striking was this argument and the elegance of the prose in which it was cast that it earned him, among the cognoscenti of the courts of Europe, a degree of literary repute. At once, he wrote Bünau a letter, tortured, subservient, yet determined: his course was clear. He longed to be face to face with what he idealised: he would leave for Rome.

It was a match. If romance could ever unfold between place and man, it did so here. He was well suited to the post of librarian-scholar. He worked for a series of cardinals, and steeped himself in archives and in texts. He was able to view the best known antique statues of the city: in their gleaming limbs his longings seemed at last to have been given a substantial form. Winckelmann, who was at that time already close to forty years old, now flowered: in a brief period he made himself the master of a new field; he became the close observer of the past in all its phases, the classifier, the taxonomist; he was the man who first saw the full sweep of antiquity; he bequeathed it an order and a system, phases and periods; in his words its descent line became clear.

Soon he entered the service of Cardinal Albani, one of the chief collectors of the age: this brought him to lodgings in the ornate Villa Albani, beside the Porta Salaria on the edge of Rome, and so into contact with the most famous painter in the city, the Bohemian portraitist Anton Raphael Mengs. Mengs had just completed a large fresco of Apollo and the Muses for the ceiling of the villa's piano nobile. The two became friends, confidantes: they began work on a treatise devoted to the artistry of the Greeks. Mengs served as a guide for Winckelmann: he showed him the treasures of Rome's princely families—the finds amassed by the Ludovisi, the Farnese and their peers.

These statues Winckelmann took not just as marvels of the past, but as incarnations of a philosophy: they needed interpretation, just as a beloved object needs a lover to perceive its qualities. He gave himself to this task: he clothed the statues in his prose. He widened his search: he made visits to Naples to inspect the excavations under way at Pompeii and Herculaneum; he travelled further down the coast, to the site of the Doric temples at Paestum, which were then still ruined and overgrown.

His was not a quest after the obvious: 'The beautiful and the useful are not to be grasped at a glance, as an unwise German painter thought after a few weeks of his stay in Rome—for the significant and the difficult run deep and do not flow on the surface.' No: they give up their secrets only to those who surrender themselves, who lose their hearts, who find in the arms of art a means of escape from the base matter of the world: 'The first sight of a beautiful statue is, to him who has feeling, like the first view of the open sea, wherein our gaze loses itself and becomes fixed, but after repeated contemplation, the soul becomes more still and the eye quieter and moves from the whole to the particular.'

Winckelmann looked: he saw deep worlds, full of metaphor and meaning, where before him the scholars and collectors had seen mere forms of elegance. He discerned the history of the statues from the clues lying hidden in their style: he came to know them as well as those who made them. Without precursors, without equals among his contemporaries, he poured out his intense, romantic prose; it still stands as a model today: fluent, in constant motion, free from artifice, poised. His masterwork, *The History of the Art of Antiquity*, appeared in 1764, printed by a court publishing house in Dresden; it made his name known throughout the world of European letters, and transformed the wider understanding of ancient art—no longer were the statues relics, unreadable in their obscurity: now they seemed to pant and breathe; they were vessels of desire. Readers passed around Winckelmann's book in their circles; they recited his bravura passages, they imitated them and learned them by heart. In his rendition, the carved muscles of a marble torso could be like the lie of hills flowing into each other, or the swell of a quiet ocean, or the undulations, barely perceptible, of molten glass—but it was the reactions to the art of the author himself, described in the most intimate detail, offered up almost as confession, that formed the most striking feature of the work.

In gazing upon the statue of Apollo in the Belvedere, he wrote, 'I forget all else, and I myself adopt an elevated stance, in order to be worthy of gazing upon it. My chest seems to expand with veneration and to heave like those I have seen swollen as if by the spirit of prophecy, and I feel myself transported to Delos and to the Lycian groves, places Apollo honoured with his presence'—but still they were far from him, still he would not see them; he was always striving, yearning, his feelings exceeded all he knew from books. 'How is it possible to paint and describe it! I place the concept of this figure that I have conveyed at its feet, like the wreaths offered by those who could not reach the head of the deities whom they wished to crown.'

Such was the trope: the new emotion Winckelmann bequeathed to the world of thought. Not love thwarted or denied, so much as love that could never reach its goal: longing that was sustained for its own sake—melancholy languishing of precisely the kind that shaped Winckelmann's tormented path in love. This jump from life to thought was next to natural for him. He had spent much of his time in Rome guiding and instructing young noblemen, to whom he dedicated monographs and learned studies, to whom he poured out tender letters, and from whom nothing of substance came back. The antique statues and the youths of the present—what were they but desire embodied, hanging before him, present only to the imagination, forever beautiful and forever out of reach. And here, abruptly, he crossed a line: in imagination, in sensibility. To be without was to be with; to deny oneself was to fulfil one's being more completely: for Winckelmann the mark of love, which was itself a sign of authenticity, was now none other than isolation, separation, anguished distance from everything one desired; and this shift inside him of the aims of romance, this preference for entangled, joyless passion, brought other transformations in its wake. If love was a lost quest, so, too, was the quest for antiquity.

With that, the past's meaning changed. The world of the ancient statues was now presented as a high, perfect realm, where thoughts were truer, bodies brighter, feelings noble, clear and pure. Gazing down into time's well, surveying the remains of Greece and Rome, and examining the marble evidence, how could one not feel regret, and a further emotion, too, more poignant still: nostalgia, which rots the present and its joys away. What, indeed, was time past but the realm of romantic love; who else was Winckelmann but its prophet, chosen by fate for this special role: an individual of the most feline charm and elegance, a writer and a thinker of the highest gifts, the sole conceiver of rich new fields of study—yet a man stamped by his birth, barred by his rank—a cobbler's son from Stendal, never able to speak his heart to those he loved. Hence the drift from the travails of emotion to the province of the intellect; hence love's slow invasion of study, and its eventual triumph: the two fuse.

In the final pages of his *History*, after a long disquisition on the collapse of art in Christian times, Winckelmann allows himself a last gaze at the vanished world of ancient Greece and its pale reflection, Rome—and he adopts a yearning persona: abandoned, classical. Antiquity has gone; the real artworks of the past have gone; only fragments and pale replicas survive. 'Just as a beloved stands on the seashore and follows with tearful eyes her departing lover, with no hope of seeing him again, and believes she can glimpse his image even in his vessel's far-off sail, so we, like the lover, have only a shadowy outline of the subject of our desires remaining'—but the copies are more potent than the originals, loss is possession, the mind's creative power is more than the strength of the world. 'One always imagines that there is much to find, and so one searches much to catch sight of something.' Irony threatens. Self-awareness descends. With Winckelmann, we step into modern times—and he could read the modern landscape very well. Coherence was fading. Splinters remained. Love was simply the way one gathered fragments up. How much had vanished!

Winckelmann lists the losses, dwelling on the details with an anguished delicacy and care. 'Treasures—the likes of which neither time nor the hands of all present or future artists are capable of producing—were destroyed in a wild fury by barbarians in their many assaults on and plunderings of the city'—and by the Romans themselves, who, when besieged, hurled down ancient statues as missiles against their assailants. Even in Constantinople, the last refuge of the empire, the handful of precious bronzes salvaged from fallen cities in the Greek diaspora were eventually all sacrificed: the Pallas from Lindos, the Olympian Jupiter carved by Pheidias, the Venus of Cnidus by the hand of Praxiteles—there is no trace of any of them after the crusader sack of the city; almost certainly they were melted down and their metal used for coin. Each one like a lost beloved, each one—and love's trials were at a peak, in those days, for Winckelmann: it was the time of his brief encounter with a young nobleman from the wilds of Latvia, Friedrich Reinhold von Berg.

They met in 1762: the flame burned bright—far brighter in recollection than in life. A romance by written word, by letter, ensued. It was one-sided. Winckelmann was just completing his *Treatise on the Capacity for the Feeling for Beauty*, a slender text. As he assured his young friend, to whom he dedicated the book, its contents were taken from the life: the form of the man allowed the writer to fulfil his task. 'The parting from you was one of the most painful of my life—may this essay be a monument to our friendship'—for the friendship was already memory; it could only flourish in the mirror of the mind. Berg had gone; he sent Winckelmann a single letter of warm feeling; a torrent came back from Rome, and these were published in due course: they secured a brief, minor celebrity for Berg's name. That correspondence held the code to Winckelmann's thought, and to his heart—for all must tell their secrets if they wish truly to be known, and every secret longs to find the light. 'Friendship arose from heaven and not from human feelings,' wrote Winckelmann in his great declaration letter: 'It was with a certain awe that I approached you; and as a result I was deprived of the highest good by your departure. What should I have had to write were a single one among a hundred of my readers to understand this sublime secret'—so Winckelmann, as if already knowing that his words would be betrayed. What else is love but an act of theft; what is beauty but the coin of its traffic: the eyes were instruments of violence; the horizon, death—and what was that gleam beyond its line? It could be nothing but the fire where all were purified and melted down at last.

Notions of this kind plaguing him, his great writings done, Winckelmann felt the temptation to see once more the homeland of his youthful sufferings. In truth, he was lost in life: he had no idea which way to go. He had received offers: from Berlin, from Dessau, from other German courts of learning where the friends of his letters held posts. He set off in April 1768, across the Alps, on the same path Bellotto had traced out two decades earlier. He reached Vienna; he was received in audience there by the empress, and decorated with a range of imperial honours, in recognition of his scholarship. Some intuition stopped him: he decided there could be no return to his own country; he turned back; the journey brought him to the Adriatic coastline, to Trieste, and there, on the night of June eighth, in the hotel where he had found lodgings, he was stabbed to death. His assailant was Francesco Arcangeli, a chancer and petty thief, who had thought Winckelmann an individual of no account. The murder was documented in vast detail by a pair of local investigators; the resultant book, translated, became a bestseller: it added a frisson of dark glamour to Winckelmann's fast-growing fame. How torn he had been in his last months; how low in spirits; how far from life. There had been true friends waiting for him over the mountains: there had been warmth of feeling, admiration too; but he drew back. He was caught in the temple of his self-made isolation—and there is a sublime match between the man and the tomb in the graveyard of Trieste's San Giusto cathedral, where his remains lie in a neoclassical vault, set apart, immured in a sarcophagus of gleaming Istrian marble with a grief-struck angel perched at its head. He had dreamed of leaving the world just as he entered it, a light-footed traveller: this dream, at least, was fulfilled.

*

The museum's doors were closing. The birthday event was long since done. Filled with solemn ideas and wild forebodings, lifted up, cast down, ancient ruins in my eyes, mind and heart both racing, I stepped out into the cold damp air. I drove, and as the kilometres flicked by I brought the story into focus in my thoughts: its reversals, its rhythms, its echoes—echoes of Armin's story, the Easterner, the pilgrim, condemned by being freed; of Specht, spinning dreams in his remembered desert—threads of stories, crossing each other, repeating, the whole world bound up in them and their interweavings; and I too, looking, retracing steps, chasing intuitions through landscapes I had once known, or imagined that I knew—all changed now. I made my way down the well-kept back roads to the destination I had chosen, somewhat arbitrarily, for that night's hotel—Halberstadt, the town at the end of the film-maker's tale, the town of rebuilt spires and destroyed munitions plants.

I arrived: it was the chill late afternoon. The smell of diesel and factory smoke was in the air. Before me was a market scene: stalls closing, vans loading, men and women farewelling each other with signs of deep affection, going their different ways. A handful of figures were headed past the low-slung housing blocks towards the older quarter of the town. I followed, through squares, and parks, taking in the streets and houses, the old and new orders thrown against each other. There was a crowd converging on a stone building straight ahead. Over its arched entrance a large banner in the style of a heraldic flag had been hung down: its edges were lifting and fluttering in the gusts of the breeze: 'As Slow As Possible', it announced—and indeed, the members of the crowd were moving slowly, in a formal, stately fashion, as if enacting the words inscribed above their heads. One by one they filed into the building, checking their watches as they went. A camera crew was filming this ceremony; a knot of dignitaries stood by. Inside, a vaulted, arcaded nave; the shell of a church, stripped of its decoration; at one end, a wooden platform, angular, symmetric, bearing tall organ pipes on both sides. Onlookers were gathered before this assemblage, from which a low, constant note was coming: a sound wave, more than a note, oddly piercing, unvarying for minutes on end—and this apparatus seemed to hold the little congregation bunched up before it quite mesmerised; they were silent; they gazed upwards with wide, marvelling eyes. Beside me was a man with a lined face, in coat and scarf.

'What's going on here?' I whispered to him.

He wheeled around.

'You don't know? Really?'

'No idea.'

He frowned.

'Well, I suppose that only makes things that much more perfect,' he said: 'Today's the day. That's the power chance holds in the work's design. There's never pure coincidence, though, is there? Absolute coincidence?'

'Isn't there?'

'No—I doubt it—I see affinities everywhere, connections: hidden ones. You: what brought you? Have you ever thought seriously about time? What it is, what kind of stuff it is, how it passes, its velocity? Ever thought about its flow? Ever wanted to slow it down?'

'I think of little else,' I said.

At which a young woman, elegantly dressed, with a hard, set expression, came towards us. 'Klemens, stop talking: it's a serious moment; it's close at hand.'

'What's close at hand?' I broke in.

'You don't know? You're here by chance? How beautiful.'

She smiled a dazzling smile; she shook my hand.

'It's art,' she said: 'Our new religion. Art in a broad frame, of course—art reconceived.'

She hurried on; she fixed her gaze on me, and gave me a low, half-whispered explanation. Halberstadt was the scene of a great cultural experiment: it was a laboratory of new ways of being, new ways of thinking.

'You surely know the name of the composer John Cage,' she went on, her voice dropping even lower, until she was speaking almost solely with her lips, and signalling, rather than speaking her words, over which the organ note could be clearly made out.

'I don't remember him being a big cultural reference point in the old East Germany,' I answered.

'Those days are over,' said she, with an air of vexation: 'Long gone. No one remembers them: no one pays that past attention any more. New times, new thoughts—and there's a performance of a work of John Cage here, under way in this space, right now.'

'That unchanging note?'

'It's not an unbroken single note, even if sounds like one—it's part of a continuing performance event. The idea came from the millennium: the year 2000. That was precisely 639 years since the first modern organ was built, here in Halberstadt—and this piece itself will take as many years to complete. In its first form, it was a brief composition—its length was measured only in minutes; the score was no more than eight pages long—so when it's performed in this way, spaced out so, with this signature in time, the notes played by the organ change only very rarely, and on the occasions when a new sound is due to be born, people gather, to mark the moment, and measure out an interval in their own experience of life.'

'And this is such a moment?'

'Exactly—now—there are only minutes left before it comes. People have been waiting a long time. The last change was more than two years in the past.'

'Slow going!'

'Don't mock,' she said, and she gave me a defiant stare: 'There were plenty of mockers in Halberstadt, when the piece began. There was nothing much here back then to treat as special, nothing to care about. No dreams; no longings. And now we have this: we have pattern inside time. Sculpture inside time. Movement; stillness; grace. Can't you imagine what it brings, when time's flow is made visible to you; when it's slowed down in this way, so you can truly grasp how sweet and precious each second in its passing is? I'm not the only one who feels great revelations have been given to me in this old building, listening over stretches of time to the sound of the single note—and when the change comes, it's like the moment when you first set eyes on someone you love: when what you've longed for is given to you; when visions become truth. When everything—past, present and future—stands in a clear pattern in your mind. Now, listen!'

There was a motion at the front of the crowd. The note changed; a new chord came. It persisted; it filled the vaulted space above us; it was as if it had always been there—regal, complete in itself. There was a murmur of appreciation: a soft noise, delicate; the members of the crowd looked around, a gentle air about them. Several minutes passed before they began to move, and speak, and filter out into the half-light of the square. One by one they went: men, women, the younger, the older; but wait—that figure, tall, dark-coated, with silver hair and a slight hunch to the shoulders. Who was it? The bearing was familiar. The heavy entrance door swung closed behind that form, more fleeting shape than solid man.

I stared: the seconds passed. There was some resemblance working at the edge of my memory, I was sure of it. The airy sense of freedom that comes in a place of strangers had a hold of me: that freedom that comes when only whims and stray thoughts can spur one on. I would go outside, and if I still could see that figure, then I would follow, pursue, overhaul him, look into his face—but even as I was making this decision, inside myself I knew: it was nothing, it would be nothing; life's joins are never where you think; it was a trick of light, no more. Out I went, into the flagstoned square under the cold sky, and glanced about— towards the new town; towards the parklands, where the road sloped down—there were children, couples walking: no one.

Then I saw him, already at a distance, beneath the last street light before the black shade thrown by the cathedral façade. He was striding away with fast steps. I gave chase. I ran. The figure swept into the cathedral. I too, and gazed up and down. The nave was dimly lit: its white stone gleamed like opals. A door banged shut: a side door—it led into the cloister. What desolation I found there: damaged tombs, crumbling stonework, roped-off sections of the arcading under repair, a garden overgrown, pale lights casting a thin glow through the murk. I walked those cloisters: the entire circuit. Empty. But still I could feel someone: a presence. I wheeled round, and in that half-second it seemed to me I caught a glimpse of a patch of movement. I went towards it. And there, beside a carved column, half-hidden, staring out, jaw clenched, just as he had stared out across the Dresden ruins twenty years before, was Stefan Haffner.

'So,' I said, lifted up by an absurd sense of fulfilment: 'It was you.'

How little changed he was. He was still tall and gaunt; his face still had an imperious air about it, his eyes blazed with a fierce alertness, there was the same bitter, anguished twist to the lines around his mouth.

'It was you,' I said again: 'Do you remember me? I've looked for you. I tried to find your traces.'

Nothing.

'I wanted to tell you: how much that talk meant to me; that talk, all those years ago, when we made a visit to your apartment, in Dresden, in the pitch of night, in the old regime days, when I was covering the East, and we had no idea what the future held. I felt it, even then: that was a night when patterns formed for me. I've been living in it ever since. I've longed to see you again, professor, to be able to tell you.'

He surveyed me, and sequences of emotions seemed to

pass across his face. Scorn, fury, a soft, pitying pondering: then resignation. He looked up at the sky, now almost black, with the haze of smoke and fumes hiding any traces of light from the moon or stars.

'To each his own,' he said, coldly. 'Everyone's longing for something.'

And that was all he said. My thoughts jumped back. They flew through the years, to the day we met. I saw him looking at me. I saw my younger self in his eyes. I saw: what? Vanity, presumption, pride—all the things one sloughs off in life, and then forgets.

'How much I learned from you then, professor,' I said, softly, almost breathing out the words: 'How much!'

'About really existing socialism,' he shot back, in a low, harsh voice: 'I had no insights. You had no need of instruction from me.'

'No,' I said: 'Not that. Of course not. About the other things. I still remember every word you told me: about the journey you made to the north, and the ideas that trip set in movement in your mind; and all those pictures and images resonated with me—deeply.'

'Images?'

'The light melting on the waves of the White Sea; the sense you had then of the way light shimmers, and dissolves; just the way you said it then: you see beyond the contours of the world, you stare through and escape yourself.'

He stared at me as if peering into a dream.

'And you've been looking for that light? Seeing it? Borrowing someone else's emotions. What a path in life!'

'It's like the closing of a circle for me,' I said: 'Seeing you again.'

I watched his face, and I was aware of doing so, in anxiety, as if I was looking for some sign there, some token, and there was some belief in me that we can reach back towards the past, down pathways through used up time.

'Indeed,' he said: 'But I scarcely remember those days you're speaking of.' He smiled, at this, almost triumphantly. 'If I remember you at all, you're like a ghost to me.'

I absorbed this remark. I felt a nameless wound inside myself.

'Of course,' I said: 'I understand. Many things have happened.'

'Changes! That whole world has gone, and all the feelings and ideas it made a home for. People disappear from you, and from your thoughts. They go like smoke.' He screwed up his face, as if what he was saying caused him great pain. 'You want to see patterns; you want to find them. And sometimes there are patterns. Sometimes we do remember, and see life's shape, but the structures that we build—they fail to hold, to crystallise: we lose them. I picture us all, in the course of our lives, like so many dust particles, pouring out of a factory chimney stack—pouring constantly out.'

He reached into his coat pocket, then stopped, as if struck, seized by something, almost against his wishes. He looked up.

'What brought you here?' he said, suspiciously: 'That note change in the organ piece? Are you some kind of music lover?'

What had? A chain of leads. Hints; cues; the need to hear chance when it calls; find links: follow them. Annihilate one's will, the better to assert it. See the core of things.

I tried to sketch this out before him: how life had turned, and swung for me, and led me there; the cascade of events, the leans and shifts that steered me on my way. I traced out the line, in all its details.

'As strange,' I said, 'as the path that took you to Solovki once.'

'You were tracking me,' he said then, abruptly, accusingly, but in a low, matter-of-fact voice: 'So that's it. Hunting me. Hunting me down.'

'No, Professor Haffner,' I said: 'Of course not—it's coincidence'—but even as I said this, the word sank into me, and it seemed to me that down the years I had been waiting for just such a search to set out on: a quest—and if I had found him by chance—the purest chance—that was in keeping with my hopes, submerged hopes—it was almost an embodiment of some half-conscious intent or will. I had been striving to find that journey, complete it, find a means of going back to that encounter—as if it had held the secrets of the world and they could only be rescued by claiming it anew.

All through this exchange Haffner had been standing, unmoving, facing the cloister gardens and the dark, resting one hand on the carved column at his side, running his fingers across the interlacings on the figures carved into the stone. Abruptly he swivelled. He looked straight at me. 'What do you want?' he said: 'Absolution?'

'For what! For caring about what you had to say for yourself so long ago, when no one cared, or knew you in the outside world? For making the trip to see you in those leaden years, and tracking you down in your little book-lined room, and listening for hours on end?'

'And what do you remember? What stood out for you, back then, in all I had to say?'

His voice was cold, still, and hostile, but a suggestion of a new tone, curious, almost sentimental, had crept in.

'Fragments: what else, but your centrepiece? The way you saw the world lying in fragments—everything lost, and wrecked, and scattered; and the task of life was in collecting up those fragments, looking, seeking for the resonances and the echoes— the shards—you said what was left to us has been exploded, pulverised, reduced to rubble; no more order, nothing, no more structure or harmony, no sequence—and the hardest thing's to find words that fit together, that hold any truth at all.'

'Yes,' he said then, slowly: 'Perhaps I did think something like that once. A doctrine. Something to live by. To make some sense of our intuitions: all the affinities that we can feel lying so buried in the world. Fragments to search for, even—even where we were then.'

He laughed, a short, bitter laugh, more yelp or catch of breath than anything.

'What a stroke of fate,' he went on. 'Old times come revolving round: at the end of twilight, in a rundown cloister, in a deadbeat, forgotten town.'

He reached into his coat once more, and pulled out a cigarette packet, and struck a match. As he did so, I reached out, and turned the pack: Belomorkanal—the blue blaze, the golden ground, the map, the modish letters in Cyrillic script. I smiled.

'The cigarette of ideology—and mourning,' I said.

'I taught you well, I see—without knowing it. That grey smoke like the haze covering the Arctic sky. You can learn to see beauty and truth in anything. Any symbol will serve. What creatures we are! How much we need!'

'Need?'

'Need meaning. Need belief. Why else would you believe in me?'

This harshly, with a sudden violence. He lifted his arm, as if to strike out—at something; someone: himself; me. He jabbed his cigarette against the column, into the carved grooving, just below the frieze of stone saints and angels, and stubbed it out.

'Not, perhaps, the act of a man of God,' I said.

'He doesn't care—care about caring,' said Haffner.

He gave a layered smile of ironies. His expression changed again. His mood swung.

'And where have you been, my western friend? You who were so young, so fresh and wide-eyed when you came to Dresden, looking for enlightenment: looking in the darkest places for the light—and thought you found it with an old, played-out dissident, under state surveillance; and the moment that you left my apartment the Stasi came to call. Where have you been since? Where did it take you, through the years and decades, your jigsaw quest for fragments to piece together. Down to hell? I wonder. Is that where life took you? Is that where you've been? Is that journey what put those lines on your face: that fretwork stamped on your forehead like a brand?'

He spoke these sentences sardonically. He spat them out and hurried on: 'You know so much, now, of course. You've got so much wisdom since then, yes—so much gathered up from all the richness of the carnival of life, the ordeal you gave yourself. But there's one thing you don't seem to know. The game never ends: it doesn't balance up. Lives don't have shapes. There aren't grand encounters when everything comes into focus—or do you think this might be one?'

'Of course,' I said, in sadness.

He scowled, and nodded: 'You have to. I, though, want to expel meaning from my life. Defeat memory, not invite it in. People come to us, with all their intensities; they blaze before us, their brilliance lights us up—then they fade, they vanish. Recollection's pointless: there's nothing to retain.'

'This was a non-encounter, then?'

'Some appointments are best left unkept. We aren't in life in a cheap movie plot. You took my knowledge. You took my stories. Now leave me: leave me be.'

And with that, before I could summon up a word or thought, he turned and walked away through the dark of the evening, which quickly engulfed him.

*

Time passed, softening the blows of life: memory threw its veil over those events; new encounters and experiences took their place. Some months later, after a chain of flights, international and domestic, I reached the little airport at Alice Springs, tired, bleary-eyed, stray thoughts running and dissolving inside my head. Heat, hot wind, bushfire smoke. I crossed the tarmac: I went through the terminal, looking, gazing, taking nothing in. Suddenly, a man approached me: he clutched my shoulder; he spoke my name.

'It's wonderful to see you again,' he said, and stared into my eyes.

This individual was tall, fair-haired, with striking features; he was finely dressed—indeed, his clothes were exquisite: jeans of dark indigo, jet-black riding boots, a scoop-necked T-shirt, body-tight. He stood out in that terminal, full of thronging tourists and men in shorts and jeans and work uniforms. We walked out into the sun, he at my side, close, still clasping my shoulder, as if a mild form of arrest had been made, or the fabric of the world was on the verge of dissolution and he felt the need to cling to a kindred being. At that point, a noise in the sky became evident: it grew. There was a vibration in the air. A dark, broad form shimmered just above the rangeline: it gained shape and definition, it swept down, it neared the runway. The noise was deep, by now, a deep bass, a grinding sensation, a force, more than a sound: closer it came; closer—the shockwave reached the trees, their branches shook; the wheels scraped, the plane rushed by on its landing run; the engines whined and cut.

'A Galaxy,' said my companion, then, in a solemn voice: 'I could feel it coming; I could feel the tension; I could tell. That's the Pine Gap plane—the transport, from the States—or maybe it was sent from some strange supply base, far off round the world—Diego Garcia, or Hawaii, or Guam. Look at it—that deep grey, as if it was aiming at invisibility, obscurity, bringing secrets out and in. I'd love to know what it was carrying— wouldn't you?'

I said nothing, and prised his hand from my shoulder.

'Where have you just come from?' he asked.

'Deep places.'

'Truly! You cosmopolitan! I go to those kinds of places too—Basel, Antwerp, Malibu, Miami—and that's not even mentioning the new destinations in the East. We're fellow travellers. Don't you remember me?'

'I'm rather jet-lagged just now,' I said.

'But you were before, too, when we first met! It must be a permanent condition. It's me—David Aster.'

'The private dealer?'

'The hawk of the art world, yes. You came into my gallery, actually, two or three years ago, in Sydney. Of course you remember me: we had a long talk! New perspectives. That was when I was just starting out.'

A recollection stirred inside me, together with the familiar, unpleasant awareness that the record we preserve of our doings is partial, flickering: pools of intermittent light in a long oblivion.

'I remember,' I said. 'I think: that vast showroom, down Parramatta Road—almost in Camperdown...'

'Yes!'

'And it was impossible to find it; you had to spend hours in the search; it had no number, and no sign—getting there was like a test or challenge, and in an inside room you had those paintings from the new wave in the Western Desert: bright reds and yellows, the kinds of things no one had seen?'

'That's right—and I told you everything; I remember it

exactly; it was a real confessional; I felt lightheaded for days afterwards—I told you all my hopes and schemes.'

'How could I forget,' I said: 'You were going to stage a revolution in the desert art trade: take things in your hands; turn the old painters into stars of the contemporary scene; shape them, guide them, bring their work to new peaks of beauty; plunge in, become a true partner to the artists, learn their language, even—I remember thinking that was a quite a plan!'

'And everything I said then I'd do, I've done. I've sold great, undying masterpieces to collectors round the world. I've turned the art market upside down.'

'And how does that feel?'

He gave a sardonic smile.

'That's not so important. Men don't act from motives of gain, or fulfilment or happiness.'

'They don't?'

'No—of course not. They act for reasons that are hidden from them.'

We had made our way across the car park, past a row of ancient, ill-starred Fords, and Kingswoods, and dust-stained traybacks, and bush Troop Carriers in varying states of decay; past the fleets of hire cars: racy sub-compacts and sleek, new-model sedans. Aster paused, an uncertain look on his face. He reached again for my shoulder. I stepped back.

'Time for me to head off,' he said.

Behind him was a four-wheel drive, new, metallic silver, glinting in the sun. There were three aerials of different designs and sizes on the bullbars, each one of them topped with a little pennant flag; two new spares and a kangaroo jack cantilevered from the rear door; mirror spotlights; a roof rack loaded up with neat-rolled red canvas swags.

'What a vehicle!' I said: 'It's like a work of art!'

'It is one: I can take you through the extras if you want—and then there's the interior!' He opened the back, with something of a flourish. 'Take a look. All customised. It's my design. You won't see anything like it on the road—not anywhere.'

'That I can believe,' I murmured. I glanced in: there were the standard splendours: chrome, flashing gauges, seats of nubuck suede.

'The back,' called out Aster.

The rear compartment had been given over to a set of storage drawers of varying widths and depths, arranged in a pleasing, symmetric pattern, each one with its own lock and clasp: the whole assemblage very like an ancient steamer trunk, swathed in leather, and mongrammed. I looked more closely.

'You have a Vuitton outback gear storage system?' I said, rather accusingly.

'Well, in a sense. It was made in Shanghai, by some craftsmen I work with: they have a strong preference for the counterfeit over the real; it's an aesthetic with them; they don't feel happy unless they're copying, improving on an original.'

'And what's that lever?'

'Don't touch that: it cuts the power: there's an Engel fridge in there. Full-size, hidden away, and all the navigation electronics as well—although out here you really don't need much help to tell you where you're going.'

'You don't ever get lost?'

'I begin from an assumption of universal, primordial loss,' he said. 'There's something I'd like to show you—before we say goodbye.'

I made a gesture. He went round to the driver's side, and came back with a dark, soft-covered book: it was a sale catalogue, in familiar livery: *Important Aboriginal Art*, said the spine.

'Always important, isn't it?' I said: 'Never just mid-grade, or of qualified significance. You can't hide from the pressures of the market.'

'Auctions!' Aster scowled: 'They're just a first approximation to reality. A guide to sentiment. The real art market's elsewhere: it's in the minds of men and women—a handful of them: a club. You have to be initiated into its mysteries to know. But sometimes even a public sale catalogue produces jewels—like this one. There's a sculpted piece in here—a desert object—old. And a detailed entry on its background—by Kim Akerman.'

'I know him,' I said, and was about to explain the link, and its intriguing convolutions, but Aster cut me off.

'You're a high roller,' he said, in an admiring voice. 'How I wish I could meet a man like that, and sit and talk. What a scholar. The depth in the things he knows—he's the real deal. Just take a look at this.'

He flicked the book open to a marked page—there was a lengthy curatorial essay, and, facing it, an image of a figurine, twice illustrated: long, thin and dark. The gloss paper caught the light and dazzled me: I shielded my eyes. The pose was striking, almost classical: the figure wore some kind of tall head-dress; its upper half was painted in bright colours; it was standing with one leg slightly bent, seeming caught in motion.

'So—what do you think?' said Aster, and then ran on himself at once. 'I think it's the most majestic, most enigmatic thing. Look—just look at the pattern in the colours—those reds, and swirling oranges, and yellows: the jet-black of the skin, the smoothness of the carved surface, the dark void where the eyes should be. I was overwhelmed when I first saw it. I couldn't stop myself. I took a flight down to Melbourne the week before the sale.'

'It's already been held?'

'It was a year ago. When I saw the statue, at the viewing, I knew, at once, for sure.'

'You had to buy it?'

'No one else much paid it any mind. All the usual connoisseurs were clustered round the usual expressionistic canvases and early boards and fashionable barks. With the statuette, I was alone—and I could hear it, speaking to me.'

'Did you just say the sculpture was speaking to you?'

'Yes—it happens to me, from time to time—I could hear sounds, noises, like whispers, half-spoken words.'

'And what were they?'

'No idea. I had a similar feeling, once, years ago, near the Stock Route, when I was driving with an old man—a man from Punmu, and we were out beyond the far shore of Lake Disappointment. It was a hot day, late in the year; there were dogs howling in the distance; the sky was full of smoke plumes—mirages everywhere: the moment you stepped out from the Toyota into the heat you felt on the verge of passing out. We climbed up to a cave in the flat-top ranges; he showed me old carved wooden figures hidden there—the creator-heroes of the lake, with lines and markings just like these: bands, and curves, and snake-meanders running up and down their head-dresses— I knew this statuette must be a companion piece of some kind. Take a look at what the essay says: it goes down the same path.'

I leaned against the white trunk of the gum tree beside us, and tried to find a patch of shadow, and coaxed my eyes to focus on the page, and read the words before me. It was a mazy text, more hints and clues than anything. Description of the object, origins, provenance.

'But he thinks it came from Docker River!' I said.

'He does—and I'm sure he's right. Max Brumby—that's the name he throws up: a famous carver of wooden figures, from long ago, almost in mission times.'

'Any relation to Daniel, and to the Wild Brumbys? You know—the group that used to play at Docker, years ago—country rock, duelling guitars—sweet, pure, full of rhythm—something like the New Riders of the Purple Sage?'

He stared at me blankly.

'You're not familiar with them, either? The Bay Area psychedelic scene—the '60s? You look like you could have stepped straight off one of their early album covers.'

'I'm not familiar with any mass-culture reference points,' he said, with a note of pride buried in his voice: 'Don't you want to know what happened?'

'At the auction with the speaking statue—of course— who wouldn't!'

'It was early evening: in the saleroom, over-airconditioned—cold. A full house: new money, fast buyers, the conspicuous crowd. I sat alone. I always do. That's the best way to gauge, and judge. There was a run of old barks and Gija works, from Jirrawun, all being sold off—the standard profit taking going on—then up came the piece, quite early in the sale: there it was, on the plinth, in the spot beams; it looked like some strange creation from distant stars. The big guns and the gallery collectors were catching their breath after the first flurry: no one made a move. I launched in: a start-out bid. I was alone.'

'And that was it?'

'It looked for a while as if it would be that way: then, after a prompt or two, another bid came, and another; they were nothing—I would have paid ten times more—but at that moment I felt a languor spreading over me, a dizziness. It was different feelings mixed into one effect: such beauty, so paraded—a contempt for buying and selling had taken hold of me.'

'Bad timing!'

'Of course, I'd always had a secret loathing for that scene, just as much as I was caught up in it: I loathed its appetites and falsities, its inability to distinguish mode and fancy from permanence and truth. And there was the sense of shame in me, too, for being there, and at the same time a longing to buy everything, to sweep up every work on view.'

'And then what?'

'Have them—hold them—burn them—I don't know. At that instant it was as if I heard the figurine, the statue, like a voice inside me, saying: Be still; freeze yourself; be still. I did nothing. It was knocked down to a low bid. The next pieces were all desert works, I remember, and it felt as though each one of them was drenched in suffering and grief. I was walking out on my own at the sale's end. There was High Street, Armadale, choked with Land Cruisers and BMWs, lit up by the shopfront lights, and beside me was one of the collectors I deal with—a real horse trader. Nothing for you, tonight, I could see him thinking, and he smiled at me. You have to wait, I told myself, wait, when something's looming before you—never buy until the signal comes. And it did. It always does. I was at home, days later, sleepless, beside myself. I was in the despair that comes from wanting beauty— a despair like love.'

'Love?'

'Yes—that piece was in my head. I was in some kind of delirium. That morning there was a sudden downpour, sharp, from nowhere, like a flash storm in the desert ranges, sheets of water tumbling down—and in the middle of it, as the rain was lashing at the windows, a call came, and I knew at once what it would be. The department head from the auction house was on the line. Did I remember that little carved wooden figure I'd looked over for so long at the viewing before the sale: it had been passed in. Did I want it, he asked me, and I told him quietly that want wasn't quite the word. And here it is!'

With a dramatic gesture he reached down, pulled out a long carrying case, laid it on the ground, undid the locks and lifted out the statuette. He held it up to me: the paint was chipped; the sun's glare seemed to bleach the colours out.

'It's perfect, isn't it?' he said, in a proprietorial voice: 'Every time I see it it's as if the breath is struck from my body.'

'Why didn't you just show me the real thing and skip the catalogue?' I asked him.

'Object and image are different,' he said: 'You know that. Sometimes it's easier to sense the aura of an artwork from its photo, rather than from the piece itself. Besides, I was just testing you out, feeling my way.'

'And?'

'What a question! What do you think—now you see it face to face?'

Aster cradled the figurine in his arms: he turned it, slowly. 'See the way the bands of red and orange wind around the head-dress? Feel the weight: it's heavy. Hardwood—it's carved from Docker River desert oak.'

'And what are you doing with it here? Do you always carry your choicest treasures round with you?'

'The most talismanic ones, of course, yes—like old desert men with their magic objects stuffed down their swags. I carry this with me everywhere. It's brought me joy—and sadness, too. I'm getting onto terms with it: coming to know it. I've been told things; I have my own ideas—about what it is, what it means. I show it to the old people, in the bush, around the fire, sometimes—in the evening, when the right time for talking comes.'

'Where?'

'Oh—down the track,' he said, with studied vagueness. 'Through the eastern Pitjantjatjara lands: that's where I'm headed; that's where the real experts are for this kind of thing: men who see the past.'

He jumped into the driver's seat, then turned back, as if an idea had just struck him. He smiled his most engaging smile.

'Why not ride along with me—for a short while. Come for the drive. I only stop at the best roadhouses.'

'You want me, after five days of uninterrupted travelling, jet-lagged into oblivion, to keep moving, keep going—to take a trip out to some unknown destination, in the hottest season of the year, in the middle of the storm time—to drive out into the Aboriginal bush without a permit, in the company of Australia's most notorious carpetbagger?'

'Well—carpetbagger! There's a judgemental term,' said Aster: 'And we were getting on so well.'

I made a waving, goodbye sign in his direction, and looked round to the glass-fronted airport building and the sky.

'But why not?' called out Aster. 'No one's going to see. After all, one man's carpetbagger is another's nurturing and prudent market maker. Put yourself in my hands. Jump in. The desert beckons. Or is there really somewhere you have to be, in the days ahead? Some vital thing you have to do? Some crucial, life-defining thing?'

'Nothing'—the word hung between us in the air—'No. And there's nowhere I have to be.'

'So—live dangerously. You won't regret it. Climb in.'

'Put like that,' I said, and laughed, 'who could possibly refuse?'

We set off, at speed; the highway took us; the talk ran on, breaking, resuming, forming itself into patterns and recurring themes: the art bazaar, the charms of desert language, its rhythms and reduplications, the intricacies of its grammar, and that grammar's lurking presence in the newer painting styles: the bush around us, too—its variations, the difference in mood and tone between the mulga scrub round Yuendumu and the gidgee landscapes of the eastern Plenty; swags, their design, the philosophy they embodied; the star-filled night sky's consoling scale. We swept past a bunched-up fleet of trucks and road trains: the sun was falling, the shadows were lengthening, the red haze deepened in the air. A turn-off flashed by.

'Didn't you see?' I said: 'That was the Victory Downs road we just passed. The way in to Ernabella and the ranges; the best access road into the lands.'

'Not the only one, though,' said Aster: 'And certainly not the one for somebody interested in life's unmarked paths and obscurities.'

He sped up. Side tracks came and went: the short-cut to Kenmore Park; the De Rose Hill entrance gate; the turn for Indulkana. Then he braked—hard. There was a dusty, unsigned road running off towards the west, almost invisible against the sunset's glare. He turned.

'What are you doing?' I said. 'This is the back way in to Mintabie, of all places.'

'I know where it goes,' he said.

'What—you need a quick resupply of hydroponic grass or something? Go slower! Marla cops are always sneaking and gliding up and down this track.'

'I doubt anyone glides down it,' said Aster, and he did

slow—he had to: the road was all corrugations; he switched to four-wheel drive. 'Anyhow—what have you got against Mintabie? It's a nice peaceful community.'

'Are you serious? Have you spent much time there? Every single deal bag of drugs and every cask of wine and whisky bottle that gets into the desert lands goes through that charming gateway.'

'Old prejudices! Stereotypes. You just don't like opal miners and their kind.'

'You do?'

'Of course: I admire that world. It's straight, unvarnished; full of men and women who can think for themselves, who talk things through. I've always loved those places at the end of the line: where the future's at a discount, where it's all a constant flashing now—where people live for risk, and profit; for adventure, and nothing else.'

I glanced across at him.

'Truthfully,' he said. 'They're my kind of crew.'

'Look out!' I called: 'Be careful.'

We were coming in sight of Mintabie: a low-slung, old-model car full of young desert men was idling on the road.

'Just a group of casual travellers taking in the scenery,' I said.

'Don't be like that,' said Aster: 'Don't judge all the time. Let life come to you—let the atmosphere around you reach you: let it all sink in.'

We passed fencelines, a maze of tracks, a generator shed: there were caravans, aerials, water towers. The sun was down below the mullock hills. The township loomed in front of us.

Aster pulled up before a brick-fronted building screened by a row of dust-stained palms.

'My God,' I said: 'I haven't been here for years—and nothing's changed.'

'The hotel? Why should it? How about a pit stop? The Goanna Grill. You hungry?'

'What for—a perentie steak?'

'Come on—try your luck. You'll know someone or other here. There's always a sweet delight in catching people up when you call in to places like this—in seeing people you've been meeting on and off for years.'

We walked in, and Aster went up to the bar and fetched the drinks. Soon the room was full. A road crew sat beside us.

One turned. 'You know me,' he said to Aster. 'We met out west. You gave me a tow—on the way in to Mount Davies, in the winter, a year back. You were with that Aboriginal friend of yours. He was something!'

'Yes,' said Aster, in a low voice, and paused a moment: 'Yes, he was.'

'He's not with you—no? How's life treating you now? Still doing battle with the chaos of the world? Still seeking immortality in art?'

The man then turned to look my way: 'That's the only way you'll ever find an afterlife. I'm a strict materialist, you see.'

I absorbed this piece of news, and nodded.

'You too? That's the way. Soon enough all superstition in the bush will be stamped out: it'll be a rational world.'

'Like Mintabie?'

'Exactly. A place of perfect harmony, give or take a feud or two. We've got everything we need. We're happy enough mining rock and being left alone. God's like the state government—always interfering.'

The faces round the table focused in.

'See,' said Aster, and looked at me.

'Some people think opal mining's got an otherworldly edge to it,' I said: 'Something like a religious quest.'

'Why?' said one of the men round the table: 'Why think that—the truth is it's the devil's stone. Just look into an opal: look closely; you'll see—it's the clouded, mocking echo of the first creation. Remember that chapter in *Karamazov*: when Ivan gets a visit from the Devil—and the Devil's a shabby young man, a little down on his luck, wearing an opal ring, or was it an opal tie pin?'

'Was it actually *Karamazov*?' said Aster.

'Well, you ought to know: you're Russian, aren't you—or something like that.'

'Something,' replied Aster. 'But I see this corner of the desert as a more Chekhovian kind of space: brief, humdrum joys, oblique sadnesses that stretch on for years.'

'Not at all, brother—it's epic! This is epic country. Mintabie is, anyway. And the only thing that's Chekhovian on the lands is the dogs.'

'The dogs?'

'The lapdogs—haven't you noticed there's a new fashion in the communities? They've all got little lapdogs now. No Borzoi or mastiffs or greyhound crosses in these parts any more.'

'True?'

'Absolutely—the chihuahua's the thing: there are tiny chihuahua camp-dog mongrels, across the lands, everywhere, yapping away. It started off at Nyapari, that little outstation at the far end of the Mann Ranges—now there's mobs of them everywhere running round.'

'Inspiring Chekhovian sentiments?'

'You may laugh—but those communities on the lands could work as Chekhovian stage sets—they're just waiting for their melancholic literary master and chronicler to appear on the scene.'

The talk flowed on; the night wound down. Our companions rose: they turned to go. The last of them paused in the doorway, and looked back: 'We're headed out tomorrow—track work—Oak Valley. Ever been that way? Good art hunting there? Should we be looking out for unconsidered trifles?'

'There's some promise,' said Aster, 'in the raw.' And he made a so-so sign with his hand. 'But heavy country. You'd know the stories.'

'Only surface ones,' said the road worker. 'We just go in and out: and not often. I remember the first time I went in there from the north: what a drive it was! Gibber stretches; washaways; red sand dunes as high as hills—you can imagine trying to pull the kind of heavy equipment we have; there were rainstorms; we were travelling for two days. We got there round dusk; we weren't expecting much: there were no staff stationed in the community. The people seemed very shy: they wouldn't come and talk to us. Back then the ground there was still poisoned, from the nuclear days: they didn't even light fires and burn their wood, not that there's much around—they just used to eat out of

233

tins, and the water tanks were all up high on stilts. Everything was quiet: I thought it was the quietest settlement I'd ever seen. We had the feeling we should keep our distance: we camped well away; then, at night, once the full moon came up, we heard voices, hundreds of voices—there was a ceremony going on: singing, chanting, dancing, right through to the dawn. What a place! Who knows why they set up there.'

'You know,' said Aster: 'You know very well. They were shifted: after the tests, down in their own land, at Maralinga.'

'Someone had a sense of humour,' said one of the road crew: 'Putting the test site down there, in that sector, so remote—it's tiger country.'

'It was for convenience,' said Aster: 'It was near the trans-continental railway line, and Ooldea siding; they could get in easily enough; all around was saltbush country—gentle, manageable. There were wells nearby, dug by explorers; there were grave markers too: spears and woomeras set up in the ground. It was a perfect spot, idyllic: even when you go there now, after everything that's happened, you can't help thinking how soft that landscape is. They built a town, an airfield—it was a whole world on its own—a closed world—strange, and foreign—it still is: as closed as the nuclear science cities in the old Soviet Union used to be.'

Aster looked across at me.

'Shall we drift on?'

'You're not stopping?' said the road crewman: 'Stay. Change your plans. You could ride with us.'

'Tempting,' said Aster—'but we're on a mission.'

'We're sorry,' said the crewman then: 'Very sorry—for your friend.'

The two of us drove out, away from Mintabie, on the track north-west, under the gleaming stars.

'What was that about?' I asked him after a few quiet minutes.

'Yes,' he said, then: 'There's something I should tell you: I'd like to. And perhaps that's why I brought you out here: perhaps I was meaning to tell you all the time. It's the story of that figurine—in a way. In a way it's the story of the whole desert. I'll set the scene. We've got a few kilometres to run.'

'Go on,' I prompted: 'You know what you said: dark's the time for telling—dark, when there's a low moon in the sky, and the night air's still warm, like now.'

'It would be five years,' he said: 'Five years since I crossed his path—when I was first going out into the desert, into the communities: I was scouring them, back then, looking for new artists to take on. I went everywhere, and I had nothing; they were the days when I built my new world up: painters, collectors; and in all those comings and goings there was one man who stood out for me: maybe you'd remember him, from the morning when you came in to my gallery; he was there then; I think I even introduced you—Mr Kilmain, I would have said; but Tjampa, that was what people called him. He didn't ever say too much, when he made his trips in to town—out in the bush with him, though, things went differently. I met a lot of desert people, in those years, men and women; I came to see their characters: how they'd present themselves, what they'd show and what they'd hide. You do, when you speak language—you pick up more of what's going on.

He wasn't like them: he was harder; he was a bedrock person. He wanted the truth of things. He didn't have any interest in being fooled or played along by the outside world.'

'He painted for you?'

'Never—we never worked together. No—he was a friend to me, and that was it: the deepest kind of friend.'

'What kind is that?'

'The kind that comforts you: tells you all your failings—sees your darknesses, and still has kindness and forgiveness for you in his heart.'

'And you for him?'

'Of course. From the very first time I met him: it was at a native title handover, at Mantamaru, in the west: there were hundreds of bush people from all round gathered for the day. He stood out; he was at ease, there, everywhere, in both worlds—you could feel it in him: he was a speaker—but in signs, in expressions, in looks. You know that old saying: man of high degree—it could have been made for him. We talked: he burned right through me with his words; after that, whenever I set out to see him there was a quickening in me: when I was with him, I became my best and truest self.'

The road forked: a light showed far ahead. Aster turned the wheel. 'Our destination,' he announced: 'Unusual place. And an unusual man who runs it: you can tell it's the last stop before the lands.'

'Unusual in what way?'

'He sees—but in another way from us.'

'You mean he's blind.'

'Wait—don't jump on, always—things have their own way of unfolding—you'll find out in good time.'

Some minutes later we pulled up. It was a roadhouse, or it had been, once, years before, and retained the traces of its origins. The frontage was low; before it was a wide verandah screened by mesh with gaping holes. A sign was stretched above the entrance—faint, weathered lettering. There was a pale gleam coming through the doorway: inside, a table or two, empty; a work desk, an iron stove, something resembling a bar. I took in these new surrounds: concrete flooring, stone walls, and on them old photographs, a series, framed, black and white, from station times—Aboriginal stockmen droving cattle; young men in the saddle, staring into the camera; a neat, white-painted homestead; a desert landscape with a sandstorm bearing down. Aster went to the verandah table, and pulled out two chairs.

'A good place to look out from,' he said. 'See that glow—over there, over the ranges, to the south?'

I followed his eyes.

'Bushfires—far off, burning through the night.'

'There's no one here,' I said.

'Yes, there is.'

Aster nodded. In the doorway, looking at us, was a man, white-haired, arms folded, eyes unmoving, with a composed expression on his face.

'Aster,' he said: 'Good to see you!'

'Snow—you too,' said Aster.

'You brought someone?'

Aster began explaining; the man broke in.

'Where's Tjampa? Not with you? But I feel him, somehow, still—around…You're right, about those fires—they've been burning all week long in the sand-dune country, and beyond, in the conservation park—when the wind's up you can smell them, and the black shards of scorched bark blow in.'

They spoke on for some minutes; the man made to go.

'Wait—sit with us,' said Aster: 'I'm just talking about him: you might want to hear'—and at that, as I watched him, the man, with studied, practised movements, came over, and reached for a chair, which Aster pushed in his direction. In the bush, nearby, a night bird was calling; the sand-brown stick insects clung to the verandah wire; moths flew and fluttered round the light, their orbits widening, then closing in.

'What's in your thoughts?' said Aster to me.

'Nothing,' I answered: 'My mind was very still.'

'It is peaceful,' said the man: 'But in the scrub, close by, all round us, the dingoes are hunting, prowling; the nightjars are on the wing. Quiet's not rest—it's stealth.'

'You hear them?'

'I hear everything: keep on. Tell your story, Aster—tell his story: he meant something to me. Tell it out.'

And Aster did. If until then he had seemed a strained, imperfect narrator, jumping between events and time horizons, explaining, amplifying, plunging into pools of details, now suddenly he was the master of his tale: he caught his subject; he caught him through gestures, through inflections; he had the rhythms of his speaking; he built a portrait for me, there, on that dark verandah—his friend seemed present to us: a compact, broad-chested desert man, with a studied way of silent staring and a taste for cowboy hats and Western gear. The two of them had travelled together, all through Aster's bush apprenticeship: they crossed the rangelands; they drove the desert highways—they made collecting trips from Wiluna to Watarru and back again; and on those journeys there were constantly repeated language lessons; there were ventures deep into empty country down half-vanished tracks.

'How far we went,' he said: 'Out to his conception site in the Hickey Hills—out into ranges round Lake Carnegie no one had surveyed and put down on the maps. And those travels were enough to change me. I thought I knew a great deal before, from books, and writing; from looking at desert paintings, dealing them, describing them: I was good at cultivating an air of knowledge.'

'Counterfeiting it?' I put in.

'The faker knows he's faking; the art expert persuades himself he knows. I can still see one scene—I seem always to be seeing it: the pair of us together, near the end of an expedition; we'd been driving in an old Mazda ute with a smashed-up windscreen and nothing much for jack or spare; we were on the hunt for an old bush campsite, out near Mount Leisler, where he'd gone when he was a boy. We found it: we stopped beneath the ridgeline, with a view across the dune fields to the mesas in the west. It was early in the build-up season: there were spinifex fires burning; the sun was setting; there were dust flurries stained deep red by the light; thunder rolling, far off; lightning flashing in the sky. And he sat cross-legged beside me, and started singing: he sang all through the night: the country, its stories, the descent lines of the men and women he'd walked it with, who'd been with him there when he was young.'

'Stop,' said the roadhouse man then, and raised up his hand: 'Quiet. Listen. Say nothing. Red-ochre men—on the way to ceremony—they'll go past.'

I waited, and turned my head. Silence—for a minute, more— then there were the faint beginnings of a sound—low, on the edge of hearing, at a distance on the road. It gained a shape, a rhythm: it persisted—it was wheels, and engines, slow moving. Lights appeared—a pair of headlights, then another, and another: a procession of them. In front was a white trayback, mud-spattered: it passed us, bumping on the corrugations; behind it was an old truck missing a side panel, with a broken, trailing bullbar, then a series of Troop Carriers—all of them full of desert men, young, old; men wearing headbands, staring out, their expressions set. The last vehicle passed. The sound died away: the night was still again. Aster shifted in his seat. There was a slight smile on his face, as if he had just seen something rare and precious, private, beyond all capture in words.

'Like a dream,' he said, in a soft voice. He resumed—or tried to—but his tale was scattered, now, it was shards and fragments once again. He stumbled: I broke in.

'Back up,' I said: 'Go back to where you were. The statuette— the carving. It's been long enough: you brought us to the edge of things. Tell us. The time's come.'

'Yes,' he said: 'It's true. But don't you understand? I'm trying to tell—and not to tell you at the same time. To keep things in suspension. Not to lead the story to its end. It was a dark day: the day when I showed him the figurine. I'd just collected it from the auction gallery in Melbourne. How proud I was! Tjampa was flying in, for some conference: art and authenticity, that kind of thing. I met him at Tullamarine, and drove him in to town. We went straight to my studio. I had the statuette set up in the back room. I'd wanted it to be a surprise. I showed it to him. There was a long, hard silence. Then he looked down. He shielded his face. He started to cry: great, shaking, soundless sobs. That wasn't what I'd expected. Why, I asked, and he began explaining to me. He'd known the carver; he'd known him well. Then he smiled at me—a smile from the pits of sadness. You've got yourself a piece of strong law here, he said, and in that instant I had a glimpse of something in him: something potent, looming there, as if a hawk or eagle were staring down. Very strong, he said again: You might want to be careful. I jumped up. I was going to move it, hide it. Wait, he said at once. And don't be sorry like that. It's not for you to be sorry—it's for us. That pulled me up short. I fell quiet. I listened: the cars were driving past, in the rain, outside; I could hear the people out on High Street, hurrying by.

'In early days, he told me, then, old men in the desert had power. Their blood had strength. They had power for the rain; power for the sun, the fire. When the rock holes had emptied out, they could call up the storms from blue sky; when the bushfires were racing, they could turn aside the flames. They could see into the future. They could travel back to the past. They could vanish right before your eyes. That was how it was, in those days. And still now? I asked him. Of course, he answered me: But things have changed. You know that. You know that very well. They cleared the desert out—or tried to—the patrol officers tried, in their white

Land Rovers, in the rocket times. And there were the weapons tests, I said: At Totem, and at Maralinga. You know everything, he said to me then: It's all there for you. It's all written down.

'How much, when I'd first known him, I'd wanted to go with him out to the old memorial sites: go out to Emu Junction, where the obelisks are set up to mark ground zero for the Totem tests. I'd never breathed a word to him—but I'd dreamed of sitting with him there, in that silent desert, beside those strange, weathered concrete shapes. I'd always felt there would be some point to that. Some circuit would be joined up. And even as I had that thought, even as it was taking wing inside me, I looked from Tjampa to the statuette—to its sightless eyes and the swirling bands like spreading shock waves on its chest, its tall head-dress and the rising circles on it, and the flashes shooting upwards—and I realised: I knew; I knew for certain—the figurine was the man of thunder; it was the atom cloud. Its maker must have been there, seen the blast, seen that pulsing light.'

Aster stopped.

'And that was it?' I asked: 'So simple: the solution to your mystery.'

'Not quite: I was on the verge of asking him—he swept on; he raced ahead of me; suddenly he began describing other stories to me, in great detail: how storms are brought to life; how the air breathes; how we endure after time's end. And I remember thinking to myself in those moments that what was happening, right then, in that little room, was the most beautiful thing happening in all the world; it was like a candle's flare; he was telling me things I could never have imagined—then he wheeled round; he looked straight at me: a kind look, in a way. You want to know the truth, he asked me, in a soft voice. The real truth? I was happy coming here, happy, on the plane, knowing I'd be here, with you—but now I see this—he picked up the statuette, and held it, and ran his fingers up and down its painted markings—and I understand: there are things I can't show you. I can't even find the words to say them. The world isn't the way you think it is. It's not the way you want it to be. It never will be. The more you look, the less you see.

'It was a bad visit from then on. I cast my mind back, and it's plain: his troubles began from that day. He went back to the Western Desert. Soon reports started reaching me: about disputes that he was caught up in, fights, feuds; there was a car accident, serious, police investigations dragging on. He'd disappear for months on end: he went on hunting trips, and he'd show up long afterwards, far away—in Newman, or Wiluna, or Jigalong.'

'You never saw him again?'

'I waited: I made plans to set out on his trail, and track him down. I'd heard he'd been down in Ceduna, and then in Mimili, heading through the lands. I decided the time had come to take a flight out to the west: I had a show just coming on in Perth. I stayed there a few days: then Kalgoorlie. Up and down its wide streets, where you feel the past so sharply pressing down. I looked through its drinking camps, and asked about. When I went back to my motel there was a message: he was in LA. You'd have been through there, hundreds of times—that little mining centre, next to where Poseidon used to be, great open-cut gold mines all around it still?'

'You mean Laverton!'

I could see the scene. I had a dull sense of how the tale was about to end: I reached out a hand to him across the table, as if to shield him from the blow.

'That's right.'

'My God!' I said: 'This isn't a story that's going to come out well!'

'It's not so much a story,' went on Aster: 'It's something else. A set of tones, or moods. Do we know, in our lives, what we go through? Do lives really form themselves into stories? I felt myself more in a movie sequence as I drove in, all the way from the Leonora turn-off on that thin, straight, level road, with the colours all slightly out of key: the green of the bush almost blue-grey, the blue of the sky too white, the red of the sand more like fire than solid ground. I reached Laverton. I checked with the police, and the loan sharks: they knew nothing. I suppose you have to look on the bright side, though: they did want to sell me some art.'

'Any good?'

'Surely by now you've noticed that my romance with the idea of purity and quality in Aboriginal art has begun to flag? I looked around the camps. It was a scorching afternoon—no one had that much appetite for talk. I found a gang of boys waiting outside the service station shop. They told me. Past the dam, they sang out: that way—past the cemetery—the golden mine. We'll take you. They jumped in—six, seven of them: my Toyota had been like a silent kingdom all the way from Kalgoorlie; suddenly it was transformed, it was full of energy and life. Out we went, into the bush, mining trucks and transports driving back towards us and kicking up thick trails of dirt. Here, said one: Put him in! He had a cassette to play: he searched the dashboard. I explained to them that I didn't think the car actually had a cassette deck: it might be just CDs, or even MP3s. They took that on board: He must be a proper poor man, they chorused. Soon the sun was sinking low in front of us. Are you all sure this is right? I asked them. We know our country, they said: That's one thing we know. We hit the outstation track: we pulled up. A house or two, a shelter, nothing more—and in the shade of the shelter, all hooped corrugated iron and hessian, there he was: cross-legged, wearing a pair of jeans stained desert-red, a shirt the same colour, a black cowboy hat, broad-brimmed, brand new. The boys scattered. He glanced up at me. Sun's going down, he said. For us all. You came to find me—but what for? Do you need me? Need me to be something for you?

'There were camp dogs, scavenging around: voices, music, from the houses, a slow beat, pounding out. I laughed—but I felt a sadness stretching over me—perhaps I already had some half-conscious sense of what was happening. We all need each other, I said back: Like the notes in a song; like the colours that make up the sky. I was waiting for you, he said. For you to show up here. I knew you'd come. Cigarette? He lit one, and smoked it, slowly. I looked around. I took in the scene. What a place! Empty tins, torn mattresses, old jerrycans: it was the usual tapestry of dirt and rubbish—but turned soft and lovely by the light: the colours in harmony; the shapes, too.

'Tjampa leaned across to me. He was talking, with urgency: telling adventures from long ago. They went flashing by. I thought to myself: how much do I really know him—then: is it really him? What do you believe happens to us, he asked me: Where do we go, when we leave this world? I'm not so sure in my mind, I told him: I have a picture where everything that's been divided in life, separated and torn apart comes back together, and time and space no longer have any hold.

'That's not what we think, he said, and took my hand for a moment, then let it go. Not at all. We think there's a white sea at the end of the world: I've even seen it, in pictures, in dreams, inside my head—it's quiet, and cold, and there are clouds over it, clouds of ice; and you have to walk there, by yourself, across the sand. It's a hard, long journey: but when you get there, then you see the sun breaking through the clouds, and that white lake gleams, and shines, and looks like fire.

'He leaned back. I stared at him, and I had the strange thought that there was something blurred in his face, his skin, his eyes. I shrugged that thought off: I kept on talking. I looked again; it was true: he was losing his distinctness—he was becoming like a shadow, in that half-light, close in front of me, close enough to touch. My friend, he said—or his voice said, softly, as though it was the wind blowing—The time has come: it has to be. I must leave you. But you won't be alone. I'll still be with you—don't you remember how I used to tell you: those who go are always still with us, if we have the eyes to see them by.

'I looked up again, and now I could make out the rocks through him in the landscape; I could see the spinifex, the trees, the sand—red and shadow out to the horizon's line. It can't be, I thought, in one part of myself—and in the other: it is. I was looking at the desert, and the falling of the night. The dogs whimpered. There was no one there: a shelter, open to the winds; a tin cup, a swirl of patterned blankets and a swag.'